THE GREAT NORTHERN WAR

JAMES E WISHER

SAND HILL PUBLISHING

CHAPTER 1

O tto Shenk sat at a desk outside Franken Manor, a sprawling mansion not much smaller than the royal palace. A ledger, its first page half filled with names, rested in front of him while a line of wizards waiting to be interviewed stretched across the lawn. The turnout surprised him. After Wolfric announced the restoration of all wizards' rights, Otto had assumed at best a third would volunteer to join the army. From the numbers on the lawn he guessed he'd underestimated by half.

The sky above was leaden and gray but at least it wasn't raining; with fall fast approaching he expected the cold wet rains to arrive soon enough. The weather this time of year controlled much of what they could do. Once winter arrived that was it, most travel would be shut down, and forget about fighting in Straken. The snow would make that impossible.

He'd had almost no rest since the king's funeral last week. Following his meeting with Lord Karonin at her tower, he had volunteered to turn the estate into a training area for the new company of wizards they planned to raise, the War Wizards. It hadn't been difficult to convince his father-in-law, the estate's owner, especially when Otto explained that, in thanks, the Crown would be refunding their property taxes.

So far Otto had found twenty-two people with sufficient power to be useful on the battlefield. Men and women who for their entire lives had been looked down upon as lesser and dangerous, now had their moment to shine.

Magic was what would win the war and see Garenland become the center of a new empire. When the ordinary people saw how valuable wizards could be, they would be quick to accept them as equals. Or at the very least they'd realize messing with them would be unwise given their power. One way or the other, Otto intended to see wizards take their proper place as respected members of society.

Now that he knew how to use them, several of the items from Lord Karonin's armory would be a great help in the coming war. But first he needed wizards to wield them—most of them anyway.

He shook the stray thought away. He could explore his new magical toys later.

A lot had to go right before he and Wolfric could see their dreams come true. A chill breeze sent a shiver down his spine. If winter came early this year, their hopes of defeating Straken before the snows fell would come up short.

Speaking of Wolfric, he had already ordered the Northern Army to deploy and secure their northern province. It would take a few days for the three legions of soldiers to march and they would have to do it without wizards to support them. At least at first. Otto figured he needed a minimum of three weeks to get a few units up to speed enough for them to be useful.

He focused on the next person in line, a woman about

thirty, dressed in grimy, soot-covered clothes. She refused to meet his gaze, instead looking a fraction to his left.

"Your name?" Otto asked.

"Tabitha, my lord." Her voice was strong and steady even if her gaze wasn't.

Otto made a note in his ledger. "Tabitha, welcome. How many threads can you wield?"

"Six, my lord."

"Splendid. Show me."

She blinked like a fish just yanked from the river. "What do you want me to do?"

"Just conjure them from your hand and make them glow. Nothing complicated, just enough to demonstrate your strength."

Her face scrunched in concentration and she turned her hands palms up. Six thin threads of ether shot up from her fingers. Not terribly potent, but good enough to make the cut.

"That's fine, thank you." Otto jotted another note. "Please take your place with the other new recruits."

She bowed and moved a little way off to the side to join the others that had passed the first test. He sighed and looked down the line. Another fifty waited to be tested. If the ratios held, half of them would be strong enough to be of use and he'd have half his unit. Maybe more, probably less.

"Next."

A boy even younger than Otto stepped up to the table. Much like Tabitha, he was dirty from working at a foundry, skinny as a fence rail, and too nervous to look Otto in the eye.

"Name?"

"Cal, my lord." The boy's voice broke halfway through giving his name and his face reddened.

"Cal, and how many threads can you wield?"

"Two, my lord."

That wasn't enough to be worth taking to the battlefield. "I'm sorry, Cal. Five is the minimum to join."

"Please, Lord Shenk. I want to serve the kingdom. His Majesty's announcement that we'd all be true citizens filled me with such pride. I would die for the king should he ask it."

Otto stood and put a hand on the boy's shoulder. "King Wolfric doesn't want your life, he wants your loyal service. Just because you aren't strong enough to join the War Wizards today, doesn't mean you can't serve Garenland. This war will be long and difficult. We will have great need for armor and weapons. Your work in the forges and foundries will feed the army the weapons it needs to win. Remember that and do your utmost to create the finest steel you can. Take pride in serving in your own way and as you grow and increase your power, a time may come when you can join the army and fight Garenland's enemies directly."

Cal had swelled with pride as Otto spoke. "I will do my best to make the king proud, Lord Shenk."

"I have absolutely no doubt about that." Otto smiled and gave Cal's shoulder a final squeeze. "Off you go."

Otto sat back down and checked his ledger. Hopefully he'd find more Tabithas than he did Cals.

"You've become quite a leader, Lord Shenk."

Otto knew that voice. His head snapped up and he found himself looking into the kind, familiar features of his former teacher, Master Enoch. The months had been reasonably kind to him. He wore a new brown robe and his beard was combed and neatly trimmed. He certainly looked better than when Stephan had chased him out of Shenk Castle.

"Master, what a wonderful surprise." Otto moved around

4

the table and they shook hands. "I feared I'd never see you again."

"It was a rough winter, but I found work where I could. When word of the king's proclamation reached me, I headed for the capital as fast as possible. I can't believe how much you've accomplished since we parted ways. And married as well I understand. Congratulations."

Otto's good mood soured at the mention of Annamaria, but he quickly shook it off. The less he thought about his blushing bride the better.

"Thank you, Master. If you're willing, I'd be delighted to have you as my second-in-command as we train the new recruits."

"I'm not sure how much help an old man like me can be, but if you think I'll be of value, then I'm happy to serve you once more."

Otto reached back to the desk and removed from its box one of the mithril rings he'd brought from the armory. He'd brought only one box of the apprentice rings after his last visit, his plan being to give them to the strongest of his new wizards both to enhance their power even more and to make sure he kept them under control.

Lord Karonin had created the rings for her apprentices and the runes running inside the band allowed one who knew how to use them to take control of the wearer's magic and turn it against them in the event of a betrayal.

Not that Otto expected his former master to betray him, but he was the most powerful wizard Otto had encountered today, so why take chances?

He handed the ring to Enoch who gave it a curious look. "Silver?"

"Mithril. If you channel your threads through it, they become thicker and more powerful."

Enoch's eyes widened. "A very valuable item. How many do you have?"

"Not enough for everyone, unfortunately. I'll be giving them to the strongest recruits once they finish their training. I'm giving you this one now as a sign of your position as my second."

Enoch nodded and slipped the ring on his right middle finger. He tried channeling a single thread through the metal. It grew about twice as thick as normal. "Amazing. I'll do my best to be worthy of it."

"If you can help me get through this line of recruits, you'll already be more than worthy. We'd best get back to it. It's good to have you back with me, Master."

"It's good to be back, Lord Shenk, though I hardly think I'm worthy of being called your master anymore."

Otto shrugged. "Old habits I suppose."

They resumed the interviews and with Enoch's help, Otto finished ahead of schedule with forty cadets. Less than he'd hoped for, but not by too much.

"Shall we retire for dinner?" Otto asked. "You're welcome to stay at the mansion if you'd like."

"I couldn't impose. I'll stay at the barracks with the other wizards. Maybe I can give them a few pointers in the evening."

"As you wish." Otto was about to insist Enoch at least join him for the evening meal when a boy came running up, a scroll clenched in his hand. "Yes?"

"Lord Shenk? Message for you, my lord." He held out the scroll.

No seal, so it wasn't from Wolfric. Who'd be sending him a message? Otto flipped the boy a penny and took the paper.

"I'll leave you to it," Enoch said. "Good evening."

Otto nodded and turned toward the mansion. As he walked, he unrolled the scroll. He read the first line and froze. It seemed someone had seen him using his magic to redirect the assassin's blade and if Otto refused to pay him ten double eagles, he'd tell Wolfric. The meeting was supposed to take place tomorrow at dawn in a park outside the city.

Clearly whoever sent the scroll had no idea that Wolfric had helped plan his father's assassination. Still, better for everyone if Otto dealt with this quietly rather than bothering the new king. Wolfric had enough on his mind at the moment. Otto didn't know who'd be stupid enough to threaten him, but whoever it was would rue the day he troubled Otto Shenk.

CHAPTER 2

Axel Shenk stood, hands clasped behind his back, in General Varchi's office. The usually perfectly ordered desk was covered with maps and lists. With the Northern Army preparing to march, there was a great deal to be done. Instead of being weighed down by the work, the general appeared invigorated.

Axel knew exactly how he felt. Since he'd arrived from the trading post where his company had holed up, they'd all been working twelve-plus hours a day. What made it invigorating was the fact that they were finally free to strike back at their enemies.

King Wolfric—it was going to take a little while to get used to that change—had ordered them to march as quickly as possible and to drive Straken's forces out of Garenland and all the way back to their capital city of Marduke. If they could burn the city down, so much the better. It was an order they'd all been waiting for but had no hope of getting from the late king.

General Varchi finished the list he was working on and

stood up. "Sorry to keep you waiting, Axel. In recognition of your outstanding work getting your forces safely clear of the Straken army, I'm promoting you to commander. You'll take charge of Braddock's three companies as he's in no shape to return to the fight. I've already ordered replacements to fill out your ranks. I'll be counting on your scout company to lead the way north."

The general pinned a silver star on his tunic and Axel saluted, fist to heart. "We'll do our best, General. My men and I are eager for some payback."

"I can imagine. Yours was the only scout company to escape the sieges. That firsthand knowledge will be invaluable. Best get back to your people and prepare. The First and Second Legions march in the morning."

"One more thing if I may, sir?" At the general's nod Axel asked, "How is Commander Braddock?"

"According to the healers' report he'll live, but given the damage he took, he'll likely never see combat again. Braddock's a good man. I'll find a place for him in the command staff when he's ready."

"Thank you, sir." Axel saluted again, turned, and marched out.

When he was outside Axel couldn't hold back a snort of disgust. The only reason he and his company had escaped the siege was thanks to his brother coming to their rescue. Otto's lightning—Axel still shivered when he remembered the damage that spell had done—not any brilliant leadership from him was why they survived and he got a promotion. Still, it was better than the alternative.

The moment he was outside the office and down the nearby stairs, Axel was assailed by shouted orders, the thud of crates being moved, and the creaking of wagons. For every ten soldiers in the army, there was another person that saw to some noncombat role, whether it be cook, wagoner, or smith. The logistics were a nightmare and Axel was glad it was the general's problem and not his. Keeping track of his own men was difficult enough.

He found Cobb snarling at the new additions while they tended their gear. They'd been bivouacked outside the wall to make room for the quartermasters to load supplies inside. Not an ideal situation, but they'd handled worse, especially during the siege. They'd lost nearly a third of their fighting force in the battles with Straken. The new guys weren't raw recruits, but they weren't scouts yet either. That took a certain amount of training and they were about to get it the hard way.

Cobb barked a final order and stalked off to meet Axel. He took one look at the silver star and raised an eyebrow. "Commander, is it?"

"The general saw fit to give me Braddock's job. He's going to live, thank heaven. How do the new arrivals look?"

"They've all got combat experience so that'll help. I suspect we're going to be doing a lot more fighting than sneaking."

"I think you're right. I'm giving my cohort to Colten. You'll be my second. The general says we march in the morning."

Cobb spat and asked, "How far do you think we'll need to march? Straken already owns half the northern province. We might run into them tomorrow morning."

"I hope we do. It'll be good to see them running for a change."

"It'll be better to see them dying," Cobb said.

Axel wholeheartedly agreed.

The throne room was packed with merchants, from the richest of the rich to a man with three wagons and six mules. Wolfric didn't bother counting them, but he guessed there were at least three hundred. Certainly enough that the twenty royal guards on duty were looking at each other and out over the throng with more than a hint of fear. If anything bad should happen, they couldn't stop them all.

Wolfric wasn't worried. He'd met most of the merchants and to a man they were cowards that cared for little beyond gold and luxury. He doubted one in twenty had the will to swing a sword in anger.

Many of the merchants seemed to think perfume was a good idea. And maybe it was under less constricted circumstances. Right now, all the different scents were making his eyes water. Perhaps the plan was to poison him. If it was, they were well on their way.

How did Father put up with them all? This morning he'd spent hours with an only slightly smaller group of nobles who feared he planned to raise their taxes to pay for the war. For now, that wasn't necessary, but unless they wanted to be ruled by Straken, they'd pay whatever it took. He'd phrased it more diplomatically of course, but they got the message.

The nobles' complaints were mostly pro forma. They felt the need to be heard and he'd listened. That should satisfy them for a little while. The merchants, unfortunately, had more serious matters to discuss. They had chosen Edwyn Franken as their representative, a man Wolfric knew well. That should make this a little easier.

Edwyn was a mammoth figure, easily four hundred pounds, little of it muscle. His white silk robe resembled a tent. At least he hadn't seen fit to wear the many gold baubles he often favored. Now wasn't the time for ostentatious displays of wealth.

"The harvest is nearly complete, Your Majesty," Edwyn said. "The problem is, we're losing a third of our grain to bandits. At this rate, we won't have enough in the city granaries to last the winter. Something must be done."

"Are they only attacking the food shipments?" Wolfric asked.

Otto had warned him that Straken agitators were controlling the bandits and while the spies in the capital had been dealt with, those in the country were still roaming free. He'd have to speak to his friend and chief advisor when they met tonight.

"No, Majesty," Edwyn said. "They attack anything they encounter. Even a large force of guards isn't always enough to discourage them. It's strange. Bandits are usually looking for an easy target, not to fight skilled warriors."

"I see. Halt shipments for the time being." A thunderous protest rose from the gathered merchants. Wolfric patted the air with his hands. "Only for the time being. Once I get this bandit situation under control things will return to normal. A few days, a week at most. After all, it's better than losing your merchandise, isn't it?"

There was a bit more grumbling, but most nodded.

"We look forward to hearing from you again when it's safe to resume shipments, Majesty." Edwyn bowed with surprising grace for a man his size and the merchants filed out.

When the last of them had gone and the doors thumped shut Wolfric turned to the court secretary, a dour man in his sixties dressed in solid gray robes that matched the few wisps of hair swirling around his head. "Please tell me that was the last of them, Jennings."

"Captain Kelten requested a few minutes of your time, Majesty. I didn't get the impression that it was urgent, so if you wish me to put him off..."

Wolfric scrubbed his hand across his face. Kelten was Father's most loyal guard. If there was anyone he needed to keep tightly to heel, it was Captain Kelten. Best to see what he wanted. "No, I'll see him. He's not a man to waste my time with a minor matter. Show him in, but after that I'm done for the day."

Jennings bowed and shuffled toward the throne room doors. The old man poked his head out and a moment later the door opened and Captain Kelten strode in. He was dressed in mail and draped with a black and gold tabard featuring the royal griffin. An arming sword hung at his side and his blue eyes looked intensely at Wolfric. For a minor matter he seemed especially serious.

Kelten bowed and said, "Majesty, thank you for seeing me."

"Not at all. You've always been a great asset to the Crown. I hope I can count on you serving me as well as you did my father."

"That's what brings me here today, Majesty. The more I think about it, the more I can't help wondering why Straken would be so sloppy in their assassination of your father. The papers we found on the dead man's body were far too obvious. All I can think is that we're missing something. With your permission, I would like to look into the matter more closely. If there is a conspiracy against the Crown in Garen, we must find it before the enemy tries to do to you what they did to your father."

That was decidedly unlikely given that Wolfric had had a hand in his father's murder. He couldn't exactly point that out to Kelten. The man was the honorable sort who would strike

Wolfric down then kill himself to atone. If that happened, Garenland would fall into chaos. It simply couldn't be allowed. He'd speak to Otto about it later. For the moment they had time.

"If you feel there's still a danger, Captain, then by all means investigate. However, given the war and threats from Straken, you'll have to do it on your own and in whatever free time you have. I can't spare you from your regular duties, not now."

"I understand completely." Kelten bowed. "However long it takes, I will find the truth."

When Kelten had gone, Wolfric rubbed the bridge of his nose. If being king was this hard, how would he manage as emperor of an entire continent?

⟲

Captain Kelten finished another long shift and slogged back to his room in the palace barracks. His command had their own building and as captain he had a small room of his own. Nothing fancy, just an eight-by-eight bedchamber with a nightstand and footlocker. He led the unit responsible for protecting the palace while his counterpart, Commander Borden, oversaw the king's personal protection. They worked well together, but Kelten always got a slightly off feeling from Borden. The man was scrupulous in his work and there were no outward signs of corruption, but something still stuck in Kelten's craw.

He shook it off and turned down the path to the barracks. The day shift was finishing up and the night shift going on duty. The cook should have dinner just about ready and he was starving. The day after tomorrow was his first free day and he hoped to get going early. He intended to begin his search for the truth about the king's assassination. What exactly he was going to do was another matter. He knew next to nothing about Lothair and beyond asking around didn't know where to start his search. Kelten's skill set didn't really translate to investigation.

He stopped in his tracks and slapped his forehead. His skill set didn't, but there were plenty of watchmen in the city. If Lothair had ever been in trouble with the law, one of them would know about it. He had a place to start anyway.

CHAPTER 3

O tto sat with Wolfric at a small table in the king's private dining room. Not the little hole in the wall where they used to meet, but a much more opulent room furnished with the finest hardwood chairs, pure silver utensils, and porcelain plates featuring the royal griffin peeking out from under the gravy. Otto found he missed the simpler room and, judging from his friend's pensive stare, so did Wolfric.

It seemed he found the crown heavy. Not a great surprise since he'd gone from one of many important court functionaries to the man around whom everything rotated. Naturally he'd need some time to get used to his new situation.

Otto polished off his chicken, sighed, and pushed his plate away. "The food is still delicious, even if the dining room has changed. Want to tell me what's got you so down?"

"Bandits to start with. The bastards are interfering with the harvest. The merchants tell me we're at risk of running short this winter unless something's done. I don't suppose you could…"

"You're in luck. My former master has just arrived in the capital and agreed to help me with the wizards' training. I can leave the basics to him while I sort out the bandit issue. I'll need to borrow Hans and his men."

Wolfric waved a hand, his face slack with relief. "Take him and as many as you need. In fact, I'm going to assign Hans and his men to you permanently, then you won't have to keep borrowing him every time something comes up. There's another matter."

Otto didn't like the sound of that. "What sort of matter?"

"Captain Kelten doesn't believe the investigation into my father's assassination is really closed. He's requested to look into it more closely and I agreed." Wolfric raised a hand before Otto could speak. "I know I should have ordered him to drop it, but if I had, he still would have investigated and he probably would have begun to suspect me."

"You did exactly the right thing," Otto said. "The question now is, how do you want him dealt with? I can make him disappear or we can let him run around to his heart's content looking for a conspiracy that doesn't exist. That's much riskier since I have no idea who might have seen what as we were working. There's no telling what he might learn."

Wolfric took a sip of wine. He'd been cutting back since ascending the throne which was a relief to Otto. "We can't kill him. The royal guards are incredibly loyal to the man and he's still loyal to my father's memory. I've been quietly moving my own people into place, but it will take time to make the change. It would be far better for everyone if he was convinced that Straken was responsible and no one else."

"I have agents that can nudge him in the right direction. If worst comes to worst we can always kill him and purge all those loyal to him. I understand it's not ideal, but one night of blood might save a lot of trouble down the road."

"Hopefully it won't come to that. Now, how goes things with your wizards?"

"Good. We've interviewed every wizard in the city that wanted to volunteer and signed up forty. More will come in from the provinces as word gets out. We should have a hundred or near enough." Otto didn't mention the extortion threat. Wolfric had enough to worry about. "Training begins tomorrow. I hope to have them on their way north in three weeks."

"I wish I could be there on the front lines when Straken sees our wizards for the first time."

"It will be glorious."

Otto raised his glass and Wolfric clinked his against it.

King Uther of Straken paced in front of the blazing hearth in the great hall of Castle Straken. Despite the heat of the fire, he wore a heavy fur cloak with a coat of mail under it. His people saw him as a warrior king and he did his best to reinforce that image. Every few strides he muttered curses against whoever had killed the king of Garenland.

Uther hated the man, hated him as much as he hated every other citizen of Garenland, but he didn't want the king dead. Not yet at least. The weakling was the perfect foe. Too devoted to peace to fight a war, he would have let Uther march right up to Garen and kick in the palace gates.

Now he had to deal with the royal brat. What Wolfric lacked in experience, he made up for in aggression. Uther's scouts reported the enemy's Northern Army had already marched. His generals were searching for a place to engage, but it would be a fraught battle. The soldiers of Garenland were angry and eager for blood. They were also fighting for their homeland. That gave men courage.

His carefully laid plans were a mess and all because some idiot killed the king. When he found out who it was, he'd wring their neck.

A small side door opened and the Lady in Red entered. As always she was a vision draped in crimson silk. Some whispered she'd reached her current position by sleeping with his former spymaster then killing him and taking his place. Uther didn't know the truth any more than he knew her real name and he didn't care. She was far more effective in her job than her predecessor.

"What news?" Uther asked.

"The bandits continue to harass Garenland's merchants." Her velvety voice was almost a purr. "I have yet to insert a new agent into the capital. With the portal closed, all visitors are checked closely. In time one will make it through."

"Hopefully whoever it is will have better luck than the last fool you sent."

"To be fair, Xavier did excellent work for years. It was just bad luck that he got caught right before the war."

"I don't believe in luck and neither do you. Do we know how he was found out yet?"

She shook her head, sending her long red hair dancing. "All we have from the capital are rumors."

"That needs to change."

"It's my highest priority. What news from the border?"

Her expression soured with that last question. The generals refused to allow a woman to join their strategy sessions, even his spymaster. It wasn't worth the trouble to argue with them.

Uther would have happily replaced the hidebound fools, but he lacked anyone of equal skill to take their places.

He gave her the gist of the meeting. "They can't decide if they want to fight it out or retreat to the forts we captured."

"If they can force a siege, it would buy us time, then winter would buy even more. By spring we'll be so entrenched, it will cost them half their army to retake their territory and they'll be too weak to threaten Straken."

"True, but I'm loath to give back what we've already claimed. One battle must be fought to test their strength and determination. After that, we'll see."

She bowed, giving him a good look at the tops of her breasts. "As you say, my king."

CHAPTER 4

Otto was up, fed, and out of the mansion before Annamaria or Edwyn had begun to stir. In fact, as far as he could tell, only the cook and her helpers were awake as they began the daily bread. Despite the troubles, the Franken coffers still had plenty of gold to maintain their lifestyle. And given Otto's position in the government, he'd be sure to see things stayed that way. Not that he cared all that much about gold but having resources at his disposal was convenient.

Beyond the gate, he found Gold Ward quiet, but the business district already hummed with activity. The incessant clanging of hammers filled the air along with smoke and soot. He ignored it all and made straight for the eastern gate. His blackmailer said morning and Otto intended to be there as early as possible. Hopefully he could get this taken care of quickly and get back to more important matters, like killing bandits and training wizards.

A few hundred yards from the outer wall, the air cleared and he took a deep breath. It had been too long since he went for a walk in the woods. Even if he was going to meet black-mailers, he'd enjoy the trip. Busy as he was, he didn't know when the opportunity would present itself again.

The fields surrounding Garen gave way to new-growth forest. A path had been cut and smoothed leading to the park. The box filled with double eagles was heavy in Otto's shoulder bag. It weighed about twenty pounds more than his mithril sword. He'd left the weapon at home. He didn't need it to deal with whoever was waiting for him and he didn't want to risk the greedy fool demanding he hand it over.

Ten minutes of hiking brought him to a clearing in the middle of the forest. There were tables with attached benches where people, mostly those with money enough to take time off but no land of their own to enjoy it, could have a meal outside. At one of the tables sat a single figure in a worn gray tunic and matching trousers. A week of stubble covered his cheeks. Hard, dark eyes glared out from under heavy brows.

Otto shifted his vision to the ether, but if this man was a wizard, he wasn't using his magic at the moment. With a shrug, Otto walked over to the table. "I assume you're the blackmailer?"

"That's an ugly thing to say to someone you just met."

Otto raised an eyebrow.

"Also correct. Put the coins on the table and sit down so we can discuss our new arrangement."

Otto moved closer and pulled the box out of his satchel.

"You should know that I saw that one weak thread you used to deflect the assassin's dagger. I can wield seven. Just remember that if you get any ideas about binding me and cutting my throat. Also…" The man snapped his fingers.

A pair of strangers in leather armor stepped out of the nearby forest and leveled loaded crossbows at Otto. They wore full face helmets and from a distance Otto couldn't tell if they were men or women. Not that it mattered. A woman could shoot a crossbow just as well as a man.

As Otto set the box on the table, the wizard across from him formed an etheric shield around his entire body. It looked like he was using all seven threads' worth to protect himself. That wasn't a technique Master Enoch ever taught Otto, though he had learned it later from Lord Karonin's spell book. It would be interesting to know where this guy learned it and who his master was. Not interesting enough for Otto to go out of his way to spare the blackmailer's life however.

"Open it," the wizard said.

Otto obliged. The ten double eagles gleamed in the morning light. The wizard's eyes grew wide as he stared.

That was all the opening Otto needed.

A twenty-thread tentacle of ether slammed through the blackmailer's shield. The moment it touched his chest, five threads' worth of lightning crashed into his heart.

Quick as thought, Otto reformed the ether into a shield.

Two crossbow bolts skipped off it and flew away.

Before they could reload, he conjured a whip and slashed their crossbows in half.

A flick of his ring bound the crossbowmen in their tracks.

And that was it for the blackmailers. Otto gathered up his coin box and slipped it back into his satchel. The blackmailer groaned and shifted.

He survived that much lightning? Impressive.

Otto dropped a hand on the top of the wizard's head and conjured ten threads' worth of lightning directly into his brain. The man's eyes exploded and smoke shot out his ears. No doubt about him being dead now.

An infusion of ether strengthened Otto's body and he

dragged the dead man over to his cohorts who were still bound and rigid. He dropped the body at their feet and pulled the right-hand thug's helmet off.

He found himself staring into the eyes of a terrified young man in his middle teens. A dusting of freckles across his cheeks made him look even younger.

Otto released the binding around his head and asked, "Who are you and whom do you work for?"

The young man looked down at the body. "My name is Eric, she's Erin. Master Anders, he hired us to provide muscle. He said this would be an easy job and promised us each a double eagle just for showing up and pointing our crossbows at you. Please, I didn't know he was trying to blackmail the king's high councilor."

"Would it have mattered if you did?" Otto asked.

"Probably not," Eric admitted. "We were desperate for coin. Please spare us, my lord. Master Anders told us nothing beyond where and when to show up."

"Is Anders his family name or his given name?" Otto walked over and removed the second thug's helmet. Underneath he found a woman perhaps two years her partner's senior. She had freckles of her own and hard, angry eyes. "Your sister?"

"Yes, my lord. I don't know which name Anders is, I've never heard him called anything else."

Otto nodded and walked back in front of the young man. "Where did he hire you?"

"The Rusty Arms, a lot of mercenaries hang out there. People come to hire guards or muscle or whatever they need. I thought we'd finally gotten our lucky break." Eric shook his head and sighed. "What a joke. If you let us go, I promise you'll never see either of us again. Please, my lord. I beg you to spare us."

Otto considered the two so-called mercenaries. They were both younger than him and Otto had just turned eighteen. They had also proven themselves his enemy. There was no reason in the world he should spare them. They didn't know much, but it was enough to make his life difficult should they choose to do so. On the other hand, if he spared them, they would be grateful and potentially useful.

"I'll let you live on one condition," Otto said.

"Anything, my lord."

"You two will come to work for me. I have a small group of loyal servants that handle things that must be kept quiet. I will see you fed and given a small wage and you will do whatever I need done. Should you make any trouble, the others in the group will cut your throats and dump your bodies in a hole so deep no one will ever find you. Agreed?"

"Agreed," Eric said.

Otto freed Erin's head as well and raised an eyebrow.

"How do we know you won't just kill us both later?" she asked.

"You don't," Otto said. "However, if you refuse, I guarantee you'll die right here and now. If you try to run or betray me, you'll wish I killed you today. You know who I am and the resources I can call upon. Not to mention my personal abilities. It's your choice."

They had a short staring match. It seemed Erin was made of sterner stuff than her younger brother. At last she looked away and nodded. "Agreed."

"Excellent." Otto moved around behind them. "Don't move."

They held their heads rigid and he carved a pair of tiny runes into the backs of their necks and empowered them. They both hissed in pain, but he ignored their discomfort. Mercy was one thing, but trust another altogether. Outside of his mother and to a lesser extent Wolfric, Otto had learned to trust no one.

"What was that?" Erin asked when he freed them from the binding spell.

"Marker runes. If you try and run, they'll let me find you anywhere in the world and kill you in an instant. A simple precaution, in case you have second thoughts after we part company." He reached into his pants pocket and pulled out a handful of silver coins. "Here, your first payment. A reward for your wise decision-making. Get yourselves something to eat and some new weapons. Are you familiar with the Thirsty Sprite?"

"I know it," Eric said. "They don't open until afternoon."

"True. I need to return home. Meet me across the street from the tavern in two hours. If you're late, you're dead. Clear?"

"Perfectly, my lord." Eric bowed.

Otto looked at Erin who nodded once. It seemed that one hadn't fully accepted her situation. She would soon enough and if she didn't, well, mercenaries weren't that hard to come by.

A stream of fire reduced Anders's body to ash. With the blackmailer done away with, Otto became one with the ether and returned home. He had a great deal yet to do today and he had already wasted enough time.

CHAPTER 5

After leaving his two reluctant new recruits to fend for themselves, Otto traveled through the ether to the Franken estate. Back in his suite, he emerged from the closet with his mithril sword belted around his waist. He'd totally given up sleeping in the same room as Annamaria. She was liable to cut his throat in his sleep at this point. Only her friendship with Wolfric and his desire to keep things calm stopped him from doing away with the woman. Perhaps after her father died and Otto officially inherited the Franken estate and all its considerable wealth.

Otto put his horrid wife out of his mind, stepped into the hall, and made his way down the main staircase to the dining room where his father-in-law was busy devouring a meal big enough for five. Edwyn was dressed in his usual billowing white silk robes. He dropped a piece of fried bread as Otto approached.

"Hello, my boy. Did I hear you up early this morning?"

"Yes, I had an errand to run for Wolfric first thing. No big deal, but he needed someone he trusts to handle it." Otto sat,

27

made himself an egg sandwich, and poured a mug of wine. "So you know, the king has tasked me with sorting out the bandit problems."

"Wonderful! As if we don't have enough issues without the murdering scum making travel nearly impossible." Edwyn took a huge bite of bread and nearly choked as he swallowed.

"I was hoping you could give me some hint about where most of the attacks have happened. At least a place to start the hunt would be helpful."

Edwyn snorted. "They're all over. Just ride around in a wagon loaded with goods and they'll find you. Though now that I think about it, a third have happened in or around Shenk Barony. I intended to write your father but haven't gotten around to it."

Otto frowned, his food forgotten. Could the attack last year have actually been an attempt to assassinate his father? If Straken was behind the bandits, it would make sense to try and throw one of the central baronies into chaos.

"Thank you, Edwyn. You've given me much to think about." He left his half-eaten breakfast on the table and marched outside.

As soon as he was clear of the house, Otto turned toward the training grounds. Leaving Master Enoch to oversee the trainees while he was gone wasn't ideal, but he trusted his former master to cover the basics with them. Offensive spells, at least the few Otto wanted them to focus on, were simple enough and now that there was no danger to teaching them, they should have little trouble learning what they needed to know.

The wizards were staying in a hastily constructed barracks that had been built right next to the guards' barracks. Otto doubted there'd be any trouble between the two groups and if there was, he'd deal with it quickly. With everything happening, he didn't have time to waste on foolishness.

A quartet of wizards were standing around outside the front door chatting. As soon as they saw Otto they bowed and said, "Good morning, Lord Shenk."

He nodded. "Is Enoch awake yet?"

"One moment, Lord Shenk," Enoch said from inside. The old man emerged a few seconds later, his brown robe slightly askew. "I was just finishing breakfast."

"That's fine. Let's take a walk." Otto led his former master away from the barracks and toward an open stretch of grass they'd designated for spell practice. "I'm going to be away from the capital for a while. The bandit problem has grown intractable and the king has ordered me to investigate. I had hoped to be here to help with training the new recruits, but it looks like the task will fall entirely to you."

Enoch waved his hand. "I'm sure I can manage, my lord. I've spoken to most of them and they all have years of practice shaping the ether. They should have no trouble taking their existing skills and applying them to combat spells. I may not be able to use fire magic to amount to anything, but I can teach them to shape a fireball."

"Good, start with that. Once they get it down, shift to defensive spells they can use against enemy archers."

"Blinding Lights might also be valuable, especially against enemy cavalry. And perhaps some basic telekinesis."

Otto hadn't considered that, but it would be fast and use a good deal less strength than lightning or fire. "Good idea. And don't forget to have them work at building their strength to their personal maximum. Good luck, Master. I leave them in your capable hands."

They shook and Otto marched off to find his new soldiers.

It was time to see if Allen was as good at gathering information as he claimed.

⌒

E ric and Erin were standing on the street corner across from the Thirsty Sprite when Otto arrived. The duo had new crossbows in hand which were drawing nervous looks from the occasional passersby. He didn't know why the locals were so surprised, this wasn't the nicest part of the city after all. Granted it might not be so bad that you needed to carry crossbows. Let them think what they wanted, Otto had more pressing matters to worry him than a few nervous city dwellers.

"Glad to see you didn't run," Otto said when he reached them.

"You made it pretty clear what would happen if we did," Erin said.

"True, but there are plenty of people who, once I was out of sight, might be stupid enough to believe I didn't really mean what I said. That you two weren't among them speaks well of your future. Come along."

They fell in behind Otto as he crossed the street. The Sprite was closed for another three hours so at least he wouldn't have to worry about customers. Otto slammed his fist into the door three times and waited.

He was just about to send a shock into Allen's rune when the door opened and Ulf glowered out. He'd trimmed his thin mustache, so it only hung down to his chin. A loose green tunic covered his thin frame. An odd, spicy smell wafted out the door. Not unpleasant, but different from anything Otto had ever smelled.

Ulf moved aside and Otto led the way in. The chairs were still up on the tables. Some concoction was bubbling on the small stove in the center of the common room. That had to be the source of the odd smell.

Once the door was closed Otto asked, "Where's your employer?"

"Still in bed," Ulf said. "I'll wake him."

Ulf went and yanked a pull cord behind the bar three times. A faintly muffled chime rang. Otto walked over to take a closer look at whatever was cooking. Ulf joined him.

"What is this?" Otto asked.

"Hangover cure. Simple alchemy but comes in handy." Ulf bent over to stir the bubbling liquid.

As he did the ether swirled around in a way Otto had never seen. Ulf was clearly affecting the potion through the ether, but as far as Otto knew, the man wasn't a wizard and he wasn't working magic the way a wizard would. Otto would have to add alchemy to the list of questions he had for Lord Karonin. It seemed he'd barely left the Arcane Lord's tower when more questions occurred to him.

The creak of a door pulled him back to the moment. He turned to see Allen emerge from the back room, shirtless, barefoot, and his hair in disarray. His eyes were closed and he was fighting a yawn. Seemed Otto had disturbed his beauty sleep.

"I told you not to wake me until an hour before opening," Allen said.

"I'm sorry the timing of my arrival wasn't convenient," Otto said.

Allen's eyes popped open and he stared at Otto before shifting his gaze to Eric and Erin. "Lord Shenk. I wasn't expecting to see you again this soon. How may we be of service?"

"It's time to see if your skill at gathering information is as good as you claimed. A man named Anders, a wizard, tried to blackmail me. He hired these two for muscle. You're going to find out everything you can about him. Was he working for someone or was he acting alone like he said? My work is too important to risk some unknown enemy derailing things. These two will help you. Should they prove less than helpful, feel free to kill them and dump their bodies. I'm going bandit hunting. I want answers when I get back."

"That's not much to go on," Allen said.

"It's all I have. You'll need to figure the rest out on your own. Oh, you might get a visit from Captain Kelten. He's not fully convinced Lothair acted just at the behest of Straken. I'm sure the man will eventually learn Lothair knew you. I recommend you be circumspect." Otto turned and stalked toward the door. Halfway there he stopped and turned. "When I return, you and I, Ulf, are going to have a chat about alchemy. The process is fascinating."

Ulf bowed. "I am at your service, Lord Shenk."

Otto nodded. At least one of his new servants knew how to show proper respect. Still, if Allen got results, Otto didn't care a lick about his attitude.

CHAPTER 6

Despite Cobb's prediction, Axel's scout unit didn't encounter the first sign of Straken's soldiers until midafternoon on the third day of their march. And even then, it wasn't men they encountered but an abandoned camp about two days old. Blackened fire pits were scattered around and judging from the numbers he guessed at most five hundred men had spent a single night in the clearing.

Axel ordered Colten's cohort to find their trail and report back. It shouldn't take the talented young man long. They needed to keep moving lest the rest of the army catch up. The three companies under his command were riding about two hours ahead of the main body of the First and Second Legions. It was their job to find the enemy and give plenty of warning to the units behind them. So far all they'd found was a lot of trees and empty road. It was impossible to think Straken's army hadn't made it this far given the complete lack of opposition they'd faced.

The Northern Army was formidable, but Straken wasn't

known for their cowardice. They'd want to fight soon enough. The only questions were where and when.

Cobb guided his mount up beside Axel. "Figured we'd have at least bloodied our swords by now. What are the bastards waiting on?"

"I wish I knew. Have the men make a thorough search of the area. Given the hour, once the rest of the army arrives, it will be time to make camp."

Cobb nodded and rode off, bellowing orders. To listen to him you'd never guess Cobb could move so quietly he could cut your throat before you knew he was there.

Axel watched as his men dispersed to carry out his orders. The worst thing about being in charge was not knowing what you were supposed to do while you waited for information.

The answer came five minutes later when Colten came racing into the clearing, his horse whipped into a lather. No way would he have abused the animal like that if he hadn't found something important.

The scout reined in and saluted. Behind him his men came rushing in behind their leader. Axel ignored them and focused on Colten. "Lieutenant, report."

"We found them, sir," Colten said between gasps. "The Straken army, a good chunk of it anyway, is dug in about five miles up the road. They picked a good spot, sir. The forest is thick on either side of their position, so we'll have to funnel through a narrow entrance to the field where they're set up."

"Numbers?" Axel asked.

"We didn't hang around to count. As soon as I saw what they were up to we hightailed it back."

"Okay. Get a fresh horse from one of the men. I'm going to have to take a look myself. Cobb!"

His second joined him while Colten went to find a fresh mount. "News, my lord?"

Axel gave him the gist of Colten's report. "If it's as ugly as it sounds, the Northern Army is in for a tough time. Send a squad to inform the general we've found the enemy and not to advance past the clearing. You, Colten, and I are going to take a closer look."

Cobb relayed his orders and once the squad was on its way, the three of them rode out, Colten in the lead. As they moved further down the road, the forest on either side grew thicker, especially the undergrowth. It would kill the infantry to force their way through that mess of briars and thickets. The Straken general clearly knew what he was doing.

Eventually the forest opened into another clearing. They reined in well back and dismounted, tying the horses to a handy tree. On foot, they snuck out to the edge of the trees. Axel slipped between a pair of trunks to better avoid detection. What he saw did nothing to reassure him.

The enemy had dug in and built a crude earthen fort, with deep trenches and rows of spiked barricades to force their movement into tight killing fields. They'd built the fort right in the middle of the road. There was no way past them that wouldn't expose the legions to archery fire. Worse, even from a distance a trio of catapults and two ballistae were visible. The heavy siege weapons would shred their formations.

Axel took his spyglass out of a padded case he kept in his satchel. The soldiers were moving around too much to allow a truly accurate count, but Axel guessed at least half a legion guarded that fort and, given the strength of their position, it would be an expensive proposition to wipe them out.

And they had to wipe them out. The army couldn't leave such a large force at their rear. The trick was going to be doing it without incurring so much damage they couldn't continue on and face the remaining Straken forces.

"Don't look good," Cobb said.

"No, it doesn't." Axel put his spyglass away and scratched his chin. "Colten, can we find a way around them?"

"Small groups can manage the forest easily enough, sir, but not the whole army. Not unless we want to move five miles a day. There are other roads, but we'd have to backtrack almost to headquarters and who knows what we'll find."

"And in the meantime, this lot will be improving their position. Okay, I've seen enough. It's the general's call. Let's go report in."

They slunk back to the horses and returned to the clearing to wait for the rest of the Northern Army. Axel didn't envy General Varchi this decision. Whatever he decided, there was going to be blood and dying, much of it on the Garenland side.

ᓂ

Axel finished his report while General Varchi paced in his command tent. The two-room tent was dominated by a folding table covered with a map of the northern province. There was little in the way of comforts beyond a cushion for his camp chair. The general took pride in living rough in the field like his men and everyone respected him for it.

The news of a large blocking force in a rough fortification wasn't exactly a shock; they'd been expecting resistance for over a day now, but an open battle had been seen as more likely. Axel wasn't as well versed on the history of war between the two countries as the general, but he knew enough to understand that Straken wasn't famous for its defensive actions. In every war since the fall of Lord Karonin, they'd been the aggressor. Finding they were skilled defenders came as a surprise.

When Axel finished his report he added, "I wish I had better news, sir."

The general stopped pacing and faced him. "It is what it is, Commander. We knew they'd try something, now it's up to us to overcome it. I want a scouting party sent out tonight. If there are hidden pits or other traps, we need to know. If possible, I'd like you to grab a prisoner. We know far too little about what Straken has planned."

"I doubt a perimeter guard will have much in the way of intel, but we'll see what we can do. Is there anything else, sir?"

"No. I'll expect your report at first light. Dismissed."

Axel touched fist to heart and marched out of the tent. As soon as he was outside, he turned toward his unit's camp. Dozens of fires burned all around the clearing and the smell of cooking stew filled the air, reminding Axel how hungry he was. He wouldn't eat too heavily with the night raid coming, though. An overfull stomach might slow him down.

A quick scouting run would be best accomplished by a small group, maybe just half a dozen. Colten and Cobb for sure, and the big man Grubber could handle a prisoner on his own, so he'd come. The former housecarl wasn't much of a scout yet, but he was quiet enough when he had to be. A couple of the veterans would round out the group. They'd leave after the sun set but before the moon fully rose, that would give them maximum cover.

Five hours later Axel and his chosen men started out for the enemy camp. They went on foot lest a stray whinny alert the enemy to their approach. As they marched past the camp's sentries Cobb said, "You're going to be one of those commanders, aren't you?"

Axel shot him a look. "Care to elaborate?"

"You know, one of those commanders who can't delegate. You have to be in the lead on every mission. One of those."

"I suppose I am. I'd rather share the risk than sit around worrying. I know, sitting around and worrying is the commander's job, but I'm not some old man"—he shot Cobb a pointed look—"who's going to slow the youngsters down. Besides, it's bad enough the general has to get his information secondhand. Thirdhand would be even worse. Any other complaints?"

Axel pretended not to hear when Grubber asked Colten, "Are they always like this?"

"Only before a dangerous mission. The banter helps lighten the mood." Colten chuckled. "If they weren't bickering, I'd really be worried."

The sun had fully set when they reached the edge of the woods. With Axel in the center, they dropped to their bellies and started to crawl. No words would be spoken until they returned to the road. Any traps would be noted for later.

Foot by foot they crawled toward the enemy fortification, only the glow of the distant torches lighting their way. Axel checked in front of him, dragged himself ahead, checked another two feet, and repeat, over and over. It was painfully slow and he found no traps along his route. Hopefully the Straken forces had focused on building the fort and hadn't gotten around to traps. It would make the approach that much less dangerous. Catapult stones, ballista bolts, and arrows were enough to worry about.

At last, after he knew not how long, Axel reached the outer wall of the fort. He was close enough to hear the men on the other side grumbling about the toughness of the meat. There were no pickets outside the fence line so grabbing a sentry wasn't happening. There was simply no way they could grab someone without getting spotted.

He looked left and right. The rest of the squad had eased up beside him. If they couldn't get a prisoner, maybe they could at least get some useful information. Axel pointed at his ears, then at the fort, then left and right. Finally he raised a single finger to indicate a one-hour time limit.

His team spread out to eavesdrop. Maybe they'd get something for their effort, but he wasn't holding his breath. Axel would remain here and no doubt learn about the enemy's culinary habits.

For the first ten minutes he didn't hear much of anything. The fires popped and crackled and someone belched, that was all. At least it was until a stern voice said, "You boys holding up okay?"

That had to be someone in charge. Maybe not the base commander, but a sub-commander for sure.

"We're okay, sir. Getting sick of dried venison, but other than that no complaints," one of the soldiers said.

"When do you think the Garenlanders will arrive?" another man asked.

"Tomorrow or the next day," the leader said. "Last our scouts reported, the Northern Army was forty miles out and that was a day ago. We'll be seeing action soon I have no doubt."

"Good," the first man said. "We've been sitting around doing nothing for a month."

There were murmurs of agreement and a few boasts but none of the overconfidence Axel hoped for. Battle was an ugly thing and these men sounded like they'd seen some of it. Their deployment had been easy up until now. But the Northern Army would change that soon enough.

"Don't get too excited," the leader said. "The men of Garen-land might be weak-kneed cowards, but their generals aren't stupid. When they come, it won't be only them that bleeds. Finish your meal, guard change in twenty minutes."

There were a bunch of "yes, sirs" followed by the faint scuff of boots. That they knew the Northern Army was coming didn't surprise Axel. They'd assumed enemy scouts were watching them the whole way. It was unavoidable.

The rest of the hour passed with nothing of interest said. Cobb was the first to return. He caught Axel's eye and shook his head. Nothing useful. The rest of the men arrived one after the other. It wasn't until Colten arrived last that he got a thumbs-up. The scout must have heard something useful.

Axel motioned them back toward the woods. It was every bit as slow and painful crawling out as it was crawling in. At last they stood, out of sight of the fort.

"Report," Axel said.

"I found a single pit lined with stakes," Cobb said.

"Same," Grubber said.

"I found one as well," Colten said. "I also overhead the fort commander talking. Straken's forces have occupied our scout fortresses in addition to building new ones right on the border."

That confirmed what they already guessed. "What about the main Straken force?"

Colten shook his head. "No mention of it. Assuming they occupied our forts and the new ones at the same strength we did, how many soldiers would that leave wandering the province?"

"We have no idea what their total force numbers, but I'd guess probably ten thousand less than it would otherwise have been. Let's get back. I need to make a map for the general then get some sleep. Tomorrow's going to be a long day."

"As opposed to today?" Cobb asked.

Axel smiled grimly in the dark. Unlike today, tomorrow was apt to be a red day.

CHAPTER 7

llen tapped his fingers together and pondered the mess his new master had dropped in his lap. Or perhaps messes would be more accurate. He glanced across the crowded taproom where the brother and sister sat at a corner table. The pair had hardly spoken to him after Lord Shenk left. Once they closed up for the night, he'd have to have a serious talk with them. If they'd held anything back, he needed to know. He'd heard of the Rusty Arms tavern, but it was a third of the way across the city. Not a short walk by any means.

And what was he supposed to do about Captain Kelten? Obviously, the truth was out. Allen was nearly as guilty as Lothair. He'd been feeding information to a Straken spy for years after all. Only Lord Shenk's goodwill kept him from the end of a rope.

He shook his head. Time enough to worry about Kelten when he came knocking. For now, Allen needed to focus on this wizard, Anders.

Ulf tugged on his sleeve and pointed at the mercenaries.

Even after getting his voice back, he spoke hardly a word.

Eric and Erin had gotten up from their table and were making their way to the door. Allen left his post behind the bar and moved to cut them off.

"Where do you think you two are going?"

"Home," Erin said. "It's been a long day and we're beat."

"Shake it off. We close at midnight then the four of us are going to have a long talk about a certain dead wizard. After that it's across the city to the Rusty Arms."

"We can do it in the morning," Erin said. "I'm so tired my eyes are crossed."

"You're both aware of what our mutual employer is capable of, correct?"

They both blanched and nodded. Good, at least they understood that much. "If we don't have this mess sorted out when he gets back, we're all dead. If that means you lose a little beauty sleep, so be it."

"The thing is," Eric said, "the Arms closes at eleven. We can't make it there tonight, even if we left now."

Allen frowned. The kid didn't strike him as a liar, his face was too open. "What kind of tavern closes that early? I close at midnight and that's considered early by some."

"The kind that opens at nine in the morning," Erin said. "It's a hangout for soldiers, people that get up early."

"Fine, we'll have our talk now and meet up again at noon tomorrow to head over. Follow me." Allen led the way back to his private office. It also served as his bedroom, but he didn't care if the pair saw his mattress. "Ulf, watch the bar."

Allen figured people would be surprised by how tidy he kept his room. There was a single neat pile of papers on one corner of his desk, a quill and ink pot, and a dirk that served as his letter opener. His narrow cot was behind the desk and fully covered by his blanket.

He sat on the edge of his desk and said, "Let's have it. Everything that happened the day you were hired until you met Lord Shenk."

"It was only two days," Eric said. "Anders hired us at the Arms last night and we met him this morning at the park."

"Walk me through it," Allen said. "Even a small detail might be important."

"We went to the Arms for dinner, same as always," Erin said.

"We go there because they offer a bowl of stew and a roll for a silver penny. Cheapest meal you can find in that neighborhood," Eric added.

Erin shot him a look and he shut up. "Anyway, it was almost nine when Anders showed up. He talked to the bartender who pointed him our way. Don't know why, but we weren't complaining. It's been three weeks since we had a job. He walks over to our table and says if we back him up in the morning, he'll give us a double eagle."

"You trusted him?" Allen asked.

"We were desperate," Eric said, drawing another glare. "It's not like we had employers beating down our door. It was worth the chance for that much money. Didn't exactly work out how we planned."

Allen knew the feeling. Lord Shenk had a way of changing your plans the hard way. "Go on."

"So we agreed," Erin said. "Anders nods and tells us to meet him at the park before dawn. When we show up, he tells us to hide and come out when he gives the signal. A little while later this rich guy walks into the clearing and they start talking. We get the signal and make our appearance. Next thing we know,

Anders is dead, our weapons are so much scrap, and we've got a seriously angry wizard bearing down on us. When he offered us a job instead of a burial, we agreed. He marked us with his magic and said to meet him outside your place. You know the rest."

Allen nodded. There really wasn't much to go on. "Would you say the owner of the tavern knew Anders?"

Eric shrugged. "No idea. They didn't seem especially friendly, but that doesn't mean much."

"He'll be the one we need to talk to. In the meantime, you two can stay in the garret upstairs. I don't want you getting any ideas about warning the wizard's friends."

"We don't know the wizard's friends," Erin said.

"So you say, but how do I know if you're telling the truth? If you think I'll risk angering Lord Shenk, you're crazy."

Erin reached for the dagger at her belt. "And if we refuse?"

"You two can kill me, no doubt about that." Allen turned and revealed the mark on the back of his neck. "But he'll know and I suspect you know what will happen next."

Her throat worked as she tried to swallow. Finally Erin put her dagger away. "Fine, a bed's a bed."

Allen smiled. He had no idea if Lord Shenk would actually know if they killed him, much less care, but the bluff worked. Now he just needed to figure out what was actually happening before the wizard killed him himself.

The commander of the Garen city watch, Norman Trask, a pot-bellied man in his fifties who'd lost an arm in some fight long ago, sat behind his desk and puffed away at his pipe while Kelten explained his theory and what he needed.

The commander wore a black and gold uniform with a griffin patch on the right shoulder. His office in watch headquarters wasn't much, but it was private and had a door.

Trask didn't answer to Kelten and any help he offered would be out of the goodness of his heart and a desire to see justice done. The city watch was its own organization and while Kelten could certainly bully a low-ranking watchman into following his orders, no way was that going to work with Trask.

In fact, there was a history of bad blood between those who served in the city proper and those who served in the palace. The watch tended to regard the palace guards as stuck up and the palace guards saw the watch as not having what it took to really protect the king. Kelten had tried his best to put an end to that sort of thinking, but he knew plenty of the old-timers on both sides still thought that way. His only hope was that Trask wasn't one of them.

When he finally finished Trask said, "So you don't buy the theory that your assassin was working for Straken?"

"I think he probably was, but I don't think that's all there is to it. I'll be happy to be proven wrong, but the king died on my watch and I have to know for sure. Can you tell me anything about Lothair?"

Trask drummed his fingers on a short stack of paper in the center of his desk and looked Kelten up and down. Finally he said, "You're not the only one curious about that incident. The king dying makes you look bad, well, just think how I feel. A ring of Straken spies was operating in my city and not only did I have no clue, but some amateur from the sticks stumbled on them and helped bring them in. He made me and my men look incompetent at best and complicit at worst."

"I've heard no talk in the palace questioning the watch's

loyalty. Certainly King Wolfric has offered no complaint in my hearing."

"It's probably more in my head than in reality, yet I can't stop thinking we should have done something."

Kelten's smile held no humor. "Then we have the same problem. I can't stop thinking about my failure either. Perhaps together we can find some satisfaction."

"Perhaps." Trask picked up the papers and held them out. "This is everything we know about the incident and Lothair himself. He had some minor brushes with the watch as a teen, but lived an honest, or at least outwardly honest, life since. He ran with another kid named Allen, no known family name, during his rowdy years. The man owns a tavern called the Thirsty Sprite. I've been debating how best to approach him. Maybe I'll just let you handle it."

Kelten took the bundle of papers. "It would be my pleasure. Thank you for your help."

"Keep me informed." Trask held out his hand and Kelten shook it.

It seemed he wasn't going to have to manage this on his own after all.

CHAPTER 8

Axel stood with his men in the clearing where the Northern Army had gathered. General Varchi had listened calmly as Axel gave his report over the pounding of nearby construction crews. Four pit traps guarded the approach to the enemy fort. They estimated two thousand enemy soldiers were stationed there. In a straight fight, they wouldn't last five minutes against the ten thousand men arrayed against them. Given their defensive position they could inflict serious damage to the Northern Army, just not enough to stop them.

The rest of Axel's meager intel was just confirmation of what they already expected. Naturally the enemy would make use of Garenland's abandoned forts, it only made sense. Retaking their territory was going to be a long, miserable slog and it would only get worse once they reached Straken itself. There, they'd have to worry about the entire population fighting them.

At least the Third Legion was expected to catch up to them in a day or two. With the Northern Army at full strength, they should be able to plow through any opposition.

The pounding stopped as the engineers finished the eight-foot-long bridges that would span the pits and serve as huge shields for the first wave to approach the enemy position. Axel was relieved that his men wouldn't be in the vanguard. They were scouts, not heavy infantry. They'd stay in the rear and help the spotters. If the enemy had any forces hiding some-where nearby, they would be responsible for sounding the alarm.

The First Legion would be leading the charge. The soldiers wore heavy banded mail and carried round shields that covered them from neck to knee. Enemy archers would have little to aim at with that much steel protecting them. It was the catapults that worried Axel. Armor or not, a twelve-pound stone slamming into a soldier would do him no good.

General Varchi emerged from his tent dressed in red-lacquered plate armor, a gold-hilted broadsword on his hip. His helmet had a crimson streak of horsehair running from back to front. He looked every bit the general. A century of soldiers fell in around him. The elite guard would keep any threat from getting too close, not that the general would be on the front line.

"Ready to give those Straken bastards a taste of Garenland steel, men?" the general asked.

A roar went up from the assembled soldiers. They knew many of them would die, but this was the moment they'd been waiting for. Now they could take the enemy with them.

"Then let's go!" General Varchi shouted.

Sub-commanders barked orders and soon the designated groups had taken up the mobile bridges. Like a great, ponderous serpent, the First Legion marched out. The general fell in at the rear. As they passed, he motioned for Axel to join him.

Axel ran over. "Sir?"

"Leave your men in camp and come with me. I don't want to risk the scouts, but your insights would be valuable."

"Yes, sir." Axel turned and used two hand signals to let Cobb know they were staying behind and that he was in command. That done, he moved to stand beside the general as they walked toward the fort. "Do you think we'll take them in the first rush, sir?"

"We outnumber them three to one. There will be loses, that's unavoidable, but I expect the First Legion to live up to its reputation."

They marched on, silent but for the crash of their boots on the hard earth and the clank of their armor. No effort was made at stealth. The legion wanted Straken's soldiers to know they were coming. Let them fear Garenland's revenge.

It took half an hour to reach the edge of the clearing. The companies with the portable bridges led the way.

Arrows arced out, slamming into the wood, but avoiding flesh. A catapult thunked, but the stone missed, passing between two groups.

The ballista bolt that followed was better aimed. It pierced two soldiers and sent them flying backward. Axel couldn't help wincing in sympathy. His time in the army had done nothing to prepare him for large-scale battle. The noise, the stink, it was all overwhelming. He gripped the hilt of his sword to steady himself.

The real fighting hadn't even started yet.

They bridged the pits, losing only ten men in the process. With the way secure, the rest of the legion marched, shields locked in the front and the men in the rear protecting the heads of the men in front of them.

Arrows were deflected.

Stones smashed through, taking half a dozen men at a shot.

The legion never stopped and never broke rank.

"A glorious sight, are they not?" General Varchi asked.

Axel nodded, not trusting himself to speak. Glorious wasn't the word he would have used, but it wasn't wrong either. The front rank reached the nearest earthen berm. Hand-to-hand fighting began. The clash of steel on steel was deafening.

Axel almost didn't hear the first arrow slam into the neck of one of the general's honor guard.

The man dropped, leaving a gap in the shield wall.

Axel grabbed the general and yanked him aside just before an arrow flew through the space he'd occupied a moment before.

"Sniper!" Axel shouted. "Close ranks! Shields up!"

The honor guard was shifting to plug the opening even before Axel's shouted order. They'd gotten their position for a reason; they knew their business.

Axel crouched beside General Varchi. "Are you okay, sir?"

"Fine, thank you, Axel. The battle?"

Axel tried to look through the openings between the guards' legs but couldn't see anything. "I don't know."

"Fighters coming," one of the honor guard called.

"How many?" the general asked.

"Fifty."

"Why would they send fifty against a hundred?" General Varchi asked. "It's suicide for those men."

"They want to open a gap in the shield wall," Axel said. "Give their archer another shot at you. I need four men!"

Four guards pulled back and the others closed ranks.

"No matter what happens," Axel said to the four, "keep your shields up and protect the general. We'll handle the enemy fighters."

The guards raised their shields and locked them together over General Varchi. A stray arrow had no hope of getting through that. Axel drew his sword and moved to join the rest of the guards.

Over one of their shoulders he could see Straken rangers approaching. They were in no rush. All they needed was a momentary lapse in concentration from the guards to finish the general. Axel had no intention of giving it to them.

"Charge!"

The honor guard roared and lunged forward, swords drawn.

They took the rangers by surprise. That was all the advantage they needed.

Axel hacked down one man and ran a second through. By the time he yanked his blade free the battle had ended.

The fight was brutal, but short. Rangers might be good in an ambush, but against heavily armed and armored opponents, their short blades were nearly useless. The honor guard took minor wounds but lost no one.

A few minutes passed and no more arrows were forthcoming. For now, at least, it appeared the general was safe. Not that anyone was going to take chances.

Axel turned his attention to the fight at the fort. It looked nearly over. Garenland soldiers littered the ground, but the day was theirs.

General Varchi straightened and stood beside him. His guards were still forming a tight circle; their gazes never stopped darting about.

"You saved my life," the general said. "Thank you."

"I'm happy to be of service, sir. And I apologize if I over-stepped my bounds ordering your men around."

"Not at all. That was quick thinking. I never imagined they'd use the fort and the men inside as bait to take a shot at me. Straken has a reputation for brutality, but using your soldiers like that... It sticks in my craw, enemy or not."

Axel nodded, but didn't really care. The more dead Straken soldiers the better as far as he was concerned. The manner of their deaths didn't concern him in the least. Their injured were being gathered and loaded on stretchers to return to camp. Axel suspected the army would take a few days to recover before moving on.

He turned to glare at the forest. The day might be theirs, but with rangers out there, it was only a matter of time before the enemy made another attempt on the general's life. Axel meant to find them and finish them before they had the chance.

CHAPTER 9

Allen rolled out of bed early, far too early for his tastes, but if he was going to have Lord Shenk's answers when he returned, there was no time to waste. Yesterday's clothes were hanging on the back of his office chair. When he pulled the tunic over his head, his hand brushed the slightly raised patch of skin where Lord Shenk had carved the magical brand on the back of his neck. He could still feel the lightning coursing through his body. That wasn't something Allen ever wanted to experience again.

He finished dressing and carried his baldric and sword out into the common room. Ulf and the mercenaries were already up and drinking steaming cups of tea. The scent of frying bacon filled the room and made his mouth water. Ulf poured a fourth mug of tea and added a little something extra from his potion flask. He handed it to Allen without a word and returned to tending breakfast. Allen sipped and sighed as strength and vitality flooded into him.

The potion cured a hangover, but it worked just as well if you were only tired. Allen drank it as seldom as possible lest he become dependent. Ulf assured him there was no risk of it, but he refused to take the chance.

Allen sat beside the mercenaries. "Anything I need to know about this place before we head over?"

Eric shrugged. "It's a hangout for mercenaries. Your questions might not be welcome, though if you offer coin for information you should be safe enough. There aren't many fights or anything."

"The mercenaries get enough fighting when they're working," Erin said. "They don't need more of it when they're between jobs. We go our own way when this is over, yes?"

"As far as I'm concerned," Allen said. "Though Lord Shenk might have different ideas."

Erin's face twisted. "How long will he keep us bound to him? We didn't do anything!"

"You pointed weapons at him," Allen said. Ulf set four plates loaded with bacon and bread on the table and sat down again. "Be grateful he didn't just kill you on the spot. There are worse jobs than serving the second-most-powerful man in the kingdom."

"Is that why you serve him?" Eric asked around a mouthful of bread. "Because he's powerful?"

"I pointed a different kind of weapon at him. Fortunately, he found himself in need of my skills. Others who threatened him weren't so lucky. I know he's young, but he was raised in the nobility. They learn to be ruthless from the moment they're born. My advice is keep your heads down, do as you're told, and give him no reason to question your loyalty."

Halfway through breakfast someone rapped on the door. Allen frowned and got up. Who could be calling this early? The Sprite didn't open for hours.

He unlocked the door and looked out. A tall, broad-shouldered blond man stood there. He wasn't dressed like a soldier, but Allen would have bet all he owned that the man was a fighter.

"Can I help you?" Allen asked.

"My name is Kelten, captain of the king's guard. I'm doing some follow-up on the assassination. I understand the killer was a friend of yours. May I come in and ask you a few questions?"

Allen stepped aside. This was the meeting Lord Shenk had warned him about. He hadn't expected it so soon. "Please. I'm happy to help in any way I can. Poor Lothair. He was always a good guy. I had no idea he'd get involved with enemies of the kingdom."

"I apologize if I'm interrupting your breakfast."

"Not at all. We were just finishing up." Allen led him to a table well away from the others and pulled out a chair. "Can I offer you a drink?"

"No, thank you." Kelten sat and Allen joined him. "What can you tell me about Lothair?"

"We grew up together, got in trouble together, nothing serious mind you. Childish pranks mostly. I got a job here and he found work in Gold Ward somewhere. We drifted apart after that as childhood friends often do. Until last spring when he showed up on my doorstep. He'd lost his job and needed somewhere to stay. Since I own the tavern now, I offered him a job as a bouncer. I thought everything was good until he disappeared ten days or so before the assassination." Allen shook his head. "I can't imagine what happened to my friend to make him a killer."

"He seemed okay while he was working here?" Kelten asked.

"As far as I could tell. He went out during his time off, but he never said what he was doing. Could he have already been working for Straken? I'd never forgive myself if there was some sign and I missed it."

"We don't yet know when he first made contact with enemy agents. That's one of the things I'm trying to pin down. Can you give me a more exact date that he started working for you?"

Allen pursed his lips and tapped his chin. "It was early spring, I'm sure of that. Mid-May perhaps? I'm sorry I can't be more exact."

"That's fine. It's a starting point anyway." Kelten chewed his bottom lip and Allen could almost see the wheels turning behind his eyes. At last he said, "I can't think of anything else right now, but if I do would it be okay if I stopped by for another chat?"

"Anytime, Captain, though I'm seldom up this early so please consider an afternoon visit."

They stood, shook hands and Allen led him to the door. When he'd gone and the door was locked again Ulf said, "You should try acting."

Allen grinned. It was a pretty good performance. Hopefully Captain Kelten bought it.

໑

His brush with the good captain left Allen without enough appetite to finish his breakfast so the four of them set out across town. The city was bustling as the forges churned out weapons to support the war effort. People were talking and seemed more upbeat than they had in a while. You'd hardly know there was a war on.

No one gave the four of them more than a passing glance as

they walked. Allen waved to the few acquaintances he saw but made no effort to stop and chat. He wanted to get this business sorted out and fast. Kelten was a problem he could have done without, but with any luck he'd seen the last of the man. Either way, he had more pressing matters at the moment.

The Rusty Arms sat in the middle of a working-class neighborhood with a dry goods store on one side and a three-story tenement on the other. A pair of toughs in leather armor stood beside a front door partially covered with chipped brown paint. The tavern's sign featured a gauntlet holding a mug, carved with greater detail than a place like this should have been able to afford. Probably the work of someone looking to pay off their tab.

The toughs looked them over as they passed but made no move to stop them. Inside, the taproom was half full of armed and armored men and women that would have looked more at home in an army barracks, albeit the army barracks of a very poor country.

Behind the bar stood a tall, stout man in his fifties, a stained apron covering a sprawling gut and a thick mustache hanging past his chin.

"Is he the one Anders spoke to?" Allen asked.

"That's him," Eric said.

Allen led the way to the bar. The barman nodded to Eric and Erin before giving Allen the side eye. "Them I know. Who are you?"

"We have a mutual friend," Allen said. "A wizard named Anders was here last night. What can you tell me about him?"

"What the hell business is it of yours?"

Allen set a silver crown on the table. "The wizard was bothering a friend of mine. He's been dealt with, but I want to make sure no one else plans to take up where he left off. Anything you can tell me will be rewarded."

The bartender slapped a meaty hand down on top of the silver coin and made it disappear. "Not much I can tell you. Anders comes in once in a while looking for muscle. The guys I've talked to say it's usually easy work, so I try and steer him toward some of our more down-on-their-luck customers."

"You don't know anything about him?" Allen asked.

"Anders wasn't exactly a chatty guy."

"Are any of the others that worked for him here now?"

The bartender looked over Allen's head at the taproom. After a moment of study, he nodded. "In the back, the three men at the corner table did a job for him about a month ago. That was the last time Anders was here."

"Thanks." Allen set another silver coin on the bar.

As soon as they moved away from the bar Erin snarled and said, "It was a pity job. He didn't really think we were the best for it."

"Who cares?" Eric asked. "Pity job or not we needed the money. Not that we got any."

"Would you two shut up?" Allen said. "You've got a new employer now and that's all you need to worry about."

They made their way across the taproom to the corner table. Three of the grizzliest men Allen had ever seen looked up at them. Each of them was missing at least a finger. One lacked a left eye and the third had a huge scar running down the right side of his bald head. They looked like they'd fought a war and didn't come out on the winning side.

"Got a problem?" Scarhead asked.

"Not at all," Allen said. He pulled out another silver coin and showed it to the man. "I'm looking for information about a wizard named Anders. The bartender said you might be able to help me."

All three of them were staring at the silver coin with a hungry look in their eyes. Whatever Anders had paid them, it appeared like they'd spent it all already.

"What do you want to know?" Scarhead asked.

"What did Anders ask you to do?" Allen asked.

Scarhead shrugged. "Nothing much. He had a wagonload of stuff and wanted some muscle to protect it. Hell, we didn't even know he was a wizard until halfway through the job he started throwing fire around. I nearly shit myself. We almost ran right then but didn't want to be roasted alive. The way he used that magic, I'm not sure what he needed us for anyway."

"What were you delivering?" Allen asked.

"Beats me. When we got where we were going, half a dozen guys were waiting to unload the wagon. We stood around and watched them load it into river boats and when we were done Anders paid us and we headed back to the city. Aside from the sons of bitches that jumped us, it was about the easiest job the three of us ever had."

"Where did you take the crates?"

"About twenty miles north of the city. There's a sandbar where the boats waited. And before you ask, no I didn't know any of the people that met us. The wagon was attacked about twelve miles north of the city. I didn't recognize any of them either."

"Last question. Where did you meet Anders before you left for the river?"

"At the north gate. He was waiting for us with the wagon, no one else was around."

Allen nodded and paid each of them two silver coins. Sounded like Anders was into more than just blackmail, though whether he was involved with the river smugglers—and they could be nothing else—Allen wasn't sure. Luckily for him he had a friend with contacts that might be able to find out.

At least getting up at this demon-cursed hour had been worthwhile. Hopefully the next lead would answer Lord Shenk's questions and he could move on. Preferably to something he could do at night.

CHAPTER 10

The roads were in far better shape in the fall than they were in the spring, so Otto and his team made good time traveling to Shenk Barony despite the creaky wagon they'd loaded with fake cargo in hopes of drawing out any bandits keeping watch. Unfortunately, none of those bandits saw fit to put in an appearance.

On the seat beside him, Sergeant Hans, once more dressed in civilian armor rather than his royal guard uniform, guided the team with practiced ease while the rest of the squad, decked out in standard mercenary gear, rode in front and back. Four guards for a single wagon should signal a relatively valuable cargo. At least that was what they were going for. They either hadn't been seen or no one was taking the bait.

The stretch of road where he and his father had been attacked was coming up soon. Otto held out hope that they might get lucky there. He restrained a smile. The idea that getting attacked could be considered lucky was a joke, but he couldn't deny the truth. They were the bait, now they just needed someone to bite.

"Are we going to call on your father?" Hans asked.

Otto grimaced. He had no desire to see his family, but if they couldn't find the bandits on their own, he might not have a choice. "We'll see. We're certainly not having much luck."

"It hasn't been that long, my lord. The bastards can't be everywhere after all."

"I suppose not. I'm going to take a look around." Otto closed his eyes and extended his sight up and away from his body. He flew across a nearby field and into the distant woods. As he continued to increase his power, his sight continued to increase its range. He could send his vision nearly a mile now in any direction. It was a useful tool, but pointless if there was nothing to see.

After a full sweep in every direction he returned to his body and sighed. There was nothing watching them except a pair of curious deer. A few days remained before they reached Castle Shenk, but it looked like he was going to have to talk to his father after all.

The rest of the day was as peaceful as the morning and near dusk the glow of a village appeared on the horizon. Hans guided the wagon toward a low, long building with a sign featuring a foaming tankard. This was the second village they'd visited. Hopefully they'd have more-useful information than the last one.

Otto hopped down. His feet had barely hit the ground when Cord said, "Look at that wagon, my lord."

He followed the soldier's extended finger. Twenty feet from them was a second wagon. Three arrows jutted out from the frame. Looked like someone had an encounter with the bandits. Maybe they'd finally get a lead.

Otto left the men to tend their horses and went inside. He was well enough known in the barony that anyone with problems should be eager to get his help, or at least to use him to carry a message to his father. He pushed through the door and into the warmth and light of the common room. The place was packed, every table taken. Some sort of stew filled the air with a savory aroma. Most of the patrons were gathered around one table in the center where a man with his head wrapped in a bloody bandage was sipping a tankard.

"They came out of nowhere," the wounded man said. "Just a damn miracle I got away. Lost three men in that ambush. Getting so a man can't travel the roads around here without risking his life. The baron has let things go to hell."

"He's doubled patrols," someone said. "Soldiers can't be everywhere. I was in Castle Town last week and there were five new bodies hanging from the walls."

Did whoever spoke actually believe his father was doing his utmost or did he just fear someone carrying word back to him? Probably a little of both. And why was a merchant bad-mouthing the baron? Even here, someone was apt to take word to his father in hopes of a reward.

"Where were you attacked?" Otto asked.

"East of here, about four hours. Ten of them shot us full of arrows. Just a miracle the horses weren't hit or I'd be dead."

"They didn't give chase?" Otto asked.

"No, I didn't see any mounts. Who the hell are you anyway?"

"Otto Shenk. I'm helping my father deal with the bandits."

A sudden hush came over the room. Everyone stared at him. Otto was used to that and ignored them. "It's not a local problem. Bandits have been attacking all over Garenland. They're working for Straken agents, trying to disrupt the kingdom and weaken us from within."

That brought a bunch of mutters, but the merchant didn't

seem surprised. Perhaps word had spread to wherever he came from. Hopefully getting them focused on the enemy would take some pressure off his father. Not that Otto particularly cared if his father was having a hard time, but in his experience, when Father was in a bad mood, his family suffered the most and not just Stephan, which was a shame.

"My men and I will head out that way at first light. Perhaps we can run them down." Hans and the others had entered the tavern while he was listening to the merchant's story. "We'll need rooms."

"We have three available, Lord Shenk," said the thin, nervous man Otto assumed owned the place. "You're welcome to them, no charge of course."

Otto nodded. They'd eat, sleep, and get an early start in the morning. There had to be tracks. They'd find the bastards and when they did, heaven help them.

Otto lay awake in the small, dark room the innkeeper had generously offered him for free, as if Otto would have had to pay for it if he didn't want to. One of the advantages of being a nobleman was he didn't have to pay commoners for anything unless he chose to.

His ether-enhanced sight rendered everything in shades of gray. Not that there was much to see. The furnishings consisted of a chair and an end table with a bowl and pitcher on it, and the hard, narrow bed. He wasn't sure how much time passed since they finished dinner and retired for the night. A few hours certainly. If he had guessed wrong, the exhaustion he suffered tomorrow would be the price of that mistake. Still, he was certain there was something off about that merchant.

At least he wouldn't have to worry about Sergeant Hans or his men teasing him. They had proven as circumspect as they were loyal and Otto appreciated that. As a reward, when they finished this mission, he was going to introduce them to the giant armor he'd found in Lord Karonin's armory. He could think of no better soldiers to man them. Such powerful weapons had to be kept in the hands of those most loyal to the cause.

Half an hour later, his patience was rewarded. The thread of ether he'd stretched across the door broke. Otto turned his head a fraction so he could watch the door slowly opening. A figure entered, a dagger held in its grip. His washed-out magical vision offered few details. That said, there could be no question about the individual's intention.

Otto flicked his ring and bound the intruder.

He agitated the ether to create light then rapped on the connecting wall to let Sergeant Hans know their unwelcome visitor had arrived. The sergeant stepped through the door a moment later, his sword bare in one hand and a lantern in the other.

Otto let the magical light fade and rolled out of bed. His would-be killer was clearly the merchant from downstairs. He had taken off the blood-soaked bandage revealing an unharmed face underneath. The bandits must have sent him in to get information and provide false leads to anyone hunting them.

"How did you know, my lord?" Hans asked.

"I've spent plenty of time around merchants, both with my father and my father-in-law. None of them act anything like this man did. They're always selling and would never bad-mouth a noble they might hope to do business with, especially when there are people around to hear."

Hans laid the edge of the sword on the intruder's neck. "You want me to carve a few chunks out of him before we start asking questions?"

"Not at all." Otto released the intruder's head from his control. "He's going to tell us everything we want to know with no trouble, right?"

"And why would I do that?"

"I assume you know my father's reputation. If you don't answer my questions, I'm going to take you to him and he's going to ask you. And I promise you don't want my father asking you questions. Now tell us where we can find the other bandits."

The false merchant glared at Otto. For a moment he feared he'd misread the man, but then he said, "There are groups scattered all over the area. The boss meets us every few weeks with new orders."

"Where can I find your boss?" Otto asked.

"He works as a tinker in Castle Town. The disguise lets him travel around and no one asks any questions."

Otto nearly laughed out loud. The Straken spy was right under Father's nose and he had no idea. Suddenly going to see the baron didn't sound like such a bad idea. Not that his father would be grateful for the information. But it didn't matter, they needed to wrap up all the remaining Straken agents in the kingdom if things were to have any hope of getting back to normal.

"I told you what you wanted to know. So let me go."

"I promised not to take you to my father," Otto said. "No one said anything about letting you go. Rest assured, your death will be painless."

"What—" Otto sent five threads' worth of lightning directly into his heart, stopping it instantly.

"What now, my lord?" Hans asked.

"You expressed interest in my father, well, you're about to meet him. We leave for Castle Town in the morning."

"What about this piece of trash?"

"We'll let the locals string him up in the village square. It'll send a good message to anyone else thinking of following in his footsteps. Drag him outside then get some sleep. We've got a long ride ahead of us."

CHAPTER 11

The Northern Army spent two days attending to their wounded and burying the dead. The healers did the best they could, but many of those injured in the assault on the fort still ended up dying.

In all his years in the army, Axel had never seen so many graves in one place. He didn't bother to count, but the dead had to number in the hundreds. It was a horrendous loss of life and still only the first of many battles. That the enemy had lost even more did little to make him feel better.

At least the Third Legion had finally caught up. With the Northern Army now at full strength, General Varchi was eager to advance and place the border forts under siege. Axel knew how he felt, but there was still the matter of an assassin lurking somewhere out in the woods. Hopefully the general would soon see reason and let him take a couple of squads out to hunt the man down.

In the meantime, precautions would have to be taken to keep the general safe. Axel was overseeing construction of one of those precautions right now. The army engineers were busy putting the final touches on a palanquin hung with chain mail curtains. The general would be safe in there from incoming arrows, the trick was going to be convincing him to ride in it at all. He feared General Varchi's pride might overcome his good sense. At least the commander of his personal guard was on Axel's side. There was simply no way to keep him safe at all times as they marched.

Cobb stomped up behind Axel and crossed his arms. "That's quite a contraption you've made. When the king sees it, he'll probably want one of his own."

"As long as it works, I don't care what it looks like." Axel glanced over at his second. "Any word from Colten and his squad?"

"The kid tracked the assassin for a way, but after about ten miles he decided to turn back."

If the assassin had retreated that far, he wouldn't be taking another shot at the general any time soon. It would also make Axel's plan to track him down nearly impossible. He trusted Colten had done everything possible to locate his prey. Sometimes things didn't go your way. He'd talk to Colten later and try to get an idea where the assassin was headed. The nearest enemy units they knew about were fifty miles north. Though there were probably more of those ranger squads lurking around.

"What the bloody hell is this thing?" General Varchi arrived and Cobb made himself scarce, the coward.

"Your transport, sir," Axel said. "At least until we find and kill the assassin."

"You expect me to ride in that? Have you taken leave of your senses?"

"No, sir. The truth is, you're the only truly irreplaceable person in this army. If anything happens to you, the men will lose heart and we'll need to find a new supreme commander. We may even be delayed until the king himself can appoint one. It's for the greater good."

The captain of the general's personal guard—Axel never actually learned the man's name—cleared his throat and said, "I'm forced to agree, sir. You'd be too exposed on horseback and we can't march the whole way north with our shields raised around you. For the time being I simply see no other option."

The general poked the chain mail curtains aside with his toe and looked into the cabin. "I'm supposed to lounge in this thing like some southern satrap, being carried around by my soldiers like I'm too weak to walk? Not only will this contraption make me look like a coward, but it will make me look like a weakling as well. I can't accept it, gentlemen. I understand the risks and accept them. You must do the same."

With that pronouncement the general marched off. Axel and the guard captain shared a look, but what could they do? In the army, the general's word was law. They'd just have to do their best to keep him safe and hope the assassin didn't get lucky.

"What should we do with this thing?" one of the engineers working on the palanquin asked.

"Put it in one of the supply wagons for now," Axel said. "If, heaven forbid, he should get wounded, we'll still need it."

They saluted and Axel went to look for Colten. Now more than ever they needed to find the assassin. If his best tracker couldn't do it, Axel didn't know who could.

He found Colten and his men sitting around a nearly burned-out fire scraping breakfast leftovers out of a kettle. As soon as the men saw him approaching, they started to rise.

Axel waved them back. After the extra work they'd been doing, he wasn't about to deny them breakfast.

"Cobb tells me you gave up the search about ten miles out. Did you see any indication about where he was headed?"

"No, sir," Colten said. "He was moving at a good clip and showed no sign of slowing when we gave up the chase. Wherever he was headed, it wasn't around here. We didn't see any other signs of enemy activity. You want us to head back out?"

"No, once the camp is broken down, we're leaving, and we'll be on point again. Bad as I want to catch the assassin, we can't risk the entire army to do it. Given your report, I'm confident we won't see him again for a while. Still, keep your eyes peeled. You see anything at all out of the ordinary, let me know at once."

Colten saluted and Axel left the men to their meal. They'd made what preparations they could but for now it looked like matters were out of his hands.

◯

The Lady in Red sat at her desk in a small office hidden deep in the bowels of Castle Marduke. Her cherrywood desk held only a quill and ink, and two small scrolls that had arrived via pigeon an hour ago. She smoothed them out again and read them a second time.

According to her agents in Garenland, the bandits were doing an excellent job disrupting internal trade. The roads had been nearly silent for days as food sat in barns and silos waiting to be moved to the cities. So far so good as far as that went.

The latest report from the front was less encouraging. Enemy forces had wiped out their most southern position and her assassin had failed to kill General Varchi. Soon enough the Northern Army would reach the stolen border forts. She held little hope that they would last long. The numbers disadvantage was just too great.

She took a deep breath, gathered her thoughts, and stood. King Uther was waiting for her report and it was never wise to keep him waiting. Not that delivering bad news was any better, but if it had to be done, better for her if she did it quickly, much like pulling off a bandage.

Outside her office, a cold, stone hall led to the king's private chambers. Unlike some sovereigns, Uther cared little for the council of his nobles. He sent orders and expected them to be obeyed. Woe to the underling that failed to do so. She found herself in the enviable position of having Uther's trust, at least as much of it as he gave anyone besides his son.

She grimaced when she thought of Uther the Second. They had never gotten along and should anything happen to his father, she held no illusions about her future at court. At best, the prince would have her removed the same day he was coronated, at worst he'd have her head on a spike.

All the more reason to keep the current king alive and happy.

She reached a heavy oak door with an iron dragon mounted on it. A quick knock and the king said, "Enter."

The door opened silently and closed the same way. Uther sat in front of a roaring fire, a tankard of wine in one hand and a smoking pipe in the other. He didn't even turn to face her.

"Well?"

"Things are proceeding well in Garenland's central district. Our agents have disrupted most of their internal trade at little cost to our own people. On the battlefront, things fare less well. General Varchi survived our assassination attempt and the fort was destroyed. Our scouts estimate they should be marching by now."

Uther grunted. "The border forts won't last long."

"No, Your Majesty. Fifteen thousand men will overrun our positions in a few days."

"What are our total forces in Garenland right now?"

"After the debacle at the fort I'd estimate eight thousand infantry and five hundred rangers."

Uther slammed his fist on the chair arm. "That's not enough! I hope whoever murdered the old king burns in hell. The weak fool never would have struck against us like this. I planned on having more time to move resources into place. Where can we muster our forces for a real battle?"

"Probably the Saber Plains. If our invasion force pulls back and we send other legions to join them, we could have twenty-five thousand ready for battle in six weeks. The rough terrain will slow the enemy's advance. I believe it's our best chance."

"The Saber Plains are in Straken." Uther's voice was low and deadly. "You're suggesting we cede all the ground we've taken and then some. All my plans, all our efforts, will have been for nothing."

She took a breath to steady herself. She'd seen Uther in a mood like this before. One wrong move and she wouldn't have to worry about the prince killing her.

"That's correct, Majesty. However, if we try to fight the Garenlanders with what we have now, the invasion force will be wiped out and the main army will have to fight them even-handed rather than with superior numbers. Once the enemy army has been destroyed, retaking the lost ground will not be difficult."

There was a moment of silence then Uther slowly stood and turned to face her. With the light of the fire behind him, he was little more than a dark silhouette. Blue eyes as hard and cold as ice chips bored into her.

Her heart skipped a beat, but she forced herself to meet his gaze. Her advice was correct. She knew it and so did he. The only question was whether or not he'd accept it. The king stepped around his chair, stood directly in front of her, and put his massive hands on her shoulders.

A long minute passed and finally Uther smiled. The expression so stunned her she flinched.

"You are quite correct. This is why you are my sole councilor. The others who came before were spineless cowards who spouted platitudes and told me what they imagined I wanted to hear rather than the truth. Each time one of them did, I added his head to the wall. I can hardly believe that I would find the heart of a true Straken warrior in such a small, beautiful woman. Prepare the orders and I'll sign them."

He took his hands away and sat back down.

Her heart returned to normal and she took a step toward the door.

"Never change, Lady," the king said. "I would hate to have to add your pretty head to my collection."

She bowed at his back and withdrew. She'd survived another day.

Perhaps tomorrow would be her last, but until then, she'd do her best to prove to Uther that he hadn't made a mistake with her.

CHAPTER 12

Around dusk, Allen, Eric, and Erin set out for the river. Much as he hated to, Allen was forced to leave Ulf behind to look after the tavern. Not that Allen expected trouble. The Riverman was an old friend and if anyone knew what was happening on the river, it was him. Even if he wasn't expecting trouble, Allen wore his sword and dagger and the mercenaries had their crossbows as well as a backup shortsword. No one ever died from being too prepared.

He led his companions toward Northgate through the rapidly darkening city. The clanging and crashing from the city's many foundries quieted at night but never went truly silent. If you had to walk through the metal district, this was the best time.

Workers were pouring out into the street to make their way home after a long day at the forges. Allen kept them to the side streets, evading the worst of the crowd, and soon reached Northgate. Today's traffic had already dwindled to nothing so they had no trouble walking out.

Allen turned up the northern trade road. It was about a mile to the Riverman's home and he wanted to get there before the sun fully set. Thrashing around through the forest in the dark didn't appeal to him.

"Why is it we couldn't do this in daylight?" Erin asked.

"The Riverman doesn't like bright light," Allen said. "He has an eye condition that makes them very sensitive. The same condition also lets them see long distances and in very minimal light. He's been watching the comings and goings on the river since long before I was born."

"Just how old is he?" Eric asked.

"Old. When I first met him ten years ago, he already had white hair, a beard, and more wrinkles than you've ever seen. Still, I haven't heard anything about him dying so I assume he still keeps watch."

"What's he do for a living? I assume there's not much money in watching the river," Erin said.

"You'd be surprised how many people want to know what is going on. Not that he's getting rich. He lives in a shack, fishes for most of his food, and occasionally trades for whatever else he needs."

"Is that why you brought the whiskey?" Eric asked.

Allen patted the satchel at his side. The cheap bottle of booze he grabbed from behind the bar before they got going should be plenty to bribe him, but if it wasn't enough, he'd also brought a bag of dried sausage.

"That's right. The old-timer likes a nip every once in a while."

They marched on in silence and after a few minutes Allen spotted the narrow trail that led down to the river. He turned off the road, ducked a branch, and generally did his best not to get tangled up in the many roots and branches that grew in the trail.

"If he wants company," Eric said, "you'd think he'd at least trim the trail."

"I never said anything about him wanting company," Allen said. "Hell, it took me over a year to actually convince him to speak to me. He's a little eccentric, so be sure to mind your manners."

After ten minutes or so bushwhacking, they emerged on the riverbank. There hadn't been any major rainstorms in weeks, so the water was low enough to expose the boulders in the shallows. Twenty yards to their left, the Riverman's shack looked just as Allen remembered. It was cobbled together from driftwood, what passed for windows were basically just gaps in the wall, and the door was made from four oars nailed together.

"What a dump," Erin said.

Allen shot her a hard glare. "What part of mind your manners do you not understand? Insulting the man's home before we even see him is beyond stupid."

"Sorry." At least she sounded contrite.

Hopefully the old man's hearing wasn't as good as his sight. Allen led the way over to the shack and rapped on the door. Silence seemed to stretch on for a long time, but finally the door opened a crack.

"Allen?"

"Evening, Riverman." Allen pulled the whiskey bottle out of his satchel and held it up. "Thought you might like a drink on this fine evening."

Allen couldn't see it, but he heard the Riverman's lips smacking. "A drink would be nice. But just you. My dump of a shack no doubt isn't good enough for your companions."

Allen winced and turned to the others. "You two are going to have to wait out here. Try not to do anything else stupid."

He stepped inside the shack and the Riverman closed the door behind him. The old man's eyes seemed to glow amber in the dark, just enough to allow Allen to make his way to a rickety table made of the same junk as the rest of the shack. He sat on the smooth stone that served as a stool and set the bottle on the table.

The Riverman sat across from him, opened the bottle, and took a long drink. He sighed in satisfaction then asked, "So what do you want to know?"

Allen knew the man well enough not to mince words. He described Anders and the three mercenaries he' brought with him as well as the smugglers he met on the sandbar.

"Do you know them and what they're up to?"

The Riverman took another long drink. "I know everything that happens on my river. That meeting happened weeks ago. Can't say what they were carrying, but that bunch of smugglers has been moving up and down the river more than any other group."

"And the wizard?"

"He met them twice, counting the time you mentioned. They seem friendly enough, but they didn't discuss much. It was just a load-and-run meeting."

"Do you know where the smugglers make their base?"

The Riverman finished the last of his whiskey and sniffed loudly. "What do I smell?"

Allen grinned and took out the sausages. The old man reached for them, but Allen pulled back. "Where's their base?"

"Ten miles south. There's a partially hidden cove on the opposite bank. They put their boats on shore and camp there."

Allen handed over the sausages. "Thanks. I'll stop in again sometime."

"I'm not so sure, Allen. You have company waiting outside."

Allen frowned. He hadn't heard anything from outside and surely either Eric or Erin would've made some noise if there were strangers approaching. He looked at the River-man's bright eyes and couldn't think of any reason he might lie.

He left the shack and found a bored-looking Eric and Erin waiting. No sign of any threat. He looked back over his shoulder and found a glowing eye staring out through the gap of the oars.

"Learn anything useful?" Eric asked.

"Yeah." Allen turned back. "The smugglers have a base ten miles south of here. We'll check it out tomorrow. Why don't you two load your crossbows?"

"Uh, because there's nothing to shoot out here?" Erin said.

"Humor me."

Allen drew his sword and dagger while his companions loaded their crossbows. When everyone was ready, they started walking for the trail.

The group only managed five steps down the riverbank when three familiar figures stepped out of the forest and unhooded lanterns. It was the mercenaries from the Rusty Arms Allen had paid for information. All three were armed with broadswords and round shields that covered most of their bodies.

Eric and Erin brought their crossbows up and aimed at the left- and rightmost men, leaving the guy in the center for Allen. The siblings set down their lanterns and separated. Before things turned bloody, maybe he could talk his way out of this.

"I hadn't expected to see you three again so soon," Allen said.

"Anders paid us to do more than escort his goods," Scarhead said. "See, we also keep an ear open for anyone asking questions they shouldn't. When we saw you heading north toward the river, it didn't take a genius to figure out where you were headed. Everyone knows the Riverman. Though not for much longer if the old man's going to tell tales he shouldn't."

"Before we start killing each other," Allen said. "Do you work for the smugglers or the suppliers?"

"That's nothing a dead man needs to worry about."

The mercenaries roared and charged.

Both crossbows fired as one.

Eric's shot struck low, piercing his target's shield, but missing flesh.

Erin took her man right in the knee. He collapsed, howling and clutching his leg.

Two against three was a little better, but the surviving mercenaries had superior weapons for hand-to-hand fighting.

Allen met his opponent with a high slash which skipped off his opponent's shield.

He dodged a counterthrust, spun, and slashed low.

The shield dropped to block his attack.

When it did, he threw his dagger at the man's exposed head.

The mercenary's broadsword flicked out and knocked it aside.

Allen grimaced. That trick had been his best hope.

"You're pretty good for an amateur," the mercenary said.

"Thanks. Now that I've earned your respect, can we call this off?"

The mercenary's smile was vicious. "'Fraid not."

Before the battle could resume, the door to the shack

slammed open. The Riverman stood in the opening. It was the first time Allen had seen the old man outside of his shack in light. His legs were made of water. They still looked like legs, but he could see through them and they sloshed around like water-filled tubes. The rest of him appeared human enough, though he clearly wasn't.

"You dare come to my river and threaten me!" The Riverman's voice sounded like the thunder of spring rapids.

He didn't exactly move. Rather his legs turned into a pillar of water and his upper body rode it over to the man threatening Allen.

The mercenary swung his sword and the blade passed through the Riverman's body, which sealed up instantly behind the swords, like it was made of water.

He grabbed the mercenary and hurled him into the river. Before Allen could react, the other two joined their companion.

The three mercenaries scrambled to their feet. The water only came to their knees.

Then the water started to climb to their hips, then their chests, and in moments all three were encased in columns of water. They fought and thrashed for long seconds before their bodies went still.

The columns collapsed and the dead men washed down the river out of sight.

A still-furious Riverman was glaring after them. Allen debated staying silent, before working up the nerve to say, "Thank you. I'm not sure we could have handled them on our own."

The Riverman shuddered and looked down at Allen from the top of the serpentine length of water connecting him to his feet which still stood just outside his door. "I can't abide being threatened, especially by some stupid humans with no idea what they're facing. I do hope you'll come again, Allen, and please bring more of the sausages. They were delightful."

The Riverman shrank until he looked mostly human again and stepped back into his shack. Allen stared at the door, not entirely sure what just happened.

"I really wish I hadn't said anything bad about his house," Erin said.

Allen nodded. "Let's get out of here. I don't know about you two, but I'm beat."

Not that he had any confidence that he'd be able to sleep, not after what they just saw.

CHAPTER 13

The wagon clattered down the empty main street. Otto's ass was numb from the vibrations and he couldn't wait to get down, even if it was in Father's courtyard. As Castle Town and beyond it Castle Shenk came into view, Otto felt only distaste. He glanced at Sergeant Hans, but the man was practically made of iron. He'd never voiced a complaint in Otto's hearing.

They passed the first house at the edge of town. It might have been a ghost town for all the people around. Only a few trickles of smoke from the inn and bakery gave any indication that people actually lived here. They'd arrived an hour before noon but despite the high, clear sky the air held a bite.

Winter would be here soon enough. Otto needed to eliminate the bandits so he could turn his attention north. Hopefully Master Enoch was making good progress with the recruits. He was a skilled teacher, so as long as his students were doing the work, things should be progressing. He wanted them ready to go as soon as he returned.

"Is it always this quiet, my lord?" Hans asked.

"In the fall it is. Everyone that can work is busy in the orchards. The apples all need to get picked before the first frost otherwise they'll freeze, get soft, and rot. Once that happens, they're only good for pig feed."

The castle sat on a small rise east of the town proper. As they drew ever closer Otto did his best to keep the memories at bay. He could count on one hand the number of happy memories he had of his family. Only his mother had ever treated him with kindness. Stephan and his father mostly used him as a punching bag. Much as he would like to return the favor, he had more pressing matters at hand.

Hans reined in before the closed portcullis. A pair of guards wearing slightly battered Shenk tabards over their mail stood just inside and shot them hard looks. A quartet of archers had gathered on the battlement directly above them. Otto hopped down and walked up to the gate.

The guards stared at him for a moment before their eyes widened and they touched fist to heart.

The right-hand guard, the older of the two, cleared his throat. "Lord Shenk. I didn't recognize you from a distance. Open the gate!"

For the life of him Otto couldn't remember the man's name. "Don't worry about it. I assume Father's around."

"Yes, my lord. The baron, Sergeant Graves, and Stephan are all in conference at the moment trying to determine how best to deal with the bandit issue. Shall I send a messenger to let them know you're here?"

"No need. As it happens, I've come to talk to Father about the bandits anyway. I've got a lead on where those operating in the barony are based."

"Baron Shenk will be delighted to hear that."

Otto seriously doubted his father would be delighted that

he was the one bringing the information, especially when he heard what Otto had to say. Still, he needed to hear it.

The portcullis clunked into the open position and Otto walked through. Hans drove the wagon behind him and the others rode along at the rear.

Otto looked back. "You guys will have to wait here. If you're hungry, I'm sure they can rustle something up for you. I'll be back as soon as I can."

"Don't worry about us, Lord Shenk," Hans said. "If there's one thing we're used to, it's waiting."

Otto left his men and marched across the yard toward the keep. If they were having a meeting, everyone should be in the great hall. That would be convenient as it would save him searching the whole keep.

Otto was about ten strides away when a tiny figure came running toward him, a wooden sword clutched in his fist. Little Stephan had grown by nearly a hand since Otto had last seen him. Despite the growth, it looked like he was still wearing the same size pants as half his calf was visible. Behind the little blond boy came his dark-haired younger brother, crawling at a good clip. Mandel wasn't walking yet but it wouldn't be long.

He looked around but was relieved to see no sign of their mother, Griswalda. The woman hated him and the feeling was mutual. If he could avoid her, Otto would be happy to do so for the entire visit.

"Halt!" Little Stephan said. It seemed the boy was on guard duty again.

Otto smiled and raised his hands. "I see you've grown since last I visited. I wish I had time to play, but I need to go in and talk to your grandfather."

Little Stephan frowned and put his wooden sword away. "Grandpa's in a bad mood."

What else was new? "Don't worry, I've got some news that will cheer him up. Have you two been behaving yourselves?"

"I think so. But everyone keeps yelling at us."

Otto knew what that was like. He bent down and ruffled the boy's hair. "Don't let them bother you. Sometimes adults just like to yell at kids. Maybe after dinner I'll show you some magic."

Little Stephan's eyes grew wide. "Really?"

"We'll see, but if I do, you can't tell your mother. You know she doesn't like wizards."

Little Stephan gave an enthusiastic nod. "I promise."

"Good boy." Otto gave him a final pat on the head and strode toward the keep door.

Otto pushed through the main doors and, as expected, found his father, brother, and Sergeant Graves seated at the dining table with a small fire burning in the hearth. They all looked up when he entered and none looked pleased. Otto ignored their glares, pushed the door shut, and walked over to the table.

"What are you doing here?" his father asked.

"King Wolfric is worried about the bandits screwing up the harvest and he asked me to help deal with them. Turns out, a lot of the attacks are happening in Shenk Barony. So here I am."

"What possible help could you be, Runt?" Stephan asked.

"A great deal. You see, I captured a bandit last night and asked him a few questions. It turns out the Straken spy running the local bandit gang is operating out of Castle Town."

Father leapt to his feet and slammed his fists on the table.

"Impossible! If the sons of whores were operating out of my town, I'd know."

Otto struggled to keep his voice even. He doubted his father went into town more than five times a year. How did he expect to keep track of what was happening?

"According to the bandit I interrogated, the spy has disguised himself as a traveling tinker. The sort of person you'd never give a second thought about coming and going."

The three men around the table shared looks.

"Does that mean something to you?" Otto asked.

"A tinkerer arrived in town yesterday," Stephan said. "Griswalda and I were out shopping and some of the items on his cart caught her eye. I thought nothing of it at the time, but he was a big, bearded man, certainly big enough to be from Straken."

Father looked like he could have happily caved Stephan's head in. It was a nice change of pace to have that anger directed at someone else. "It didn't occur to you to mention that given everything that was happening?"

"There are plenty of big, bearded Garenlanders as well, Father," Stephan said, as if a logical argument had ever worked on Father.

"Perhaps, my lords, we should go arrest this tinker and find out for sure who he is," Graves said.

"My men and I can handle it if you'd like, Father," Otto said. It was a twist of the dagger more than anything, but he just couldn't resist.

"I think not." Father stood and said, "Assemble the garrison, Graves. We move as soon as they're ready. Otto, you and whoever you brought can stay out of the way. If we find anything, I'll let you know."

Otto bowed and took his leave. As he walked out of the

keep, his mind raced. He needed to keep Father from killing the spy long enough to extract whatever he knew about the rest of Straken's activities. If Father wanted to torture him to death after that, he was welcome.

The moment he was outside he caught Hans's eye and made a circle with his finger. The sergeant and his men quickly gathered around Otto.

"Lord Shenk?" Hans asked.

"Father's going after the spy. He's ordered me to keep out of it. That said, we need to be near enough that we can search his property and hopefully keep the man alive long enough to question."

Hans nodded. "Orders?"

"I wish I had some. We'll follow the garrison, keep back, and stay alert. If the tinker is really a Straken spy, he might have a few surprises in store."

Otto offered up a silent prayer to any angel or demon willing to listen that Father would keep his temper under control. The last thing Otto had time for was a complete reset of his search.

CHAPTER 14

After their harrowing visit with the Riverman, Allen had no desire to work in the tavern. He went directly to bed and stared at the dark ceiling. After all the years he'd known the Riverman, he never guessed he was anything but an eccentric hermit who liked living by the water. Instead he turned out to be some kind of monster, albeit a monster that saved Allen's life. If you had to deal with monsters, that was the best sort.

He couldn't have said how long it took him to finally fall asleep, but he woke up far too soon. When it became clear he wasn't going to sleep anymore, Allen got up, dressed, and went out into the common room. Ulf was already up and preparing something on the stove. It smelled better than his usual concoctions.

Ulf looked up from the pot he was stirring. "You're up early."

"We've got another full day. The tavern will have to close for today. I need you with me for this one."

Ulf nodded. He never argued with Allen. Granted, he only

gained the ability to speak a little while ago, but even so, Allen appreciated the silent support.

"What are you cooking, some sort of alchemy potion?"

"Tea. Want a cup?"

Allen grinned. "Sure. I'll get the mugs."

He fetched a pair of tin cups from behind the bar along with a bottle of brandy. Ulf poured the tea through a strainer into both cups and Allen added an unhealthy dose of brandy to his own. Despite working in a tavern, he'd never seen his silent barman take so much as a sip of alcohol.

When he'd finished the slightly bitter, but still tasty drink Allen said, "We're going up against a smuggling gang. Got any tricks we can use to reduce their numbers?"

"How many are there?" Ulf asked.

"No idea, but I'll wager it's more than the four of us can handle in a fair fight. I thought maybe some of that stuff you used to put out the guards last summer. If you can dart a few of them before they know we're there, it would even the odds."

"I have a spare vial of sleep potion, but only six darts. If we need more than that…"

"It'll be enough, hopefully."

♌

A ride that was supposed to be ten miles ended up taking four hours for Allen and his companions. First they had to go an extra mile downstream to find a ford, then they had to ride back on the opposite side where there were no roads and barely a dirt path, and finally they ended up turning away from the river proper and traveling most of another mile through thick undergrowth along a narrow but deep offshoot of the main river.

But now, at last, they were gathered twenty yards from the smugglers' camp. The sun was low in the sky and soon it would be dark. They couldn't hit the camp in broad daylight. Allen counted fifteen men gathered around a bubbling pot waiting for dinner. A flat-bottom barge was tied up at the edge of the firelight. Dozens of boxes littered its deck.

The smugglers were as motley a collection of scoundrels as you could hope to find. All of them would have looked right at home in Crane's band of cutthroats had they still been among the living. They were all dressed in battered leathers and had at least two weapons jutting from their belts. They looked more like pirates than smugglers.

Not that they couldn't do a little thieving when time allowed. Allen didn't know them well enough to guess how they spent their free time. Nor did he want to. He just wanted to know about Anders. If he went to all this trouble and these slobs didn't have any useful information, he was going to be pissed.

Erin crawled over beside him. "Even if your friend takes out six of them, there's still no way we can handle nine on our own."

Her voice was tight and anxious, and he didn't blame her. "We'll think of something."

"I already have," Ulf whispered. He pointed at a branch hanging over the camp. "If I climb up there, I can pour the potion into their stew. That'll get all of them at once."

Allen eyed the branch and frowned. It looked awfully skinny. "You really think it'll hold your weight?"

"I think we have limited options if we want to do this without getting killed."

Allen couldn't argue with that. "Good luck."

Ulf slid away from them and crawled out of sight toward

the tree's base. He didn't make a sound as he slipped through the undergrowth. Allen shook his head. His friend was a man of many hidden talents. Hopefully his aim was as good as his stealth.

As Ulf made his way to the tree, Allen tried to listen to the smugglers' chatter. He picked up a word here and there, but the rush of the river drowned out most of it. What he did hear was disjointed and made no sense. Erin and Eric had shifted their crossbows into position just in case this went badly. Allen wished he thought to bring one of his own, but he had little experience with the weapons and would probably just end up missing anyway.

Time seemed to crawl as they waited, but finally he spotted Ulf inching his way out across the limb. The further out he went, the more it bent, but there were no cracks, thank heaven. Ulf eased three-quarters of the way out on the branch and waited.

The bearded fellow tending the pot finally turned away to get something from a basket behind him. The moment he did, Ulf poured the potion. Only a few drops went wide.

Allen restrained a victory cry and waited with bated breath for dinner to be served.

Fortunately, he didn't have long to wait. After a final sprinkle of salt, the smugglers lined up, each with his or her own bowl, to be served. The cook ladled thick, brown stew into each bowl and they settled in to eat. Before, when Ulf darted someone, the poison kicked in immediately. Allen wasn't sure how long they'd have to wait for it to work when it was eaten.

The answer came ten minutes later when the first person clutched his stomach, groaned, and fell over, unconscious. His companions had just time enough to be concerned when they started falling over as well. The cook was the last to go but go he did.

Ulf dropped down from the branch and landed between the fire and an unconscious smuggler. He reached down and touched the side of the woman's neck. "She's alive."

Allen blew out a sigh. It would've defeated the purpose if he'd killed them all. Allen needed answers, not bodies. He stood and his back popped. Lying on the forest floor wasn't the most comfortable thing in the world. He couldn't wait to get back to the city. Roughing it was not for him.

The three of them joined Ulf in the clearing. Allen looked around and asked, "How long will they be out?"

"Not long," Ulf said. "The potion isn't as effective when eaten."

"What the hell are we going to do when they all wake up?" Eric's voice was shrill with fear.

Before Allen could respond a voice from the barge said, "Hey! Where's our food?"

"Damn the luck." Allen bent down and grabbed two bowls. "You two follow me. As soon as you see the boat guards, let 'em have it."

The mercenaries nodded and hefted their crossbows.

Allen coarsened his voice and said, "I'm comin'. Keep your pants on."

He walked over, holding the bowls in front of him. Standing in the front of the barge was a tall, slim man with a scar across his face. The smuggler looked down at Allen. "Who the hell—"

The rest of his question was cut off when Erin fired her crossbow. The bolt drove into his neck and came out the other side.

"Bart!" A woman came running toward the fallen man.

Eric fired but only grazed her side.

The woman snarled and pulled a hand axe from her belt.

Allen tossed the bowls and drew his sword.

He turned aside the first heavy blow from the axe. The female smuggler was strong if not skilled.

Behind him Eric and Erin rushed to reload their crossbows.

Allen turned aside another strike and his counterthrust took her in the left shoulder. It was a deep wound, but she was so enraged she didn't seem to notice.

He barely dodged a backhand slice before lunging in again. His blade found her stomach this time and she collapsed.

Behind him one of the crossbows fired again.

Someone groaned further down the barge. Partially hidden by the crates was a third man, a throwing knife at his feet. Hopefully he was the last guard.

They made a quick sweep of the barge while the female smuggler bled out. Looked like they were in the clear.

"Sorry about that first shot," Eric said. "When I saw it was a woman I flinched."

Allen shrugged. "All's well that ends well as the saying goes. Let's grab some rope and get the others tied up before they come to."

When they got back to camp with two coils of heavy hemp rope, they found Ulf already tying up his third smuggler with a thinner cord he'd found in the smugglers' supplies. The three of them joined in and before the first person came moaning back to consciousness, they had them all bound and stripped of weapons.

"They'll need a little while to recover before you'll get any useful information," Ulf said.

"Keep an eye on them." Allen grabbed a burning brand from the fire. "I'm going to take a closer look at their merchandise."

He motioned for Eric to join him. The younger man set his crossbow down and the two of them returned to the barge. It was easier to see with the makeshift torch to light their way. The crates were simple wooden boxes without merchants' marks on them. Not that it meant much. If they were shipping stolen goods it was only natural that they'd transfer the items to unmarked crates.

"Pry the top off one," Allen said.

Eric drew his dagger and set to work. The lid was attached very well and it took a few seconds to get it off. A dozen long items wrapped in oilcloth filled the crate. Allen handed Eric his torch and pulled one out. It was clearly a sword. Fine steel gleamed in the torchlight.

The weapon had a round pommel, an upswept guard, and an oak hilt. It was a common design in Garen, one you could buy from any of a dozen forges. It certainly wasn't something you'd need to smuggle. There weren't even any internal taxes on blades.

It took about ten minutes to check the rest of the crates. They all held either swords or armor, all in a common style, and none of any great value. There was exactly nothing remarkable about these items beyond the fact that they were on a smuggler's ship.

What was the point?

"They're about ready," Ulf called.

It was time to find out.

Allen and Eric returned to the camp and Allen brought the sword with him. The smugglers were all sitting up and looking more or less alert. A couple of the brighter-eyed ones were staring holes in Ulf and Erin.

Well, no sense beating around the bush. "Who's in charge here?" Allen asked.

His question was met with silence, so Allen chose one of the smugglers at random and crouched down in front of him. "Who are you working for and what are you doing with these weapons?"

The man bared a mouthful of rotten teeth. "I don't know anything."

Allen straightened and said, "That's unfortunate."

A casual backhand swing with the sword cut the unfortunate smuggler's head half off.

Dead silence filled the clearing.

Allen looked all around. "Now that we're all clear on what happens to those who don't know anything, I'll try again. Who are you working for and what are you doing with these weapons?"

The smugglers were all looking at each other. Allen took that to be a good sign. Hopefully one of them would speak up and answer his question.

Half a minute passed and it became clear his hopes would not be answered. He chose another smuggler at random, a woman this time, and tapped her on the shoulder with his bloody sword. She looked up at him with fear in her eyes.

"Nothing to say?" Allen asked.

"Okay, look. We were hired to move the merchandise downriver to the border. We were told someone would meet us there and we'd get paid the rest of our gold. It was supposed to be a simple job, easy money."

If they kept to the river, the only border they would reach was Lasil's. The question was, why did anyone need to use smugglers to move merchandise there? Garenland was still on reasonably good terms with them, at least compared to some of the other countries. It didn't make sense.

"Who hired you?" Allen asked.

"I don't know who they are, I swear," the woman said. "We've delivered small loads for them before. I think they might be thieves, but I can't prove it."

If the merchandise came from thieves, it made more sense that they needed to use smugglers. It shouldn't be too hard to figure out which merchant had a load of swords and armor stolen lately.

Now he just had to decide what to do with the smugglers. Marching them back to the city in the dark didn't especially appeal to Allen. Besides, the watch would only hang them anyways.

A bloody few minutes' work and the smugglers were all dealt with. Hopefully he had enough information now to satisfy Lord Shenk. As soon as he thought it, Allen knew it wasn't going to be enough. He needed to hunt the thieves down and find out if they were involved in Anders's blackmail scheme.

But tomorrow would be soon enough for that. Right now, he needed to get home and get a drink.

CHAPTER 15

Otto and his squad tagged along behind as Father and Stephan led twenty men, half the castle garrison, out the front gate toward Castle Town. Some might think twenty men was excessive to capture a single target, but Otto was relieved. If Father was bringing this many men, he had to be hoping the spy would see them and simply surrender. Of course, depending on how devoted he was to Straken's cause or how well he knew Father's reputation, he might kill himself as soon as he saw them coming.

That would be the worst-case scenario. Otto had learned a great deal of magic in the past year, but speaking to the dead was still beyond him, assuming such a thing was even possible.

At least they'd chosen a good time to make their move. It would be hours before anyone returned from the orchard. If there was a battle, they wouldn't have to worry about anyone getting hurt. Not that Father or Stephan was apt to give a commoner a second thought if they got in the way.

When they reached the main street, Stephan pointed left and the group turned.

Otto frowned. The town market was the other way. Surely the tinker would have set up there to avoid drawing attention. He needed to have a better look around.

"Hold a moment, Hans." Otto stopped and closed his eyes. A moment later his sight flew free and over the rooftops. From on high it wasn't hard to spot a solitary covered wagon at the edge of the village. A mule was cropping grass twenty feet away. It was a very idyllic scene. Hardly the sort of place you'd expect to find an enemy of the state.

Otto pushed his sight through the canvas side of the wagon. Inside was a collection of pots, pans, and other odds and ends. A small anvil and a collection of tools sat in one corner, just as neat and tidy as you could hope for. What was missing was a big man with a beard.

Where the hell was the tinker?

"Your father and his soldiers are getting further away, my lord," Hans said.

Otto ignored him. Finding the tinker was what mattered. Where would he be if he wasn't at his wagon?

The view expanded as Otto pulled back. He flew around a nearby tree but came up empty again. There was nowhere else nearby to hide.

He flew high enough to see the entire village. Father and the others were only a minute or so away from the wagon.

A hint of movement on the baker's roof caught his eye. A closer look revealed a bearded man armed with a crossbow hiding behind the chimney.

In a moment Father and Stephan would step into view.

Otto formed a hand out of ether and pulled the bolt out of the crossbow, gently, so it would look like it slipped. He would have bound the man in place but feared him falling and breaking his neck.

Next he connected his voice to the ether and flew down by his father's ear. "He's on the bakery roof and armed with a crossbow."

Father stopped and barked orders Otto couldn't hear.

Otto dissolved his ethereal senses and returned full awareness to his body. "Hans, let's check out the wagon. Father and his men will capture the spy."

Hans nodded and Otto led the way to the tinker's wagon, being careful to avoid the bakery and the many shouts coming from that part of the village. They reached the wagon without incident and without being seen, at least as far as Otto could tell.

The wagon looked exactly the same to his physical eyes as it did to his magical sight. The canvas was a little rattier up close, but other than that he saw nothing out of the ordinary.

"Someone check under the seat." Otto climbed up into the back of the wagon. There was a faint noise coming from somewhere. "Do you hear that, Hans?"

"I hear something, my lord."

Otto pulled his dagger and started tapping the floor. It sounded hollow under the center board.

He backed out of the way and said, "Pull that board loose."

Two of the squad knelt and jammed their own daggers into the cracks between the boards. A little wiggling and prying and they soon had it loose. There was a small opening underneath and inside were three cages holding a trio of black birds.

Otto pulled one out for a closer look. "Do these animals look familiar to you?"

Hans eyed the birds and nodded. "They look just like the ones we found back in the city. This guy's a spy for sure."

"Indeed." Otto frowned and asked, "What did you ever do with that bird we took from the rookery?"

"We kinda made it the squad mascot. I asked a couple of the guards back at the barracks to feed it while we were gone," Han said.

"You know if it gets out of its cage it'll fly straight back to Straken," Otto said. Since they were at war now, he could think of a way to use that. "Keep this one but don't get attached. I've got a job for it for later."

Hans took the cage and handed it off to one of his men. Otto zapped the rest of the birds just to be sure and they set to work searching. Ten minutes later when Father and a bleeding but still breathing tinker showed up, Otto had found three hidden compartments. The contents were rather disappointing: writing materials, some gold and silver coins, and a nice selection of weapons.

Otto climbed down out of the wagon. "Congratulations on capturing your first Straken spy."

"No thanks to you," Stephan said.

"I could have let him shoot you with the crossbow," Otto said. "Don't think I didn't consider it. Only the fear that I'd end up as Father's heir stopped me."

"Enough, both of you," Father said. "I'm going to question him at once. Do you want to sit in?"

"Yes, thank you. Hans, keep searching. Tear the wagon completely apart if you have to."

Hans nodded and got back to work. Otto fell in behind his father and brother and they set out for the castle. As they walked, Otto darted a few looks at the injured spy. The blood was coming from a deep gash in the man's side. His rib bones were visible and only the efforts of two soldiers kept him upright.

He certainly looked the part of a poor traveling tinker. If Otto hadn't found all the hidden items in his wagon, he would have doubted the information he got from the bandit yesterday was accurate.

"You've taken my command to get close to the new king to heart," Father said.

"Not really. Wolfric is a good man and a good friend. Our friendship was more his doing than mine. It's an honor to serve as his advisor." It was also a handy way to steer him in the direction that would make Otto's dream of becoming the next Arcane Lord a reality, but he saw no reason to tell his father that last part.

When they reached the castle, Father dismissed all the soldiers save those half carrying the prisoner. They made the short walk to the basement torture chamber. Three braziers filled the room with ruddy light.

Someone had already set the coals to heating and put a trio of irons in them. On the right-hand wall hung a dozen different blades in various shapes and sizes. In the center sat a rack fixed with a heavy winch and thick, leather restraints. The almost-black stains on the wood gave silent testimony to Father's frequent use of the room.

"Strip him and strap him down," Father said.

The spy's rags were ripped away and thrown in a corner. While the soldiers were strapping him to the rack, Father selected a glowing iron rod that ended in a wide, flat stamp. As soon as he was secured, Father slapped the iron to the spy's wound.

He screamed as the hot metal seared the injury shut. At least now he wouldn't bleed to death. Otto left his father to do his thing. If experience was any indicator, he'd torture the spy for a while before asking any actual questions. Otto wanted a closer look at his clothes.

He conjured a light and started with the man's bloody shirt.

It was slashed and soaked through, nothing written on the inside or outside. He tossed it aside and moved on to the cheap canvas pants. The prisoner let out a few more screams but Otto ignored them. Before his time in the capital, he would have cringed and fled as fast as he could. But now the man's pain meant nothing to him. Whether that was an improvement or not he wasn't ready to say.

A blade of ether slashed both pant legs so he could look at the inside. Not encouraging. As he was about to toss them aside, Otto noticed the cuff was folded up and sewed shut. Not unusual if your hand-me-downs were too big, but his gut said to check them anyway.

Using magic to pick threads was tricky, but he treated it like a control test and in short order had the threads loose. When he unfolded them, a small, tightly folded piece of paper fell out.

Unfolding that without tearing it was nearly as tricky as picking out the threads, but he eventually managed to get the four-inch square smooth. In a crisp, neat hand someone had written orders for his followers should anything happen to him. The bandits must have known to look in his cuff.

The instructions indicated the next contact was based in a town called Grunewald and that the bandits could get new orders there. Otto didn't recognize the name of the town, but he doubted he'd have any trouble finding it.

CHAPTER 16

The spy finally expired after what Otto suspected was the longest three hours of his life. If Father understood the concept of mercy, he showed no sign of it during the interrogation. In the end, the spy told them everything, the location of all the camps in Shenk Barony, his orders from Straken, everything.

When he was finished, Father led the way outside. The clean, fresh air was a welcome change from the stink of blood and burnt flesh. Other than the soldiers manning the walls, Otto, Stephan, and their father were alone. Sergeant Hans and his squad should have finished up by now, but they might have decided against returning to the castle. Otto would have to find them when he was done.

"What will you do now?" Father asked.

"That depends," Otto said. "Will you need assistance dealing with the bandits?"

Father snorted at the suggestion.

"In that case, I'll leave at first light to find the next link in the chain. Are you familiar with the town of Grunewald?"

Father shook his head. "Never heard of it, though it sounds like the sort of name they'd use in the south."

Hopefully not too far south. Otto had more pressing business than running all over the kingdom hunting spies.

"Will you be joining us for dinner?" Father asked.

The invitation surprised Otto and he took a moment to answer. Mostly it came down to whether having to tolerate Griswalda was outweighed by getting to see Mother and sneaking a little magic show in for the kids. In the end he decided it was. "I'll be there."

Father nodded once and he and Stephan stomped off toward the keep. Otto turned for the gate. The same pair as when he arrived was on duty and Otto asked, "Have you seen my squad?"

"No, my lord," the older guard said.

Maybe they were still searching the wagon. When the portcullis was high enough, Otto ducked under and headed east. It didn't take long to make the trip and sure enough he found Hans and the others seated around the covered wagon, a stack of papers between them.

"Find something?" Otto asked.

They started to stand but he waved them back.

"I'm not sure what we found, Lord Shenk," Hans said. "These are all records of where the tinker visited and did business. I can't decide if they're real and he kept them as a cover, or if there's some kind of code."

"Do any of them mention the town of Grunewald?"

"Not that I've seen," Hans said.

"I've got one," a young man named Lute said. He held out the paper and Otto started reading.

About six months ago, the spy had visited Grunewald, repaired a tea pot, and sold three frying pans. Looked like he stayed one night before moving on. Interesting. Otto handed the paper back.

"I want you to sort those by town. Everything in Shenk Barony in one pile and everything out of it in another."

"Of course, my lord," Hans said. "May I ask why?"

"I think this guy was more than the commander of a local group of bandits. I think he was a messenger between the Straken spies. The fact that he was in Grunewald and the town was mentioned on a hidden note as the location of another spy can't be a coincidence. Anywhere else he visited is potentially a target. Oh, and where's that bird? It's time to send Straken a message."

The cage was resting on the ground behind the wagon. Cord got it and handed it to Otto. He set the cage down and collected a blank scrap of paper from the pile. Switching his vision to the ether, Otto set to work charging the paper with fire magic. When it nearly glowed in his magical vision, he rolled it up and set a thread across the edge as a trigger.

"Get the bird out."

Hans gently pulled the black pigeon out of its cage and held it while Otto slipped the paper in a small leather holder attached to its leg.

"Let it go."

With a rush of wings, the pigeon took off and headed directly north. Otto grinned as it disappeared from sight. With any luck the Lady in Red collected her own messages. If she did, this would be the last one she collected.

Hans and the men were looking at him but asked no questions. "I need to make a couple stops then I'm joining my family for dinner. When you finish, head back to the castle. You can find bunks and food in the barracks."

Hans saluted and Otto took his leave. As soon as he was out

of sight, he became one with the ether and shifted to Lord Karonin's tower. Her green-tinged face filled the mirror that was the top floor's sole decoration. She looked exactly the same every time he saw her, same high cheekbones, same dark hair floating around her face, same cold, emotionless eyes. He shouldn't be surprised. The dead didn't age any more than immortal spellcasters did.

"I hadn't expected to see you again so soon, Apprentice."

Otto bowed. "Master, I was hoping you could help me with something. I need a way to see beyond the mile or so I can extend my sight through the ether. Do you know a way?"

"My, but you do have an appetite for secrets. Of course there's a way. There's a way to do almost anything if you know how to shape the ether properly. Farseeing requires something extra. In the armory you may have noticed a clear crystal ball sitting on a pillow."

Otto thought back. He'd been so focused on all the wondrous things he couldn't actually remember a crystal ball. Still, if it was there, he'd find it. "What purpose does it serve?"

"If you connect it to the ether, you can use it like a window to anywhere you can imagine. The view will be warped by the crystal, so you can't see details like you could by extending your own sight, but for observing troop movements, or the comings and goings of a town, it works wonderfully."

"What's the process for connecting it to the ether?" Otto asked.

"It's complicated. Go to the armory and fetch it. You can make your first attempt with my guidance. I doubt you could get it on your own."

He wasn't about to turn down the chance to learn directly from his master. "I'll be right back."

CHAPTER 17

The Lady in Red paced in front of her office door. The general of the southern army was late in making contact and she hadn't heard from several of her agents in over a week. The lack of information was making her nervous. It wasn't doing anything to improve Uther's mood either. The king was snarling more than usual, though happily not at her. Still, his temper was making the entire castle staff uneasy. The keeper of the pigeon coop was due to make his report anytime now. She wished he'd hurry up.

She stopped and turned to make another trip around her favorite worrying spot. Before her foot came down an explosion shook the castle. She staggered but caught herself. What in the world could that have been?

The noise sounded like it had come from the eastern wing of the castle near the coop.

She hurried down the hall anxious to find out what was going on. Nervous servants looked at her as she passed but she had no time to waste. She rounded the corner and found herself staring at open air. The pigeon coop was gone. The door and frame that led to it were a mangled mess of wood and shattered stone. A catapult stone making a square impact on the castle wouldn't have done that much damage.

She moved closer, testing each step to make sure the floor wasn't going to collapse underneath her. She made it to the entrance and peered around what was left of the room. The stone was blackened and all the birds were dead. A charred body was smashed up against the wall. Only magic could have done this.

"What the hell is going on?"

She turned to find Uther stomping his way down the hall toward her. The king's face was red and he kept his hand on the hilt of his sword as though expecting to find someone to fight.

"We received a message, Majesty," she said. "It seems the wizards of Garenland have entered the war."

Uther brushed past her and peered into the ruined room. "You think magic did this?"

"I can't think of anything else that might have. It appears the rumors are true. The new king really has given his wizards the freedom to use their magic offensively."

"That boy is a fool. Taking the wizards off their leash will lead to his destruction." Uther turned to face her. "I've always believed that the only good wizard is a dead one. This just reminds me why. We'll need to set up new lines of communication. Can you handle it?"

"Of course I can, but anything I devise will be far slower than the pigeons. We'll probably need to use relay riders."

"Do whatever you must. And get this mess cleaned up." Uther stomped off back the way he'd come leaving her to handle the details the same way he always did. Not that she minded. The more he relied on her, the safer she was.

CHAPTER 18

Dinner with his family went better than Otto feared
it might, mostly because Griswalda pled sick and
ate in her room. It was a kindness he hadn't
expected, though he assumed it was because she couldn't stand
looking at him.

Well, the feeling was mutual and he was happy not to have
to deal with her. Stephan was on his best behavior and even
Father was in a good mood now that he knew where to find
the bandits. No doubt he would find hours of entertainment
with those unfortunate fellows in the torture chamber. Not
that Otto had much sympathy for bandits, especially ones that
threw in with Garenland's enemies.

He'd barely made it home in time since it took hours to
learn how to make the crystal ball work and, even now, he
couldn't get a clear image through the blasted thing. Still, it
was good enough to find bandit camps and that was all he
needed. All in all, Otto couldn't complain about his day back
home.

But he had to get back to work. He left early the next

morning to avoid goodbyes, pausing only long enough to leave a letter for his mother. He would have liked to give her a final hug, but that would have meant dealing with Father, Stephan, and heaven only knew who else. No, a note was definitely the way to say his goodbyes.

Outside, he found Sergeant Hans and his men up and getting their mounts ready. Otto had found a map with Grunewald marked on it. It was well to the south, but the roads were clear this time of year and it shouldn't take the men more than a week to make the ride, probably less.

As soon as Hans spotted him approaching, he saluted fist to heart. "Morning, Lord Shenk."

"Hans. I trust you have all the supplies you need?"

"The quartermaster was most generous, even trading the wagon for a fine gelding." Hans's forehead crinkled. "Are you not going with us, my lord?"

"No, I'll join you when you arrive." Otto took a rune-marked coin from his pocket and handed it to Hans. "When you reach Grunewald, get rooms at an inn, set this in a large open space on the floor, and tap it hard with your dagger hilt like you did before. I'll sense it and come join you. Just make sure you stay at least six feet from the coin until I arrive. I'm not sure what will happen to you if the ethereal energy hits you and I don't want to find out."

"That makes two of us." Hans accepted the coin and slipped it into his pocket. "We'll make good time, my lord. You can count on it."

"I have no doubt about that, Sergeant. Safe travels." Otto offered his hand and after a moment of hesitation Hans shook it.

Otto waited until the men were mounted up and riding out the front gate to become one with the ether and travel to

Franken Manor. He appeared in his closet amidst his clothes and boots. The rune on the floor appeared as bright as ever in his magical vision. Lord Karonin had never said whether they needed renewing, but so far none of the ones he'd prepared appeared to have weakened.

He stepped out of the closet and extended his sight into the hall. The coast was clear both ways, so he turned invisible and slipped out. Otto snuck downstairs, careful to keep his footfalls as quiet as possible. By good fortune he made it out one of the servants' exits, circled around, turned visible, and walked up to the front door.

The butler opened after his first knock, bowed, and said, "Welcome home, sir. Master Franken is in the dining room. Shall I have a place set for you?"

"No need, thank you." Otto shrugged out of his cloak and made his way to the dining room.

Edwyn was seated at his usual place at the head of the table, a feast surrounding him. Maybe it was Otto's imagination, but the feast looked a little smaller than usual, only five platters of food this morning. Still enough for ten men, but a mere snack for Edwyn.

The master merchant spotted him, started to rise, thought better of it, and slumped back in his chair. "Please tell me you have good news, my boy."

"Some." Otto sat and fixed a bacon and egg sandwich. "Father is cleaning up Shenk Barony as we speak. In a couple of days, I'd say travel through there should be ready to resume. After I check on a few things here and speak to His Majesty, I'm heading south to root out the bandits there."

"That is wonderful news. If Shenk Barony is secure, we can at least resume bringing in the harvest. Have you spoken to

Annamaria yet? She seldom leaves her room, but I'm sure she'd be happy to see you."

Otto seriously doubted that. Part of him was tempted to tell Edwyn exactly how things stood, but he didn't. Otto's father-in-law had enough to worry about with bandits and trade issues, no sense shattering all his illusions. If Annamaria wanted to tell him she could, but it wasn't Otto's job.

He finished his breakfast and said, "I need to go check on the trainees. I doubt I'll be back before setting out again."

"Best of luck in your hunt, my boy." Edwyn hesitated then asked, "Could you ask them to practice a little more quietly? By the end of the day, all those explosions have given me a splitting headache."

"Training for war is a noisy business, I'm afraid. Don't worry, it shouldn't be long before we all head for the front. Until then I'm afraid you'll just have to bear the noise."

Edwyn sighed. "I feared you'd say that."

Otto left him to drown his sorrows in food and wine. He had so much to do it wasn't funny.

○

Otto's first stop was just a few steps out the mansion's side door. It was still early and the trainees hadn't begun practicing yet. And while he wanted to see how much they'd improved, Otto really wanted to talk to Master Enoch. He dearly hoped to find things progressing quickly despite his absence. When he'd offered to train wizards to serve in the army, he hadn't paused to consider how much time it would take nor how many other claims he'd have on his attention.

All around the hastily built barracks, the grass was trampled down and dead. The smell of charred earth filled the air. It was a good smell, one that meant they'd learned to hurl at least basic fire magic. He went to the barracks door and pushed it open. Inside, the trainees were seated at two long tables where they devoured a breakfast much less appetizing than the one Otto had just enjoyed.

Enoch sat at the head of the table, a half-eaten bowl of oatmeal in front of him. It seemed today was to be Otto's day to talk to people over food. As he walked toward the far end of the barracks, he drew a few curious looks. He didn't bother counting, but Otto would have sworn there were more people here than when he left.

As he got closer Enoch finally noticed him. His former master hastened to stand. "Lord Shenk. I'm sorry, I didn't notice you enter. When did you get back?"

"Just this morning. Please, sit and enjoy your breakfast. I only wanted an update on your training before I went to speak to the king. I see some new faces have joined us."

"Yes, my lord. Six new arrivals from beyond the capital have signed up. Everyone has shown great promise despite my lack of ability with fire magic. They can all now cast a fireball safely and accurately every time. We moved on to defensive magics just yesterday."

"Excellent." That was actually better than he'd hoped. The spells were fairly simple, but still it was good to hear they were making progress. "When do you think they'll be ready to march?"

"The most promising group should be ready in a week to ten days at most. Have you heard how the army fares?"

"Not yet. I expect I'll get a full briefing at the palace today. I'll leave you to it then. I plan to be in the city for a few days so maybe tomorrow I'll join you for some practice."

"We would be honored to have you, my lord." Enoch offered a seated bow.

Otto left the wizards to their meal and headed across town. It was time to find out if his new spymaster had learned anything interesting about the would-be blackmailer. The streets of Gold Ward were quiet this early in the morning, but once he entered the business district, the streets grew crowded. The familiar sound of hammers on steel filled the air along with shouts from vendors offering cheap meals for the workers on their way to their jobs.

No one paid much attention to Otto and soon enough he reached the Thirsty Sprite. The tavern was closed and locked up tight. No surprise there as they didn't open until later in the day. Otto wanted to get his business taken care of before the crowds arrived.

He knocked a few times and waited. When no one answered after nearly a minute, he extended his sight and went to have a look around. First, he found Allen asleep in his bed. Next he flew upstairs and found the mercenaries he'd spared in the garret. It took a moment of searching but he finally found Ulf asleep behind the bar. It seemed his servants had put in a long night. Pity he couldn't let them sleep in.

He sent a single thread to the runes on the back of Ulf's and Allen's necks. A weak shock zapped both men awake. Otto knocked again and this time the door quickly opened. Ulf looked as tired as Otto expected but he stepped aside so Otto could enter the tavern.

Allen emerged from his office a moment after the outer door closed. He rubbed the back of his neck and said, "That's a hell of a way to wake a man up."

"I have business at the palace and I want to be able to give the king a full report. Now, what can you tell me about the blackmailer?"

"Not as much as I was hoping. It seems Anders was working with a bunch of thieves. They stole some weapons and gave them to a group of smugglers who intended to deliver them to the Lasil border. The smugglers didn't know much about the thieves, but I'm hoping to track down the manufacturers of the stolen weapons and see if they knew who might have taken their goods."

Sounded like Anders was just hired muscle for the thieves. He probably saw the assassination and thought he could make some easy gold. At least Otto hoped that was all it was. They needed to find the thieves to make sure.

"Did you bring one of the weapons back with you?" Otto asked.

"Of course." Allen went behind the bar and came back with a sword wrapped in oilcloth. He unwrapped it and handed Otto the blade. "If you need more, there's a whole barge full of them downriver a ways."

Otto ignored the comment and studied the weapon. It was a common design made in a number of smithies in Garen. There was one easy way to tell who made this particular sword, assuming it really was stolen and not custom-made for the thieves. Otto made a blade out of ten strands of ether and sliced off the peened-over end of the pommel. With it unsecured, he pulled the pommel off and then the hilt. Stamped on the tang was a stylized anvil, the number four, and a decorative capital F.

He shook his head. This couldn't be right. The sword had been made at their fourth forge. The F marked it as a Franken blade. It was unlikely to be counterfeit since the maker's mark was very specific. Edwyn hadn't mentioned any shipments going missing, so either he was hiding something from Otto or the manager of forge four was keeping secrets. Either way Otto needed to know.

"Lord Shenk? Does the sword mean something to you?" Allen asked.

"It does. I'll be joining you in your investigations today. You've done well. It seems keeping you alive was the correct decision. Tell me, how did the newbies perform?"

"Eric's a little nervous, but he did okay. Erin is a stone-cold killer. She was a great find, though I wouldn't trust her to watch my back on her own."

"I'm glad they proved useful. Make whatever preparation you must. I'll return in an hour and we'll head out."

CHAPTER 19

Otto spent an hour practicing with his crystal ball while Allen and the others prepared to confront the manager of forge four. He still couldn't get an especially clear picture, but he did see Sergeant Hans making good time as he rode out of Shenk Barony toward Grunewald. His gaze next turned north. The army was on the move and getting closer to Straken by the second.

As much as he searched, Otto could find no sign of Straken's army anywhere in their vicinity. There was no way they could retake the entire northern province that easily, but he also couldn't deny what he saw.

Using the crystal ball was surprisingly taxing and he wanted to be at his best when he approached whoever was in charge of the forge. On the plus side, Otto was now able to easily command twenty threads' worth of ether and, if he pushed, twenty-four, though that would exhaust him in minutes.

When he returned to the Sprite, he found everyone armed and ready to go. Eric and Erin both nodded to him but showed no particular deference. Hopefully they wouldn't get any ideas about defying him. Having extra muscle available in the capital when Hans and his squad were out of town was useful, but not so useful that he wouldn't kill them both at the first sign of rebellion.

"Where are we bound, Lord Shenk?" Allen asked.

"The forge where that sword was made. It's a Franken piece so we won't have any trouble getting to whoever's running the place."

If Allen had any thoughts about him not knowing what was going on at one of the family's businesses, he was smart enough to keep his opinion to himself. The truth was, the Frankens owned so many businesses, Otto doubted Edwyn even knew everything that happened in them all.

The forge wasn't a long walk away and ten minutes after they set out, they came to a halt in front of a sprawling brick building. The crash of metal being shaped was nearly deafening. Otto used ether to partially plug his ears. The others had pained expressions, so he took pity on them and plugged their ears as well. The magic didn't leave them totally deaf; it only brought the noise down to a bearable level. If it was this bad outside, inside was bound to be worse.

He was right. Inside, a dozen smiths hammered away at swords, axes, daggers. The heat from the many forges made Otto instantly break into a sweat. He scanned the work floor. There had to be someone that wasn't doing anything useful. That would be the manager.

Allen tugged on his sleeve. Not bothering to try and talk over the noise, he just pointed up and to the left. Otto followed his finger and there was a man standing on a bare metal catwalk looking down at the workers. That had to be who they were looking for.

Otto waved, trying to get his attention. It was a waste of time. The man never looked their way.

A quick peek around revealed a set of stairs leading to the catwalk. Otto stalked off with the others behind him. He clanked up the iron steps and worked his way around to the manager.

Up close he was a skinny little man, with a short salt-and-pepper beard. "You can't be up here!" he shouted over the noise.

"We need to talk," Otto said. "Right now."

The manager glared at Otto, who debated throwing him off the catwalk. The fall was only about twenty feet. At worst he'd break both his legs. Restraint won out and Otto settled for crossing his arms and not moving. Having four, armed people behind him probably helped convince the manager to relent and lead the way to an office built into the side of the building.

The instant they were all inside and the door closed, the noise cut back to almost nothing. Otto looked around with his magical sight and sure enough there was an ethereal barrier blocking the sound. Interesting, and no doubt expensive.

The manager settled into a battered chair behind a metal desk that were the office's only furnishings. "Look, we don't sell to individuals here and we don't keep any gold on hand if you're thinking of trying to rob the place. If you want to buy blades, we have a stall in the market."

Otto kept his composure and in an even tone said, "We're not here to buy swords or to rob you. We're here to find out if any of your merchandise has been stolen lately and if so when."

"I don't see that it's any of your business. None of you look like members of the city watch."

"You don't recognize me, do you?" Otto said.

"Should I?"

"My name is Otto Shenk." The manager's face turned white and he clenched the arms of his chair. "I see I have your attention now."

"Lord Shenk, forgive me. I've heard your name of course, but I've never had the opportunity to see you in person. My name is Lorenzo and I'm honored to have you in my humble forge."

"Lorenzo, let's get one thing straight. This isn't your forge; it belongs to my father-in-law. You just look after things for him. Now, talk to me about stolen merchandise."

"I'm not aware of any stolen merchandise, my lord."

"Show him, Allen," Otto said.

Allen dropped the sword they'd recovered from the smugglers on Lorenzo's desk. "We found this and plenty more just like it in the hands of smugglers who said they were bound for the Lasil border. They claimed a group of thieves provided the merchandise."

Lorenzo checked the maker's mark and said, "This is one of ours, though I can't say from which batch. If it was stolen, it didn't happen here. We pack and load wagons on the dock out back. After that I have no control over what happens to them."

Otto frowned. If the weapons weren't stolen here, they must have gotten hit on the road. He'd have to talk to Edwyn later. "I assume you keep records of what you ship out."

"Of course, every blade that leaves here is recorded."

"I'll need to see the records for the last month." Otto looked around at the empty office. "Where do you keep them?"

"In a storeroom off the loading dock. I'll show you."

They followed Lorenzo back across the catwalk and down a different path to the rear of the building. Another set of iron stairs descended to the floor and a few feet away a heavy door waited. He pulled it open and a blast of blessedly cool air rushed out. They stepped through and once more the ear-splitting clang was dulled down to a bearable level. Otto released the spell that blocked their ears.

Beyond the door was a wide walkway that wagons could back up to for loading. There was no one waiting at the moment. Lorenzo led the way down the walk to a door that led to a room filled with cabinets. A woman in her early thirties, rather plain with brown hair and eyes, sat behind a wood desk and scratched away with a crow quill. She looked up when they entered and her eyes widened.

"Lord Shenk," Allen whispered.

"I noticed. I'll make sure she doesn't do anything foolish; you keep an eye on him."

Lorenzo had been watching their inaudible discussion with a nervous little smile. When it was clear they were finished he said, "Val, this is Lord Shenk. He's checking on a load of merchandise that went missing. We'll need the paperwork for the last month."

"Yes, sir." Her voice shook, more than it should for simple nerves.

When she started to stand, Otto said, "Stay there, please. Just tell me where the manifests are kept and I'll get them."

"I couldn't ask you to." She kept moving, edging her way to the left, toward the nearest cabinet.

Otto flicked his ring and prepared a binding spell. "You're not asking me to do anything. I'm telling you not to move another inch. Sit down and be still."

Finally sensing the mood, Eric and Erin set their crossbows on the floor and started to load them. The sight of the weapons getting cocked sent her over the edge.

Val lunged for the cabinet.

She managed three feet before Otto's spell locked her in place.

Lorenzo took a step, but Allen had his sword at the man's throat in a blink. "Keep your distance."

The manager nodded and raised his hands before stepping back against the wall.

Otto turned back to Val, releasing her head and asking, "What did you do?"

"I didn't think anyone would notice." Tears ran down her face. "We've lost so much to bandits I figured why shouldn't one wagonload go to someone who needed it. He was so handsome and kind. When he looked at me, my knees got all wobbly."

Otto wasn't overly interested in her wobbly knees. "Tell me everything and if you don't lie, I might not have you hung."

"Hung?" The word came out in a squeak.

"In a time of war, stealing military equipment is an act of treason. I'm getting the impression that you're less a thief than you are an idiot who's easily manipulated. For the last time, what happened?"

"We met at a tavern one night. Thomas sat down beside me and smiled. I think I fell in love a little. He told me about his financial troubles and couldn't I help him? He knew people who would pay good coin for Garenland steel. He said after it was done, we'd run away together. It was stupid, but I agreed. I faked a signature and when he showed up with a wagon and some men, I ordered the crates loaded."

"Have you seen him since?" Otto asked.

She closed her eyes so she couldn't see Otto staring at her. "No."

Her answer was barely audible and told him all he needed to know. "What did Thomas look like?"

"Tall, blond, pretty blue eyes. He dressed in plain but clean clothes, nothing fancy. His voice was soft, gentle, and caring. He was so different than the other men I've met. He acted like he really cared about me."

"That's all it was," Otto said. "An act. Where did you meet him?"

"The White Pony."

"I know it," Allen said.

"Is there anything else you can tell us that might help locate this man? Your life might depend on your answer."

"I'm sorry. Now that I look back on it, he really didn't tell me that much about himself. That should have been a warning sign, shouldn't it?"

Otto just shook his head in disgust and released his spell. He turned to Lorenzo. "You don't make armor here, do you?"

"No, my lord. We're only set up for bladed weapons."

"I was afraid of that. I suggest you put a system in place to prevent this from happening again. I or one of my agents will be checking in later. If things aren't running smoothly when they arrive, you'll be looking for a new position. Clear?"

"Perfectly, my lord."

"Good." Otto started to go, paused, and turned back to look at Val. "You're fired."

Otto jumped down from the loading dock and led his companions away from the forge. When they'd gone a little ways down the street he said, "This Thomas has pulled the same trick or something similar elsewhere. That must be where he got the armor. I don't suppose you got the maker's mark off the mail?"

"No," Allen said. "I assumed it all came from the same place."

Otto waved his hand. He could count the number of places

that made armor on one hand. The process was much more complex and time consuming than making weapons. It wouldn't take long to track the missing mail.

The more Otto learned, the more certain he was that Anders had been acting on his own. Nevertheless, he wanted to deal with these thieves. Having someone running around stealing from his family's business made them look weak. And that was something Otto couldn't allow.

CHAPTER 20

The White Pony reminded Allen of his own tavern. It was situated in a similar neighborhood and the building had an almost identical layout. He could have felt at home here. They even had a pretty good crowd considering it was only ten o'clock in the morning. Over half the tables were occupied by groups of men and women in their later years. Maybe he should try appealing to that group. They had plenty of free time and hopefully money.

The smell of coffee and baked goods mingled with bacon and sausage. It made his mouth water. Not that he imagined Lord Shenk would be happy with him if he took an extra fifteen minutes for a late breakfast, especially considering he was waiting outside in an alley. Allen scanned the room and quickly spotted Ulf seated at a corner table sipping a cup of coffee. Eric and Erin were at another table trying to look inconspicuous and failing miserably. They were the only ones in the place wearing armor. Only Lord Shenk's order had gotten them to leave their crossbows behind.

Speaking of their leader, he elected to remain outside

both to ensure Thomas didn't escape and to avoid drawing too much attention. There were plenty of people that knew him both as the king's chief advisor and the son-in-law of the richest man in the city. Not everyone of course, the incident at the forge proved that, but plenty. There were times being rich and famous was useful and times it was a nuisance. Allen was willing to give it a try just to see if he liked it.

There was no sign of Thomas, but someone had to know him. Attractive people tended to leave an impression. He settled at an empty table and soon enough a cute young woman in a black tunic and white apron walked up to him.

"What can I get you?" the server asked.

"A cup of coffee for now. I'm supposed to meet a friend of mine but he's late. Tall blond guy named Thomas, you haven't seen him, have you?"

"Not this morning. He doesn't usually come in until later in the afternoon. Does he owe you money or something?"

Allen chuckled. "Or something. He insulted my sister and I mean to have satisfaction."

"That sounds like Thomas." Her face twisted in distaste. "He has a new girl every couple weeks. He's handsome enough and charming when he wants to be, but deep down is a real shit."

Allen sent a silent prayer heavenward at his good luck. "It sounds like you have first-hand experience."

"More than I'd like."

He put a silver coin on the table. "How would you like to help me teach him the error of his ways? That coin has friends if you can tell me where to find him."

"How many friends?" she asked, never taking her eyes off the coin.

Allen took out three more and put them in a neat pile on

the table. "I also promise to punch him once in the face for you."

"Make it two punches and you got a deal."

He grinned and nodded. "Where is he?"

"He keeps a love nest above the barbershop on Saint Street. If he's not there, I can't help you."

"Thanks." Allen stood and left the coins behind. He caught Ulf's eye and gave a slight shake of his head. He found Lord Shenk waiting outside across the street. "I have an address but there's no guarantee that he's home."

"If there's one thing I've learned," Lord Shenk said. "It's that there are no guarantees in life. Let's go see if we can find him."

"What about the others?"

"They can stay here in case he shows up. The two of us should be able to handle a single fop."

Having seen Lord Shenk's power firsthand, Allen figured he could handle an entire army of fops. Saint Street was only a few blocks over, so they went on foot. His employer—Allen refused to think of Lord Shenk as his master even though that was probably closer to the truth—seemed disinclined to talk.

"It seems we are coming to the end of this job," Allen said. "Do you have something else lined up for us?"

"This business was a distraction. As soon as it's dealt with, I want you to get busy building the spy network we discussed when I first decided not to kill you. It seems we will need to expand beyond the original scope I intended. There's far too much going on in the city that I know nothing about, these thieves for instance. Imagine what's going on in the rest of the kingdom that's escaped our notice. There are simply too many outside threats for us to have chaos internally. It needs to stop and it needs to stop as soon as possible."

Allen tried to swallow but found his throat dry. Lord

Shenk's grim tone made it clear that whoever was causing the chaos he didn't like was going to regret their choices in life. It made Allen happy that he was on the right side of that anger.

"On another subject," Allen said. "Captain Kelten paid me a visit the other day."

"And what did you tell him?"

"The truth, just as you suggested, though heavily edited."

"And did he seem satisfied?"

"For the moment. He said he may have more questions later on. I can't imagine him finding anything to make it worth coming back to talk to me."

"Let's hope so. He is yet another distraction I don't need right now. Don't all these people understand that there's a war on? That we're surrounded by enemies who want to see us all dead? All this foolishness just makes our enemies' job easier."

Allen didn't have anything to say to that and they completed the short walk in silence. They had no trouble spotting the barbershop; it had a six-foot red, white, and blue pole out front. There was an alley separating it from a dress shop next door. A set of steps running along the outside of the building led to a door that he assumed opened into Thomas's flat.

By some miracle they made it to the top of the stairs without them creaking. Allen tried the door but found it locked.

"You want me to kick it in?"

"No need." Lord Shenk put a finger on the wood and a moment later said, "Give it another try."

Allen tugged and the door opened easily. He glanced down and found the latch had been sliced cleanly in half.

Putting the magic firmly out of his mind, Allen stepped into the flat. The curtains were drawn, but a little light leaked through the cracks, enough to reveal a small sitting room with a couch and table and a cold hearth. A door led to another room out of sight. Not a sound could be heard.

"He's not here," Lord Shenk said. "Let's have a look around, maybe there's a clue to his whereabouts. And close the door, we don't want to scare him off should he return home."

Allen obliged then set to checking the sitting room while Lord Shenk disappeared through the inner door. He threw the curtains open to let in more light and went to the couch. The cushions were a little worn, but not too much. He tossed them aside but found nothing underneath. The table held only an empty wine bottle. There didn't appear to be a kitchen.

He frowned. If he were a gigolo that worked for thieves seducing women in useful positions, where would he hide his valuables?

Allen turned at once to the hearth. He knelt, reached up the chimney, and felt around. Nothing but sooty bricks.

He reached as far as he could and his nail ticked off of something metal. At the risk of hurting his shoulder, he stretched enough to grab a metal box and pulled it out. The thing was filthy, but Allen didn't let that bother him.

The box's lid fit tight, but it wasn't locked. With a grunt of effort, he yanked it open. Inside was a pouch and two sheets of paper. The pouch clinked when he shook it. Allen grinned and pocketed whatever coins Thomas had collected. Now the papers.

The first one was written in some sort of code. The words were legible, but the message made no sense, at least not to him. He checked the second paper. It was a love note from some poor, deluded soul that imagined Thomas cared about her. Allen frowned. Why would he keep this note given the number of women he'd seduced? Maybe there was more to it than he thought.

"Did you find anything?" Lord Shenk emerged from the back room empty-handed.

"Perhaps, I'm still reading. You?"

"Just clothes. Let me see what you have."

Allen handed him the coded paper and kept reading the love note. It was signed by someone named Sin. There were plenty of names that might be short for, or it might be a nickname. He went to the top and read it again. There were the usual confessions of eternal love, a promise that he would be well rewarded for his work, and another promise to meet soon at the Nest for a night he wouldn't forget. The Nest might be important, but it wasn't a name he was familiar with. Could be an inn or tavern or anything really.

"Can you make anything of the code?" Allen asked.

"Given time I'm sure I could decipher it, but I'm not wasting my efforts right now. What about the other note?"

"It's a fairly generic love letter. The only thing of interest is the mention of a place called the Nest and a promise to meet."

"The Nest?" Lord Shenk scratched his chin.

"Does that mean something to you, my lord?" Allen stood and brushed himself off.

"There's a modest villa in Gold Ward that's called the Nest. It's short for The Crow's Nest. It's owned by the Crow family, a newly wealthy clan that only moved to the ward a few years ago. The older families like to sniff at them, but I briefly met the matriarch during the party before my wedding. She struck me as a sharp woman, too sharp to be mixed up with thieves. But that doesn't guarantee some other member of the family isn't."

"What should we do now, my lord?"

"We'll have to pay them a visit. But first you need to change your clothes. You look like a chimney sweep."

Allen grimaced but asked, "May I keep the coded letter? Ulf is good at that sort of thing."

Lord Shenk handed it over. "By all means, take it. I hate puzzles. Meet me in front of the portal at two. The Crow's Nest isn't far from there."

Allen bowed. He'd never visited a home in Gold Ward during the day. It should be interesting.

CHAPTER 21

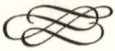

Otto sat at a small cafe near the portal and sipped a glass of white wine. The huge mithril construct still crackled with ether in his magical vision, but it wouldn't activate. He'd been thinking about ways to change that, but Otto understood so little about how the magic worked that his ideas were rudimentary at best. Someday he was going to have to bring it up with Lord Karonin, but there was so much else to do, he didn't know when he'd get the chance.

His irritation with the obstacles in his way had built to a dangerous degree and he needed to get it under control before they went to see Mrs. Crow. He'd get nowhere if he went in there frothing like a mad man and barking orders like his father. Rich matrons had their pride, especially those with new money who hadn't fully won the respect of their peers. Hopefully he could use that pride to his advantage.

He took another sip of his wine. It was an excellent vintage. One of the things he loved most about Gold Ward was that no one sold cheap wine. In fact, no one sold cheap anything.

He yawned and closed his eyes. A moment later his vision was flying up over the nearest houses and toward the Crow's Nest. Just because he wanted to be polite, didn't mean he wasn't going to scout out the area before he approached. If his enemies were operating out of the villa, he didn't want to walk into a trap.

The Crow's Nest was painted dark gray with gold accents. They didn't have any guards patrolling the small yard and no fence separated them from the street. The villa itself was only two stories with no wings flaring out to either side. It was still a beautiful home even if he could've easily fit the whole thing in a small corner of Franken Manor.

Otto tried to fly through the dark-red door, but something stopped him. He shifted his vision and found an ethereal barrier blocking his way. It surrounded the entire house and while he could easily tear it apart, he decided not to risk alerting its creator. The barrier had to be new since the house itself was only fifty years old. He was surprised that there were any wizards currently capable of making such a spell. He barely understood the process himself, not that he'd spent any great amount of time studying protective magics. This little episode was making him think maybe he should.

He returned his sight to his body and opened his eyes. If nothing else, the magical protections gave him confidence that there was something untoward going on at that house. After all, you didn't hire someone to protect your home from prying wizards unless you had something to hide.

And exactly what wizards did they have to hide from? As far as Otto knew, he was the only wizard capable of extending his senses and he didn't exactly advertise the fact that he knew how. If it wasn't him they were hiding from, who was it?

"Lord Shenk?"

He glanced right and found Allen, dressed in a fine tan tunic and matching trousers, standing a few feet away. He hadn't worn his sword which was unfortunate. Otto nearly sighed at his lack of awareness. If some enemy had snuck up on him like that, he'd have been dead before he knew there was danger.

"Allen. Are you ready?"

"Yes, my lord. Ulf is working on the code as we speak. He seemed optimistic that he could crack it in a reasonable amount of time."

"Good." Otto didn't really think the code was that important, but every little bit of information they could get helped. "Are you armed?"

Allen pulled up his right pant leg revealing the hilt of a dagger jutting from the top of his boot. "I didn't think we were expecting combat. Should I go back and get a sword?"

"No, and I didn't expect combat either, then I found a magical barrier protecting the house. Now I'm not sure what to expect. Come on." Otto stood and tossed a silver coin on the table. "The only way to find out for sure is to introduce ourselves. For the record, you'll be playing the part of my personal assistant."

"Why am I not going as myself?" Allen asked as they left for the Crow's Nest.

"Because why would I be bringing a tavern keeper with me to visit my neighbors? Dragging a servant along at least makes a little sense. I could say we're going shopping later and I need you to carry my purchases. I've seen a few people doing that. I doubt it will come up, but I wanted you to be ready."

Allen nodded and asked no more questions. It took just over five minutes to reach the villa. It looked exactly the same as it had during his magical investigation. To his ethereal sight it appeared surrounded by a rainbow-colored dome not unlike the one that protected Lord Karonin's tower, though far weaker.

They stopped in front of the door and Otto looked at Allen. "What?"

"Knock. That's one of the jobs a nobleman's servant performs."

"Okay."

Allen rapped on the door and a few seconds later it opened. A middle-aged man dressed in all black looked from Allen to Otto. "Can I help you?"

His voice oozed the sort of disdain Otto took special pleasure in knocking out of people. "My name is Otto Shenk. I need to speak with the master of the house on a matter of Crown interest."

"What sort of matter?" the servant asked.

"Are you the master of the house?" Otto asked offering his most arrogant sneer.

"No, sir."

"Then it's none of your concern. Fetch your employer. Or shall I return to the palace and inform His Majesty that the Crow family is uninterested in helping the Crown in a most serious investigation?"

"One moment." For a second Otto wondered if the servant was going to slam the door in his face, but instead he stepped aside and gestured for them to enter. "Wait here."

"Here" was a small entry room that held a coat rack and table, but no chairs or other decoration gracing its off-white walls. It was extremely plain compared to Franken Manor. It almost felt like someone had started decorating, got sick of it, and stopped halfway through.

When the servant had gone to get his master Allen said,

"Not terribly hospitable, are they? You'd think they'd want to suck up to the king's closest advisor."

They should want to and the fact that the servant at least didn't made Otto all the more nervous. "I'm going to try and have a look around. As soon as you hear someone coming, let me know."

Otto closed his eyes and tried to extend his sight again. He succeeded this time and began flying around the house. He examined a number of well-appointed bedrooms, several closets and storage rooms, and a fine kitchen where a cook and three helpers tended a large stove and the many pots and pans covering it. Another servant was cleaning upstairs.

He only got three-quarters of the way through his search when Allen said, "My lord."

Otto opened his eyes and a moment later the servant in black returned with Mrs. Crow following along. She looked just as Otto remembered, portly, with perfect gray hair, a strand of pearls, and dressed in all black.

"Lord Shenk, this is a surprise." Her voice was deep for a woman, but still pleasant.

"Mrs. Crow." Otto offered a shallow bow of apology. "Please forgive the intrusion, but I was investigating a matter for the king and some information led me to your door."

"I'm happy to be of any help I can to the Crown. Won't you come to the sitting room? Bartram, be a dear and get us some tea."

The servant in black bowed and departed. Otto and Allen followed Mrs. Crow to the next room to the right which held a selection of velvet-cushioned chairs situated around a square table. A cold hearth filled half of the far wall. A painting of a stern, hatchet-faced man hung over it.

"My late husband, Evenrude," Mrs. Crow said when she

noticed Otto looking at the painting. She sat and Otto took the chair across from her while Allen stood behind him. "How may I be of assistance?"

"During an investigation into the theft of military supplies, specifically weapons and armor, I came across a reference to your home and someone I assume lives here. Does the name or nickname Sin mean anything to you?"

A tiny flinch was the only indication that she knew what he was talking about. It came and went so fast Otto almost thought he imagined it.

Before she could form an answer, Bartram returned with a silver tray bearing a tea pot, two cups, sugar, and milk. He set them on the table, poured, and retreated to the corner of the room. Otto took his cup and stirred it with a strand of ether.

The thread instantly turned a sickly green.

Poisoned. Any doubts he might have had about the Crow family's involvement disappeared.

Otto pretended to take a drink then set the cup back down. "You were saying?"

She stared at him and he stared back. The moment stretched to the breaking point. At last she said, "It might be referring to my eldest daughter, Alison. She sometimes goes by Sin, even though I've told her many times how much I hate that nickname."

"I see. Is she home? I'd like to have a word with her about a gentleman of her acquaintance named Thomas. Tall, blond fellow, perhaps you've met him."

She was getting more nervous by the second; the fine wrinkles round her eyes tightened and a single bead of sweat rolled down her face and stuck in a fold of fat on her neck.

"Bartram, go see if Alison is in her workshop downstairs.

The dear girl has a fondness for carving, but I won't have the mess in the main house."

"Yes, madam." The butler left through a door partially hidden behind a wall hanging.

Otto wasn't sure what was stupider, a noblewoman that enjoyed carving or a noblewoman that would care about making a mess for the servants.

"I hope my silly daughter hasn't gotten into anything untoward." Mrs. Crow's laugh sounded brittle.

Otto stayed silent. Whatever was going on, he was certain the woman knew all about it and was stalling for time. Time to do what was the question.

A few minutes later Bartram returned and said, "Mistress Alison would be delighted to meet with the king's agent. If you'll follow me, sir."

Otto stood and looked at Mrs. Crow. "Do join us, madam. I may have questions for you as well."

"Oh, no, I have trouble with the stairs."

"I'm sure you'll manage," Otto said in a tone that made it clear he wouldn't accept no for an answer.

Her brittle smile fractured, but she got up anyway. Otto motioned for her and Bartram to lead the way. He and Allen followed them through the side door and down an undecorated hall to a flight of steep steps. Flickering firelight from the basement illuminated the steps enough that they could descend without fear of misstep.

At the bottom was a room holding a scarred wooden table, a chair, five men counting Bartram and two women counting Mrs. Crow. The second woman was stunning, maybe five years older than Otto. She wore all black leather including pants that appeared painted on. She looked like sin, that was for sure.

Two of the men were rough-looking thugs and two more had ether glowing around their bodies. The thin protective barrier marked them as wizards of modest power, he guessed six or seven threads' worth of ether protected them. They were above average in strength for wizards that hadn't broken through their personal barrier, but nothing he couldn't handle.

There was a strangled noise behind him.

Otto turned to see a tall blond man, Thomas he assumed, holding a knife at Allen's throat.

"Well, your lordship, you said you wanted to talk." He turned back to find the younger woman smiling a wicked smile. "Let's talk."

CHAPTER 22

Otto studied the collection of characters surrounding him. It was an odd group for sure. Cleaned up and put in proper clothes, Alison would fit right in at a noble's ball. Her thugs, on the other hand, wouldn't find work answering the door in Gold Ward. The wizards were the biggest surprise. For some reason, Otto had never considered that wizards might work for an illegal organization like this. Though given how they were treated, he couldn't be too surprised.

He gathered a little ether in his hand. The instant he did, one of the wizards smashed it with an ethereal whip. "None of that, now," the wizard said.

"Best behave yourself if you want your friend to live through this," Alison said.

"I don't especially care if you kill Allen." Otto shrugged. "He's a useful ally, but hardly a friend. It wouldn't be the end of the world if I had to replace him, but it would be a nuisance. If your blond boyfriend does cut Allen's throat, I'm going to gut him like a hog and roast him over an open fire.

Now, if we're finished with the threats, let's get down to business."

"You're hardly in a position to be giving orders," Alison said.

"Why, because you've got two wizards watching over me? I assure you those two weaklings can no more stop me from killing all of you than your threat to murder Allen can. The only reason I haven't done it yet is the hope that we can settle this in a peaceful manner. Your organization might be of use to me. If you prefer to skip straight to violence, I'm happy to oblige."

Alison stared at him as though not entirely sure if he was insane or serious. Clearly this wasn't how she imagined the discussion going.

"Don't pay him no mind, Sin," one of the wizards said. "Anders says he can only use a single thread of ether at a time."

"Did you send him to blackmail me, Anders I mean?" Otto asked. "Was he acting on his own or was that one of your schemes?"

"What happened to him?" Alison asked. "Anders is my second and a valuable asset."

"He's quite dead. I melted his brain and burned his body to ash."

"Liar!" the second wizard shouted. "Master Anders would never lose to someone as pathetic you."

"Shut up," Alison said before turning back to Otto. "He's really dead?"

"He really is."

"What a waste. I warned him not to get involved with the nobility. Nothing good ever comes from it. They have too many resources and the power of the law behind them. It's never worthwhile." She sighed and shook her head. "Poor

Anders. He never listened. You understand I can't allow you to get away with killing one of my people?"

Otto raised an eyebrow. "Violence it is then?"

"Boys."

The two wizards forged the ether into tentacles and lashed them at Otto.

He conjured a barrier and the tentacles shattered against it.

Before they could recover from their surprise, he wove a twenty-thread whip and slashed at their necks.

One tried to block and failed.

His head went flying in a fountain of blood.

The second tried to dodge and failed.

Otto cut him in half at the waist.

In the stunned silence that followed, Otto flicked his ring and bound Allen's captor. He walked over, removed the knife from Thomas's hand, and repositioned the arm holding Allen in place, freeing him.

"You okay?" Otto asked.

"Perfectly, my lord." In a lower voice Allen asked, "You were just kidding about not caring if they killed me, right?"

He actually sounded pained at the suggestion that Otto wouldn't value his life. Otto had pegged him as more practical than that.

"Of course. If they thought I cared, you'd have been in even more danger." Otto offered him the dagger. "Kill him if it makes you feel better. He's certainly of no use to me."

"It's a little close to dinner time for murder."

"Suit yourself."

Otto turned back to find the other thieves still standing where he'd left them. No one had even tried to draw a weapon. A wise decision on their part.

"Now that we all know where we stand," Otto said. "Perhaps we can try to have a civil conversation."

Alison's arrogant smirk was long gone now. The blood had drained from her face making her appear even paler than before. "Let me start by apologizing for stealing from you. It wasn't personal. The female clerk was just too easy a target. If you wish, I can try and recover your goods."

"The weapons and armor have already been recovered and the smugglers you hired executed."

She winced. "Our buyers will not be happy."

"Tell me more about these buyers. They're from Lasil I understand. Where did you meet?"

"We've never met them directly."

There was a creak on the steps behind him. Otto spun and found Mrs. Crow looking to make a quick escape.

"Where do you think you're going?" Otto asked.

"You two have so much to discuss. My legs are getting tired, so I thought I'd rest upstairs. You don't expect an old woman to stand on this hard floor forever, do you?"

"You're welcome to sit on the floor," Otto said. "Move another step higher and I'll make you drink your own tea."

She blanched and dropped back to the floor.

Otto turned back. "Is she actually your mother, Alison?"

Alison laughed. "Hardly. She's just some stupid actress I hired to be the face of the family. And my name's not Alison, it's Sin, just Sin."

The thugs behind her were getting restless. One started inching his hand down to the shortsword on his belt. After Otto's demonstration earlier, you'd think they'd have known better. Then again, the muscle was seldom hired for their brains.

"You might want to warn your people not to do anything stupid," Otto said.

Sin looked back. "Knock it off, you two. I'm trying to get us out of this alive."

The thugs slumped and sat on the floor.

"Now, about the buyers," Otto said.

"Right, we never met them. An old business associate of mine mentioned some buyers in Lasil were looking for good-quality weapons and were having trouble buying them thanks to the portal being shut down. There was good money in it if we could get the goods past the tax collectors on the border."

"Hence the smugglers." Otto was starting to get the picture now. "And who is this associate of yours?"

She laughed though it sounded strained. "You'll never believe it. He's a tinker that travels the country. You'd be amazed what he picked up here and there."

"Let me guess," Otto said. "Big guy with a beard and covered wagon?"

Sin's eyes widened. "You know him?"

"My father tortured him to death yesterday. Your associate was a Straken spy. I doubt there was even a buyer in Lasil. He just wanted to deprive the kingdom of weapons to help his masters. And you played right into his hands."

"But the smugglers had our payment," Sin said.

"No doubt spoils from the many bandit raids over the past weeks. It seems you have less to offer me than I'd hoped. How large is your organization?"

"If you count the pickpockets and cutpurses that pay us a percentage maybe fifty. The numbers change depending on who's in jail. My main crew is fifteen, twelve now, not to mention I'm all out of wizards."

Otto brightened. "Speaking of magic, how did your wizard create the barrier surrounding this villa? It's excellent work. I assume Anders handled the spell."

"Not exactly. Anders found this ugly statue in a shop. He said it was magic and that it would protect us." She barked a laugh. "What a joke."

"He was right to a certain extent. The magic creates a barrier that prevents wizards from spying on this house. It's possible he didn't fully understand what he'd found. So much knowledge has been lost since the time of the Arcane Lords. Show it to me."

Sin started for the steps then paused. "What about Thomas?"

Otto looked at Allen. "You're certain you don't want to kill him?"

"Yes, but..." Allen punched Thomas twice in the face then kicked him in the groin. "The first two are from the serving girl at the White Pony. The kick was from me."

Otto grinned and ended his spell. Thomas collapsed and curled up in a ball. Sin continued on her way. At the top of the stairs she let him catch up and walked along at his side toward the center of the villa.

Sin stroked his arm. "Thomas isn't going to be much use for a few days. Do you have plans for tonight?"

Otto pulled away from her. He already had a wife that hated him, he didn't need a mistress that might cut his throat in his sleep. "The statue?"

She pouted but opened an oak door. Beyond it was a large, nearly empty room. The only decoration was a round end table with a foot-tall statue of a knight in armor that crackled with ether. Threads ran into it then back out the shield and up into the barrier.

Remembering his lessons, Otto conjured a plug and placed it on the foot of the statue. The flow of ether stopped and over half a minute the barrier vanished. When the statue appeared fully normal, he picked it up and tucked it under his arm. It seemed this wouldn't be a complete waste of time after all.

To Sin he said, "Here's my offer. Your thieves will stay away from anything related to the war or owned by the Frankens. Any information you pick up that might be of value, you pass to Allen. Work against me, my family, or the Crown and I'll find you and kill you along with anyone that's ever worked for you. It's a one-time offer. Pass and I burn this villa to the ground with you and your fellows inside."

"You are a tough negotiator, my lord. Of course I accept. My people are at your disposal." She licked her lips and ran a hand down her ample chest. "As am I."

"Good. Turn around and lift your hair off the nape of your neck."

She gave him a slightly confused look but complied. It really was a lovely neck, pale, smooth skin over lean muscle. He formed a thin blade of ether and carved a rune into her neck, drawing a pained hiss. Next he charged it with magic until he could sense it in the ether.

"There, all done," he said. That was five people he'd marked, each with a unique rune, plus the three runes he used to mark teleportation sites. Too many more and he'd have trouble keeping track of everyone.

"What have you done to me?" Sin asked.

"I put a mark on your neck, a magical one. With that I can find you anywhere you might run or simply kill you with a thought. It's not that I don't trust your word, but after all you are a thief. Check in with Allen once a week at the Thirsty Sprite, and welcome to the team. I have every confidence we'll have a long and productive relationship."

Her smile was sour and beaten. Otto hoped she stayed beaten. It would be a shame to have to kill someone so lovely.

CHAPTER 23

After a long, exhausting day, Otto made his way to the palace. There was only an hour until sunset and long shadows lay over everything. A chill hung in the air, arguing that winter would be here before they knew it. All the magic he'd used had left him on the edge of exhaustion. Nevertheless, he dared not skip meeting with Wolfric. If he got word that Otto was back in the city and hadn't come to see him the first day, he'd be upset. Besides, a meal at the palace was bound to be more pleasant than one at home.

At the side entrance he usually used, the two men on duty snapped to attention and ordered the portcullis raised for him. Gone were the days of him having to explain himself or bind his sword. His new title made everyone snap to when he showed up and his magic made them afraid, even not knowing exactly what he was capable of. Had they known, he doubted anyone would have been able to meet his gaze.

Otto put the guards out of his mind and resumed his trudge across the courtyard to the main keep. Just inside the massive structure a servant appeared to take his cloak and guide him to the library where the king waited. He barely registered the journey and next thing he knew he was surrounded by books.

"You look worse than I feel." Wolfric stepped out from behind a bookcase. He was dressed in a fur-lined robe of the finest blue velvet. "You have news?"

"A great deal, Majesty. Would it be alright if we sat and talked?"

"Of course and please, it's just us here. I get enough of Your Majesty this and Your Majesty that from the servants and nobles. I need at least one person I can talk to like a normal human being."

Otto slumped into an overstuffed leather chair and offered a silent prayer that he could stay awake long enough to deliver his report.

"We killed the Straken spy running the bandit groups in Shenk Barony," Otto began. "Father's hunting down the strays, and grain shipments should be safe to resume in a few days."

"That is wonderful news. Everyone's crying about how we're all going to starve this winter." Wolfric rubbed the bridge of his nose and sighed. "I really don't know how Father put up with them. Everyone has a complaint or, worse, a suggestion. Forgive me, continue please."

"Hans and his men are heading south to find the next group. I'll join them in a few days when they arrive. The wizards are shaping up, at least according to my former teacher who I've put in charge of their training. I'll observe them myself tomorrow. With any luck we'll have twenty or so to send north by the end of the week."

Wolfric nodded and leaned back in his chair, seeming to finally relax a fraction. "They might not have much to do. According to the last report I got, after some initial resistance, the army hasn't fought so much as a skirmish. By the way, your brother saved General Varchi from an assassin so not executing him turned out to be a good thing."

Father wouldn't have agreed but wasting a soldier as skilled as Axel was stupid. The war was going to be a long one and they'd need everyone they could get before it was over.

"That's a relief." Otto said.

"Captain Kelten hasn't seen fit to trouble me again about Father's assassination, but he's still investigating." Wolfric sighed. "Like a dog with a bone that one is."

"I still say we should arrange an accident for him. The man's more trouble than he's worth."

"No, there'll be too many questions if Kelten dies while investigating a suspicious death. We'll just have to be patient. He'll hit a dead end soon enough and that will be that."

Otto dearly hoped his friend was right. Even though he had his doubts, he was too exhausted to argue about it now. If there was a problem, they'd deal with it when they had to. Otto was finding he had a knack for solving problems.

CHAPTER 24

Axel crouched in the forest across from the fort that he used to call home. Even though noon had just passed, the air was chilly. Their window for war, especially as they went further north, was closing. He figured a month at most before they had to hunker down until spring.

All around the fort, blackened spots dotted the ground where Otto's lightning had scorched the earth. It would be a wonder if anything ever grew there again. He shivered and not because of the cold. Otto had always been a joke to him and Stephan, a runt to push around. Axel pitied anyone that tried to push him around now. They were liable to end up fried.

He put his younger brother out of his mind and focused on his job. The Northern Army had been marching steadily for a week and would catch up to his scouts in a day or two. Every day Axel expected to encounter enemy forces and every day he was surprised to find their path undefended.

Now they were back to where it all began, at least for Axel and his men. The fort was the closest thing he had to a home after leaving Shenk Barony and fleeing had been a bitter decision.

Unavoidable, but still, bitter.

"I don't see any movement," Cobb said.

Axel had dispatched his troops to check the other forts and right now it was just him, Cobb, and a single squad spying on their old home. Prudence said they should wait for General Varchi and the rest before approaching the fort, but everything he'd seen argued that they were alone out here.

Hell with it.

Axel stood. "Let's go take a peek."

He looked at Cobb, but his second didn't argue. That probably should have worried him. Instead the small group stepped out into the killing field.

No archers stood up on the battlements. Infantry didn't pour out of the open gate. The clearing stayed as quiet as it was before they broke cover.

Encouraged and confused, Axel led the way across the field. His hand never strayed more than an inch from the hilt of his sword. Not that they had any hope of defeating even a small garrison, but if he ran into the enemy, Axel planned to take as many of them with him as possible.

The yard was empty and the keep door open. Axel pointed at two of his men then made a circling gesture around the keep.

They nodded and hurried off to check the rear of the building.

Axel led the rest inside. The dining hall was empty, the kitchen stripped of food, and the armory sacked. The enemy had definitely been here, but what he couldn't figure was why they didn't either occupy the fort or burn it down. The upstairs was much the same. The Straken soldiers hadn't even bothered with Braddock's military books, though they did drink his emergency stash of whiskey. Pity, Axel could have used a drink just then.

"What now?" Cobb asked when they finished checking the last room.

"Now we wait for the other squads to report and the main body of the army to catch up. If the rest of the forts are empty, we should have a smooth path to the border. Once we cross into Straken, all bets are off."

"You think they'll just let us cross the border without a fight?" Cobb asked.

"Looks that way. Remember, it's not a few hundred scouts they have to stop this time, it's three legions of the finest soldiers on the continent. I don't know Straken's full strength, but I doubt they sent fifteen thousand men into Garenland. I'd guess half that at most. It would have been plenty if the army hadn't mobilized, but now..."

Cobb knew as well as Axel that the Northern Army would roll over any lesser force and Uther had to know it as well. The Straken king must have been counting on old King Von Garen being unwilling to fight it out. Having Wolfric in charge changed everything.

"Commander Shenk!" one of the soldiers called from outside, panic in his voice.

Axel and Cobb shared a look. He knew it had been going too smoothly.

They ran outside and found a trembling rookie whose name Axel couldn't recall waiting outside. He was one of the two that had gone to search the rear of the keep. That he was alone wasn't a good sign.

"Where's your partner?" Axel asked.

"Dead, sir. The man in black came out of nowhere and cut

his throat. Next thing I knew he had his sword at my throat and I couldn't move."

"If he had you," Cobb said. "Why are you still breathing?"

"Because he said he wanted me to give the commander a message. He said you cost him his kill and you were going to pay for it. Unless you want all your men to die in your place, you have to face him in single combat, a duel."

"Who did you piss off this time?" Cobb asked.

Axel could only think of one person. "It's got to be the assassin that tried to kill General Varchi. He's the only person I've saved. But who ever heard of an assassin challenging someone to a duel? That's the kind of thing a knight might do, but an assassin would just put an arrow in me and be done with it. When does he want to fight me?"

"In fifteen minutes at the main gate. He said if you refuse, he'll hunt down every scout you send and bring you their heads."

"You're not actually considering fighting the madman, are you?" Cobb asked.

"Of course I am. No more of my people will die in my place. Once we get started, take the men up to the battlements and break out your bows. Win or lose, the son of a bitch doesn't walk away from here. Clear?"

Cobb nodded. "Good luck, Lord Shenk."

Axel drew his sword and walked toward the gate.

CHAPTER 25

Just outside the gate Axel found himself face to face with a young man, who couldn't have been more than a year or two older than Otto, dressed in all-black leather armor. He held a pair of curved shortswords that were the signature of the Straken rangers. His brown hair was cropped close to his skull.

"I expected someone older," Axel said.

"You're not the first to say that," the assassin said. "I had the general dead to rights. Thanks to your interference I was ordered back to Marduke. I may even face a rebuke from the king."

"You were ordered back yet here you are, many miles from the Straken capital."

"Yes, I couldn't return with nothing to show for my efforts. Even if I can't kill the old man, your head will be a small consolation."

Axel raised his sword to high guard. "If you had a bow and I didn't know you were coming, I might be worried, but one on one, in a fair fight, I like my chances."

"I have heard that before as well." The assassin crouched and lunged toward Axel.

Axel stepped back and slashed down, turning aside a blow aimed for his chest.

Steel clashed as Axel used every trick Graves had taught him to avoid getting his guts spilled. The assassin might be young, but he was well trained. The curved blades moved so fast they looked more like flashes of light than swords.

The initial rush left Axel panting but uninjured. He'd fought plenty of rangers over the years, but never one this good. It was no surprise that he'd been sent to kill General Varchi.

He managed two deep breaths before the assassin came barreling in again.

Axel spun away from a double low thrust and countered with a heavy overhead chop.

The assassin leapt and rolled away.

With his opponent finally on the defensive, Axel pressed ahead, trying to use his heavier blade to overpower his opponent.

Try though he might, the assassin was every bit as good on defense as he was on offense. The twin blade twirled and spun, turning aside Axel's every cut and thrust.

Come on, Cobb. His second had to be nearly in position.

No sooner had he thought it than a crash sounded from inside the fort.

The assassin did a back flip and spun to face him. "It seems your men found the battlement I weakened. I will not be interfered with again."

So much for plan A. Axel just wished he had a plan B.

His opponent wasn't going to give him time to come up with one.

The man in black charged again, even stronger this time.

Axel turned aside one blade, but the second screeched across his mail coat. It didn't penetrate, but the weight of the blow staggered Axel back.

He caught himself and lashed out with a two-handed slash.

The heavy blow sent the assassin reeling.

Axel kept going.

Defense wasn't going to save him now.

He either overwhelmed his opponent or he died.

And Axel didn't plan to die.

Two-handed blow after heavy two-handed blow rained down on the assassin, forcing him back.

One of his curved blades shattered and went flying.

Axel's shoulders screamed for a rest. He ignored the discomfort and pushed on. It was now or never.

He thrust at the assassin's chest.

And missed.

The younger man twisted out of the way, flexing his spine in a way spines weren't meant to bend.

Axel stumbled and fell to his knees. The instant he hit he dove and rolled.

When he came to his feet, the assassin was there, already inside his guard.

The curved blade arced up toward his neck.

There was nothing Axel could do, not at this range.

A fraction of a second before the blade would have struck home, the assassin shuddered and collapsed. An arrow stuck out of his back.

Axel followed it back to the source and found Colten at the edge of the woods, a bow in his hand. He let out a long sigh. That had been far too close.

Then he remembered Cobb and the others. Axel waved Colten and his group over.

"You should be ten miles east by now," Axel said as he led them toward the fort. "Not that I'm complaining."

"We were making good time," Colten said. "But about three miles out we cut a trail headed this way, reasonably fresh too. Just one set of prints and faint ones at that. I thought it might be the assassin and rushed back to warn you. If it turned out to be nothing, I figured a few hours more or less wouldn't matter, but if it was important..."

"It was a good call. Now we need to dig Cobb and the others out."

Just inside the gate, an eight-foot section of battlement had collapsed. Arms and legs jutted out here and there amid the broken timbers. A few muffled groans escaped the mess. At least everything visible was moving. Hopefully there was nothing more than bumps and bruises.

Everyone teamed up to toss timbers off the trapped soldiers. The first two had bloody but shallow gashes on their scalps. Number three could barely stand or focus, he must have knocked his head extra hard, but a few days' rest should see him recovered.

When they finally found Cobb, he came up cursing and snarling. That more than anything assured Axel that he'd be fine.

Cobb finally stopped for a breath and Axel asked. "You okay?"

"Can't believe I fell for such an amateur trap. The damn thing was creaking like a hundred-year-old man's knees and I still led the guys across. How could I have been so stupid?"

"Forget about it, Cobb. Everyone survived and that's what

matters. Better yet the assassin's dead so General Varchi won't have to worry about taking a stray arrow."

"You beat him?" Cobb asked.

"No, I lost, but Colten came back in time to pull my fat out of the fire. Speaking of which…" Axel turned to find Colten helping the last man out of the rubble. "Lieutenant, I think we're good here if you want to get back on the trail."

Colten saluted, rounded up his men, and took off. He was a good man. Soon enough he'd probably have Axel's job. Though it would be a waste of his talent to have him out of the forest.

"What now?" Cobb asked. He seemed no worse for having half a ton of logs fall on him. Probably because his head was so hard.

"Now we get everyone to the barracks, button up the gate, and wait for General Varchi to arrive. I can safely say that I've had enough for today."

"I'll second that," Cobb said.

No argument from Cobb for the second time that day. Maybe he'd hit his head harder than Axel thought.

CHAPTER 26

The signal indicating Hans and his squad had arrived in Grunewald reached Otto an hour after lunch and since he had no meeting scheduled for the afternoon he'd gone at once. Otto emerged from the ether in a small room surrounded by Hans and his squad. There was only a foot of space between him and the bed on one side and him and the wall on the other.

When he told Hans to find an open space to place the enchanted coin, he meant bigger than this. Still, he'd squeezed in without materializing in something solid and nothing else mattered.

He bent and picked up the coin. The rune still glowed strong and bright in his magical vision. Sending someone to run an errand then joining them when they arrived was far easier than wasting a week on the road. Speaking of which, the first batch of war wizards should be setting out tomorrow morning to join the Northern Army. Otto had selected three squad leaders and gifted them a mithril apprentice ring. They'd swelled so with pride he feared they might burst. If they knew the real reason he gave them the rings was to keep their power under control, they probably would have been less excited.

"Lord Shenk," Hans said. "We did a little preliminary scouting before calling you. Grunewald is an interesting town."

"The way you say that, Sergeant, makes me think it's not interesting in a good way."

"That depends on your point of view. There's no law here, not really. There's no town watch, mayor, or other noble overseeing things, and everyone goes around armed. I haven't seen any kids and the women aren't exactly ladies."

Otto scratched his chin. "How far are we from the Rolan border?"

"Maybe a day's ride on a good horse," Hans said.

The Rolan border wasn't really marked. At some point the plains on the Garenland side turned into Rolan as you went south and west. There'd been a few squabbles over the border over the years, but not many. There really wasn't much out here to make a fight worthwhile. The grazing was fair and there were wild horses that could be caught and tamed, but that was about it. Otto had learned next to nothing about this part of Garenland and now he was regretting his tutor's lack of instruction. Hell, he didn't even know which noble ruled this part of the kingdom.

"Did you pass any fortifications on your way south?" Otto asked.

"There was a walled town about thirty miles north," Hans said. "But that's all I remember. What are you thinking, my lord?"

"I'm thinking that focusing all our attention to the north has emboldened our other neighbors. I suspect Rolan has taken a bite out of our southern province, whether they've done so with the complicity of the local lord or not remains to be seen."

"And the spy we're hunting?"

"I assumed it would be someone from Straken, but now I'm wondering if our friend the tinker carried messages to other members of the conspiracy. So many questions and so few answers. Well, that's why we're here. The first matter of business is to figure out who runs this town. Because someone does, you can be sure of that."

"How will we find them?" Hans asked.

Otto grinned. "Simple, we'll ask. I assume this place has a common room?"

"Yes, though it wasn't terribly busy when we arrived a few minutes ago."

"As long as the person running the joint is around, I don't care about customers. Let's go and keep your weapons handy."

Hans and the men shared a look then loosened their swords in their scabbards. Otto didn't really expect trouble in an inn's common room, but better to be prepared than not.

He led the way downstairs, the floorboards creaking with every step. The railing looked like it might fall off if he put any weight on it and the paint was chipped and flaking. Clearly Grunewald had seen better days. In the common room, two tables were occupied by bronze-skinned men sporting beards and scars. One of them looked hard at Otto through his single eye. Otto stared back and he finally looked away.

Behind the bar a gaunt woman in a red dress that might have been attractive on someone thirty years younger stood and watched them approach. Otto doubted she was the owner since women weren't allowed to own property, but then again you never could say. Out on the frontier, the laws tended to be less well enforced. As long as she answered his questions, he'd be happy.

"Didn't see you come in," the woman said when Otto stopped in front of her. She coughed up something and spat in a spittoon behind the bar.

Otto suppressed a shudder. "I came in another way. I was hoping you could direct me to the local lord. King Wolfric has tasked me with determining the situation on the Rolan border."

"You from the capital?" she asked.

"That's right. The new king is curious about his subjects and I'm here to get him the information he needs."

Her laugh led to another coughing spell. When she'd spit and wiped her mouth on her sleeve she said, "No king has ever given a bent copper about us. Why does this one care?"

"Given the current difficulties, His Majesty wants to be sure all his people are safe. Though things are bad in the north, he has no desire to ignore the rest of Garenland. So, do you know where I can find the local lord?"

"Probably in the capital. Lazy turd never stays around here, too crude and poor. The tax men come real regular, but his high and mightiness just spends the coin on wine and whores."

"That won't do at all. When I deliver my report, rest assured you will have a new lord soon enough."

She shrugged. "We get along fine on our own. One turd or another, don't make no difference. If you want to know who's in charge, that'd be Mendelson. You can find him and his boys at the Exchange, it's the only stone building in town. You can't miss it."

Otto nodded his thanks and slid a silver penny across the

bar to her. When he turned back, the one-eyed man was gone as were the rest of his tablemates.

◯

T he Exchange might have been the only stone building in Grunewald, but that didn't make it impressive. It was built out of mortar and field stones, with no windows and a slate roof missing half its tiles. The building's door, at least, was good, solid oak. Mendelson looked like he didn't want any unwelcome visitors just walking in. If he was what Otto thought he was, his prudent precaution wouldn't save him.

The single-story building huddled in the center of a row of businesses lining the main, and only, street in town. Assuming you could call a dirt path a street. Shenk Barony wasn't the richest in the kingdom, but even the poorest town in his father's domain appeared rolling in wealth compared to this place. Aside from not wanting to give bandits a base of operations, Garenland might be better off letting Rolan have the town.

"There were more people on the streets when we arrived, my lord," Hans said.

Considering there wasn't a single person visible in either direction, there wouldn't have had to be many. The emptiness of the streets set Otto's teeth on edge. It felt like they were walking into a trap. After the one-eyed man had fled the inn, he'd been sure they were walking into a trap; the silent streets just confirmed his feeling.

"Watch the rooftops," Otto said.

"We don't have bows," Hans said.

"You don't need bows; you just need to tell me someone's up there and I'll handle them. Shall we knock?"

Hans hammered his fist against the door and when no one responded, drew his sword and slammed the pommel into it. At last the door opened a crack and a single beady eye looked out.

"The Exchange is closed." He tried to slam the door but Hans jammed his boot in the crack.

"We are representatives of the king," Otto said. "I wish to speak to Mendelson."

"He's busy."

"I fear I must insist. Hans?"

The burly sergeant put his shoulder to the door and shoved. The owner of the beady eyes sprawled on the floor and stared up at Otto when he walked in. "You are dead."

Hans and his fellow soldiers chuckled and the last one through shut the door behind him. The first room held little beyond a chair and the unpleasant man that had no doubt been sitting in it. A door led deeper into the building, though given its size, Otto doubted there were more than two rooms.

"Is Mendelson back there?"

Beady-Eyes scrambled to get up, but Hans kicked him over and put his sword to the man's throat. "Lord Shenk asked you a question."

Before the man could answer, the back-room door opened and a whip-thin man in tan leathers stepped out. He had a curved cavalry saber at his waist and a thin mustache decorating his lip. Both the sword and mustache were popular in Rolan. Maybe it was a coincidence, but Otto doubted it.

"You wish to speak with me, yes?" He said each word precisely, biting each one off before moving on to the next. "Would you mind letting Dermot up? The poor man has a delicate constitution."

Hans looked at Otto who nodded. The sergeant stepped back but didn't sheathe his sword.

"Thank you. As you no doubt guessed, I am Mendelson. I run this town. I understand you are messengers from the new king. What does His Majesty have to say?"

"To a Rolan bandit?" Otto asked. "Nothing. I will say that you have one hour to collect your trash and get back across the border. Should you or any of your flunkies still be here at the end of that hour, we'll kill you all and hang your bodies from the nearest tree."

Mendelson threw back his head and laughed. "If you wish to drive me from my new home, you should have brought more than six men. My new friend. I fear you misunderstand the situation. This is now Rolan and you are trespassing. Here is my counteroffer. I will allow you and your men to leave so you may carry a message back to King Wolfric. Tell him the Rolan border now extends thirty miles north of its former position and should it be necessary our army will defend our new territory. I doubt your king wishes to fight a war on two fronts."

"Since when does a bandit speak for Rolan?" Otto asked.

He tried to put up a brave act but Mendelson had a point. Garenland would be pushing its luck trying to fight two nations at once. The Southern Army wasn't as large or skilled as the Northern Army. On the open plains against Rolan's cavalry, it wasn't a fight they wanted.

"What made you think I was a bandit? I am Captain Mendelson of the Rolan First Cavalry."

"I will take your message to the king," Otto said. "If you give your word of honor to end the bandit attacks outside of your new territory, he may look favorably on your proposal. Should the attacks continue, the Southern Army will march. Maybe you'll win the war, but Rolan will bleed."

Mendelson's confident smile turned cold. "I swear in the king's name that as long as the Southern Army stays in its barracks, the attacks will stop."

Otto nodded, turned on his heel, and marched out with Hans and the others behind him.

CHAPTER 27

Captain Kelten had been working his way through every house in Gold Ward trying to figure out which one employed Lothair prior to him turning assassin. Twenty-three houses down and everyone claimed to have no idea who he was. The only ones he had left to check were the big shots. And if he was going to bother them, Kelten figured he might as well start with the biggest. Thus he found himself approaching the gate to Franken Manner.

The two guards on duty snapped to attention when he got close. Technically Kelten was investigating this matter during his off-hours, but he still wore his armor and tabard as he'd found they opened a lot of doors. Hopefully no one complained to the king. His Majesty was already at the edge of his patience with Kelten's efforts and lack of results. If he didn't find something soon, Kelten feared he'd be ordered to quit the investigation altogether.

"How can we help you, sir?" the right-hand guard asked.

"I'm investigating the assassin that murdered our late king. I have it on good authority that Lothair worked for someone in Gold Ward. I'm asking at every house and business if anyone remembers him."

The guards shared a look then the spokesman said, "Aye, he worked here for a few years."

Kelten straightened, his excitement rising. "What can you tell me about him?"

"Not much, sir. He did his job, didn't complain much, then one day he just run off and never came back. Next we heard of him was when he… well, you know."

"Rumor is he liked to moon over the master's daughter," the left-hand guard added, drawing a glare from his partner.

"Lady Shenk is a beautiful girl," the right-hand guard said. "She would catch any man's eye."

It seemed there was more here than he'd first hoped. "Is Master Franken in? I'd like to speak to him about Lothair."

"He is, though whether he'll see you or not I can't say." The right-hand guard motioned to his partner and they pulled the gate open for him. "You'll have to inquire at the mansion."

"Thank you very much for your help." Kelten hurried through and wound his way up a dirt path toward the mansion.

He'd barely taken a step when the first explosion sounded. Kelten spun back around but the guards just waved him on. Not overly reassured, he set out a second time. He passed under trees that were partially green and partially bright orange. When he cleared them, he spotted a cloud of dust rising from the side of the estate. More explosions followed shortly thereafter.

That was when he finally remembered. This was where the wizard recruits were training. He'd overheard some of the guardsmen talking about them. Kelten wasn't sure how he felt about giving wizards the same rights as normal people much less having them serve in the army. Then again, no one had asked his opinion and they probably didn't much care what he thought.

He reached the front door and rapped several times with a heavy bronze knocker. The door opened a few seconds later. A thin, scowling man in a servant's black and white uniform looked him over and asked, "Can I help you, sir?"

Kelten gave the same speech he'd given the guards and said, "I'd like to speak to Master Franken."

"Lord Franken is busy arranging grain shipments."

Kelten frowned. "I thought the king had suspended shipments until the bandits had been wiped out."

The butler's look of disdain would have curdled milk. "Lord Shenk eliminated the bandits a week ago. Any further delay may result in the harvest not reaching Garen before winter."

Kelten was about to argue that five minutes wouldn't delay the harvest arriving when a short, round man with a bald head, dressed head to toe in silk robes came strolling into the entry hall.

"Is there a problem?" the newcomer asked.

"Master Cotton, I was just explaining to the gentleman that Lord Franken is indisposed."

Cotton smiled and said, "Yes, the master wouldn't appreciate any interruptions. Perhaps I can be of some assistance? I oversee much of the day-to-day business of the Frankens' affairs."

"Thank you. I'm here to inquire about a former mercenary in your employ. His name was Lothair and he murdered the late king."

"Ah. An ugly business that. Follow me, please. We can speak in my office."

Kelten fell in behind Cotton and after a short walk down the most exquisitely decorated halls he'd ever seen, including those of the palace, they arrived in an unassuming office. Cotton settled behind a desk made of dark wood that had a neat pile of papers on one corner and a gold ink pot and quill.

Kelten sat in a leather chair that probably cost more than he made in six months. He hardly dared move for fear of scratching something.

"Would you like a drink?" Cotton asked.

"No, thank you, just information."

"Very well. There's little enough I can tell you about Lothair. He wasn't terribly remarkable. He worked for us for a few years then walked off in the middle of his shift, not to return. It's just as well you ended up talking to me as Lord Franken has nothing to do with the guards."

Kelten was about to ask another question when someone knocked softly on the door and pushed it open. "Alaric? Do you know…"

A beautiful girl in a blue dress, her round belly just starting to hint at the new life growing there, looked from Cotton to Kelten and back. "I'm sorry, I didn't realize you had a guest. I'll come back later."

"Not at all, Annamaria. What did you need?"

"I wondered if you knew what Father wanted for lunch. He didn't tell me this morning and I hate to bother him."

"He said nothing to me. Perhaps a selection of his usual favorites?"

"That would probably be best. Excuse me."

"A moment, Lady Shenk." Was it Kelten's imagination or did she wince at that name? "I was told a mercenary in your employ had an infatuation with you. Can you tell me if Lothair ever did or said anything that might give you the impression he planned something violent? Please, anything you can tell me would be helpful."

Annamaria put a hand to her lips. "Excuse me, I have to go."

When the door closed behind her Cotton's good-natured expression went flat. "You should be ashamed of yourself, troubling a girl in her condition. I will bid you good day and offer you my promise not to mention your rudeness when Lord Shenk returns."

"Actually, I was hoping you could tell him I was here and ask him to seek me out when he has a chance. I'd like to ask him some questions as well."

"You want me to tell Lord Shenk that you were rude to his wife and that a commoner, whatever his rank might be, wants to talk to him? Not only talk to him but that he should go looking for said commoner. Have you never dealt with the nobility?"

Kelten grimaced. Maybe he had gotten a little carried away. "You could phrase it a little differently than I did."

"Or maybe you could ask the king to pass your request on. Lord Shenk would actually listen to him. Good afternoon, sir. I believe you can find your own way out."

Kelten quickly made his way out of the mansion. He hadn't learned much of value and he'd upset one of the most powerful families in the kingdom. At this rate, he'd be lucky if he didn't end up as dead as the late king.

CHAPTER 28

Otto and his team took a different route back north. After the unsatisfying conversation he had with Mendelson, Otto was keen to reach the capital. He could have teleported through the ether, but he wanted to make a stop on the way. Lord Karonin's armory was two days south of the city and he wanted to collect the giant suits of armor, one for Hans and each of his men. Activating them was going to be tricky, but hopefully by the time they reached the battlefield, Axel would have enough prisoners that he could spare a few.

A day ago, they'd swapped their horses for wagons at a military supply depot and once again Otto found himself bouncing along on a hard seat. At least they'd gotten a final gasp of summer. It was warm enough that the men had shed their heavy cloaks. The weather wouldn't last of course, but that was no reason not to enjoy the moment.

"How do you think the king will take your news?" Hans asked. The good sergeant had been tiptoeing around the question ever since they left and Otto was relieved to have him finally speak his mind.

"Not well, I'm sure. Knowing Wolfric, he'll probably want to order the Southern Army out at once. Hopefully I can dissuade him."

"Would it not be best to dislodge Rolan before they get too dug in?"

"Of course, if we weren't fighting a war on our northern border. Mendelson knew what he was talking about. A war on two fronts isn't where we want to be. First, we crush Straken then we see if Rolan still wants to fight. With any luck they'll just slink back where they came from, giving us time to consolidate. Then we can deal with everyone else who betrayed Garenland."

Otto closed his eyes and focused. They had to be getting close to the armory. He'd visited a number of times, but always via teleportation. This would be the first time he arrived at the front door, assuming he could find it. When he finally attuned himself to the marker's vibration, he found they were nearly on top of it.

"Keep your eyes peeled for a turnoff. We're getting close. It should be on our left."

They rounded a bend in the road and off to the side was a faint path, now mostly grown over with shrubs and bushes. If you didn't know what you were looking for, no one would ever spot it.

"I'm not sure if we can force the wagons through that mess," Hans said as he reined in.

"I'll open it up."

Otto wove a hoop of ether two feet wider than the wagons and three threads thick. In all it took fifteen threads' worth of ether to make the spell. He set the hoop to spinning and guided it down the path.

Brush flew every which way, neatly cut off at ground level. When Otto had cleared two wagon-lengths of undergrowth, Hans flicked his reins and followed the now-open path. The process wasn't a quick one, but after nearly an hour they reached a clearing big enough to turn the wagons around.

"There's nothing here," Hans said.

"That's where you're mistaken, Sergeant." Otto let his spell vanish and focused on the power directly in front of them.

The armory's magic screamed in the ether. He was only feet away.

Soon enough he found the outline of a set of massive double doors hidden by the background emanations. Otto reached out through the ether, forming a hand of pure magic, and twisted the door's handle like Lord Karonin had instructed him. The ether scattered and the physical doors were revealed.

They measured twelve feet by twenty and were made of enchanted steel. The doors had been set into a cement frame on the ground. Otto had suspected after his first visit that the armory was underground, but now he knew for sure.

"Shall I open them, Lord Shenk?" Hans asked.

"No, don't touch them. They aren't meant to be opened by physical contact and anyone that tries will trigger defensive magics. I'll handle them."

Otto poured ether into the doors' hinges and they swung silently open.

"I'll bring the weapons up," Otto said. "Get the wagons turned around."

He hopped down to the ground and made the short walk into the armory. The fresh air helped cut the mustiness, but

Otto didn't have time to linger. He went straight to the massive suits of armor and once more channeled the ether. This time he charged the mithril bands running through the first suit.

Instantly he felt connected to it. At his command, the suit clanked out of its cubbyhole and marched up the stairs.

"Bloody hell!" Cord swore when he saw the armor.

Otto ignored him and guided the suit to the nearest wagon and had it sit in the bed. It slid back as far as it could go then he ordered the legs tucked up close, so they didn't hang off the back. With the armor loaded, Otto let out a long breath. He was running down and still had five pieces to go. He allowed himself five minutes' rest then went back to work.

One after another the suits of armor clanked up out of the armory until all the wagons were loaded. That was it for the magic and thank goodness for that. Otto was at the end of his rope.

"We still need a couple more things. Follow me and touch only what I tell you."

Hans fell in behind Otto and they all entered the armory. A few feet from where the first suit of armor had stood was a stack of six pieces of a cage made of mithril and a long, heavy chest. Those were the final components he needed to activate the armor.

The men lugged them upstairs and loaded the pieces into Hans's wagon. Everything was covered with heavy tarps they'd brought for exactly that purpose. With a final burst of ether, Otto sealed the armory and hid the doors. Unless they knew how, even someone stumbling on the clearing wouldn't be able to get inside. And if they tried, they'd end up very dead.

"Let's be on our way, Sergeant. The sooner we get back to the capital the better."

"Yes, my lord." Hans hesitated then asked, "Are you okay?"

"Just tired. Using too much magic will do that to a wizard. Should we run into trouble, you'll have to deal with it."

Hans saluted, seeming pleased at the idea of finally being able to protect Otto instead of being rescued by him. "Count on us, my lord."

Otto would do exactly that. Right now, he didn't really have a choice.

CHAPTER 29

Axel led his men north toward the Straken border. The main body of the Northern Army had reached the abandoned fort yesterday along with the scouts Axel had dispatched. As he expected, all the border forts were empty. General Varchi hadn't given the news more than a passing thought before ordering Axel to find out where the enemy forces had gathered.

They'd been riding for a couple hours and were only five miles from the northernmost villages and fifteen miles from Straken itself. So far, they'd encountered nothing more dangerous that an angry, growling squirrel. Though they had to confirm his theory, Axel was certain all the enemy forces had retreated back across the border.

He didn't blame them given the size and power of the Northern Army. In an even fight, their legions would defeat Straken's and anything less than an even fight would be a slaughter. Still, Axel was surprised King Uther had the discipline to retreat. That wasn't his reputation.

For his part, Axel wished they'd turn and fight. Wiping out the forces that had invaded Garenland would make taking Straken that much easier. Wish as he might, he clearly wasn't going to get what he wanted.

"Does this stretch of road look familiar, Lord Shenk?" Cobb asked.

Axel looked around at the mixed pine and hardwood shading the road and making it feel colder than it had any right to be. It did look familiar. "Our last patrol went through here."

"Yes, sir. About a mile further is where we met the logging crew that had been enslaved."

"Looks like we'll get to keep our promise to free them without having to swing our swords. Do we have extra provisions? I doubt Straken left much behind for them to eat."

"We've got enough for a few days. Depending on their condition, we might need to bring them back to the main army so the healers can check them over."

Ten minutes later they reached the skid path that led to the village. Axel turned his horse down the trail. On either side the trees had been harvested and hauled away. They'd gotten a lot done in the few months since Axel was last here. The enemy forts must have been nearly complete. He smiled to himself. It must have galled the Straken general to leave so much behind. Served the bastards right for trying to take what didn't belong to them.

It didn't take long to reach the outskirts of the village. Not a soul could be seen moving in the streets. The collection of simple log cabins appeared frozen in time. Beyond them, the wall of the fort they'd been building towered twenty feet above the cabins. The keep appeared nearly done. Only a pair of guard towers looked half complete.

"This feels wrong," Cobb said.

It did feel wrong, but Axel couldn't do anything about it. Instead he loosened his sword in its scabbard and guided his horse past the first cabin.

No ambushers came howling out nor did any grateful citizens. They reached the forest without seeing a soul; no villagers, no soldiers, no nothing.

"Fan out," Axel said. "I want squads to check every cabin. First squad with me, we'll check the fort."

His men dismounted and set to work. Axel, Cobb, and six men walked through the open gate, swords drawn. If there was going to be trouble, this was where it would happen.

Axel's heart skipped a beat when he looked at the dirt yard. Bodies dressed in rags, covered in horrible wounds, lay scattered everywhere. Iron shackles still bound them.

"I'll kill them all," Cobb growled. "Every no-good one of them."

Axel knew exactly how his second felt, but they still had work to do. "Let's finish our sweep, though I don't expect we'll find anything."

He was right. They checked the fort and found it empty. The enemy hadn't even had time to bring in furniture. Axel would have happily burned everything to the ground, but he didn't have anything that would light the green wood.

They left the fort and found Colten waiting for them. The scout was paler than usual and Axel almost didn't want to ask what he'd discovered. "Report."

"We found the women and children dead in their cabins. No survivors, sir."

Axel nodded, disgusted but no longer surprised. "You all know the drill. Collect firewood and bodies. We'll give them a proper pyre before we move on."

The men saluted and Axel left them to their grim duty. Heaven knew they'd done it often enough over the past few years. Just this once, Axel had wanted to arrive in time to save someone.

It seemed he was doomed to a life of disappointment.

CHAPTER 30

Captain Kelten rounded a corner after checking the guards stationed outside the throne room. They were his best men and always on alert, that was why he chose them for such an important position. Today had been no different: they snapped to attention at his approach, nodded that all was well, received a nod of recognition from him, and that was it. If only all his work was so simple.

The investigation into the king's murderer, for example, had run dead into a wall. He'd spoken with the watch commander, but that man had no more information to offer. He wasn't sure what his next move was supposed to be. Deep down he was starting to think the new king was right and he should just let it go and move on with his work, which was keeping the current king alive.

He sighed as he approached the next guard post. Things had been much quieter since the bandit raids in the central kingdom had ended. Whatever else Kelten might think of Otto Shenk, the man had proved his worth to the kingdom many times over. King Wolfric favored him over all others, which worried Kelten, but there was no evidence that Otto had used his position in a way that undermined the king or the kingdom.

Kelten twisted his neck from side to side, trying to work out a kink. One of the servants that served as a message runner came barreling out of a door to his right, his blond hair flying behind him. The boy was about twelve, dressed in a black and gold smock.

He spotted Kelten, skidded to a halt, bowed, and held out a sealed scroll. "Message for you, Captain, from the guards at the front gate."

Kelten accepted the scroll and nodded to the boy who ran off. When he was alone in the hall, he took a moment to examine the seal. It was a stylized capital F. Everyone in the city knew the Franken mark. Perhaps Mr. Cotton had thought of something important. Of course, considering how he'd left, Kelten doubted the man would go to the trouble of sending him a message.

More curious than ever, Kelten broke the seal and unrolled the scroll. It was a short letter, only a few lines written in a neat hand. He skipped to the bottom. It was signed Annamaria Franken.

So the daughter had sent him a message. Interesting.

He started reading. Apparently, she thought her husband knew more about the murder than he let on. There was no real evidence other than him telling her about it before the public announcement. That meant exactly nothing, since Otto had seen the murder when it happened. All he had to do was go home and tell her as soon as he arrived and it would have been before the announcement. It wasn't the sort of revelation that he could take to the king or even use in a confrontation with Otto.

Just to be sure there was nothing of value, he read the note again. No, still nothing useful, but he did get the impression that Annamaria didn't like her husband. He heard enough about the goings-on in Garen to know their marriage was arranged and neither of them had a say in it. Was she trying to cause trouble for a man she didn't like or was there something more?

He didn't know, but when he next saw Otto, he'd be sure find out.

☾

After a long, rough ride, Otto and his men finally arrived back in the capital late in the evening two days after collecting the magical armor. Hans and the others were exhausted and Otto wasn't in that great a shape himself. He'd used too much magic securing the armor and while he had mostly recovered, he still wasn't at full strength. A good night's sleep in his own bed should see him set to rights.

But first he needed to talk to Wolfric. The king wasn't going to be thrilled when he heard about Rolan's annexation of a chunk of the southern province. Hopefully he wouldn't blow his top and order something foolish.

Otto yawned as they pulled through the palace gates. So much to do and so little time.

"Orders, my lord?" Hans asked.

"Secure the wagons and get some sleep. We leave tomorrow for the front."

Hans saluted and Otto jumped down. The wagons clattered off and he trudged toward the keep. With any luck Wolfric would have finished for the day and he could get right in to see him. The guards let Otto in without comment, bless them, and he made his way toward the throne room. If the king wasn't there, the guards could give him directions.

Three-quarters of the way there, a voice called out from behind him. "Lord Shenk!"

Otto turned to find Captain Kelten hurrying his way. He grimaced. Kelten was the last person Otto wanted to deal with right now. Bloody pain in the ass. Maybe Otto could kill him and make it look like his heart gave out.

No, satisfying as it would be, killing Kelten in the middle of the castle wouldn't be a good idea.

"Captain. I need to speak with the king. Whatever you want will have to wait."

"Please, my lord, I need only a few minutes."

"Fine, speak."

"I learned recently that the assassin worked at Franken Manor for a time. Did you know him?"

"No, I believe he disappeared shortly after I arrived in the city."

"That's what Mr. Cotton told me as well. Earlier today I received a letter from your wife claiming you knew about the assassination before it was announced to the public."

Otto scowled. What was Annamaria playing at? "Of course I knew about it before the announcement. I was there when it happened. You'll have to excuse my wife. She's with child and you know how women get when they're pregnant."

"No, I don't, but I'll take your word for it. From the tone of the note, I got the impression that you two don't get along."

"Did you? And when, exactly, did my family life become your concern?" Before Kelten could answer Otto plowed on. "You've wasted enough of my time. Have you actually found any, I don't know, evidence, that Lothair killing the late king was anything other than what it appeared?"

Kelten's strained expression told Otto everything he needed to know before the man spoke. "No, I haven't. But I haven't given up hope of finding something."

"Bury your hope, Captain, and stick to the facts. As far as I can see, you've accomplished nothing beyond pestering me and my family. When I speak to King Wolfric, I intend to advise him to order an end to your pointless investigation. The only grand conspiracy is in your head, Captain. Let it go and move on to something more useful."

Otto spun and left Kelten standing in the hall. He was going to have to have a chat with Annamaria tonight, much as he preferred to avoid the woman. If his blushing bride was going to be a problem, he'd have to put a stop to it. Fortunately, he had plenty of means at his disposal.

Leaving that unpleasantness behind, he resumed his trek to the throne room. From there he was directed to Wolfric's private chambers. That was another hike that felt like miles but was really only a hundred yards or so. Finally, he reached an oak door carved with griffins and knocked.

"Go away." Wolfric's voice was muffled by the thick door, but still clear enough to understand.

"It's Otto. I have a great deal of news, little of it good."

The door opened a moment later. Wolfric stared at him as if expecting him to disappear. The king was trying to grow a beard with little success. He had a few patches of hair clinging to his cheeks and that was all.

"You look horrible," Wolfric said. "Come in."

He moved aside and Otto strode through. The king's private suite was luxurious and bigger than many people's homes. They sat at a table on the opposite side from the huge bed. Wolfric poured wine for them both and Otto gratefully drank.

"If the servants knew you were pouring your guest wine, they'd have a fit," Otto said when he'd washed away some of the road dust.

"They're always complaining about something I do differently from Father. I no longer care. So, what's the news from the south?"

"We're dealing with more than bandits. Rolan has claimed about thirty miles of the southern province."

"What!" Wolfric slammed his fist on the table, making their glasses jump.

"The one running the raids is a captain in the Rolan cavalry. He said as long as the Southern Army stays in their barracks, he'll end the raids. It's a good deal for us right now. I warned him that if the raids didn't stop, we'd attack and while we might lose, they'd bleed as well."

"Do you think they could beat us?"

"In open combat on the plains, Rolan's cavalry is the best in the world. Our infantry is skilled, but the Southern Army is half the size of the northern and less well trained. The assumption was that any war would be fought with Straken not Rolan."

Wolfric scrubbed a hand across his face. "How do you know all this? I mean, I was raised in the capital and trained to be king and you still know as much or more about our forces than I do."

"Father has few interests, but war is one of them. He insisted that, in addition to my worthless swordsmanship lessons, I learned the history of the kingdom's military, its strengths and weaknesses, battles fought and won or lost and why. I always enjoyed reading and our family's modest library was well stocked with books on strategy and history. Having seen your library, I feel confident that you had a wider range of subjects to study than I did."

"My father encouraged it as well. He always believed problems could be solved with diplomacy rather than steel."

"Pity he was wrong about that last theory." Otto poured another glass of wine and took a drink. "I dislike fighting but understand its necessity. First, we crush Straken then we move on Rolan. When we do, my wizards will have real combat experience to draw on. That will be a huge advantage."

Wolfric nodded. "Agreed, though I don't like it. Anything else? Some good news maybe?"

"More bad I fear. On my way to talk to you, I ran into Captain Kelten. Somehow, he tracked Lothair to the Franken Estate. He got little from his discussion with Edwyn's business manager but now he thinks I might have some information he can use. I told him otherwise, but I'm not sure he believed me. I suggest you have a talk with the good captain, make him admit he has no new information, and put an end to his search. His sniffing around is a distraction neither of us needs."

"I'll speak to him tomorrow. I've been patient long enough. You should go home, Otto. I've seen day-old corpses that look better than you."

"My very plan. Tomorrow I'm heading to the front. Have you had word from the army?"

"Last I heard they'd had no contact with the Straken army and were making good time toward the border. They should be crossed over by the time you join them."

"That's good. Surprising, but good. Before I leave, with your permission, I'd like to place a marking rune somewhere secure in the palace. Should there be an emergency and you need to contact me you can strike it with a hammer or hilt and I'll sense it."

"By all means. In fact, I know the perfect place."

Otto stood. "Excellent. I'll pop in tomorrow and take care of it before I leave. Good night, my friend."

They shook hands and Otto withdrew. Much as he wanted food and sleep, first he needed to talk to Annamaria. She was another distraction he didn't need. The only reason he let her live was that her death would throw both Edwyn and Wolfric off and he needed both of them focused.

Maybe it was time to reconsider.

CHAPTER 31

Otto left his mithril sword behind when he went to talk to Annamaria. Not that he really feared he'd lose control and cut her head off, but why take chances? His suite was halfway across the mansion from hers, so Otto had time to decide how he was going to go about convincing her not to cause trouble. She had a few vulnerabilities, but the child would be his strongest argument.

It wasn't that late, but the house was quiet all the same. The only sound was his footsteps on the hardwood floors. He could have been alone in the world and sometimes he wished he was. The quest for greater magical knowledge would be far easier if he didn't have all these other considerations holding him back. How had the Arcane Lords even learned anything new when they had whole empires to rule? Maybe everyone was so scared of them that they didn't dare bring any problems to their attention. Must have been nice.

Mimi stood in the hall in front of Annamaria's room. The maid was dressed in her black and white uniform as she paced silently back and forth in front of the door, her stockinged feet making not a sound.

She spotted Otto and hurried to meet him, bobbing a curtsy before saying, "She had a stressful day, Lord Shenk. Perhaps you could come back later?"

"Did you deliver the letter, or did she send someone else?"

Mimi looked away, answering his question without words. "I knew it was a bad idea, but she insisted. What could I do?"

"You could have smiled and nodded then held on to the letter until I returned. She'd never know the difference."

"I couldn't do that. Lady Fran...I mean Lady Shenk trusts me to do as she says." She looked back with pleading eyes. "If she can't depend on me, who can she depend on?"

"There's that charming loyalty again. If only my wife was as loyal as her maid. I could dismiss you just to hurt her, perhaps provide a maid more obedient to my needs. But I suppose even Annamaria deserves someone like you. Now go away. If I find you listening outside the door, it will be the last thing you do in this house."

"Yes, Lord Shenk." She fled like a mouse before a cat.

Otto dismissed Mimi from his thoughts and pushed the door open. The room looked just as he remembered from those dreamy days when he'd shared it with her. It was all red silk and lace and feminine appeal. How wonderful he'd thought she was. When in reality he was stupid and blind to her true intentions. He really should thank her for the lesson. Annamaria had been kind enough to really teach him something he should have known all along: that no one can be trusted.

Annamaria turned slowly over on the bed, her smile turning to a scowl when she saw it was him in her doorway. She was still beautiful; he couldn't deny it. The thin silk nightgown she wore clung to her curves in a way that once would have set his heart racing. The modest swell of her stomach did little to diminish her beauty.

Looking at her, he felt nothing but disgust. He could have loved her if she'd given him half a chance. Oh, well. No sense dwelling on what might have been.

Otto secured the door with a thread of ether then wove a dome of silence around the room. Whatever happened here, would stay here.

"Get out!" Annamaria shouted.

Otto ignored her, crossed the room, and sat in a chair beside the bed. "We need to talk."

"I have nothing to say to you."

"That's fine. All you have to do is listen. I had a visit with Captain Kelten today. The man seems to think I know something about your darling Lothair beyond the fact that he was an assassin and traitor to the kingdom. I've convinced him otherwise. Whatever you hoped to accomplish with your letter was a failure. Should you attempt such a foolish stunt again there will be consequences."

Her laugh was bitter and devoid of humor. "You've already taken the man I love. What more can you do to me?"

Otto cocked his head. "I didn't say the consequences would be for you."

Her hand went to her stomach.

"Good, I see you understand. Lothair's bastard has no standing beyond what I grant. Your actions are enough to get the marriage annulled and I could demand compensation from your father for the dishonor. Of course, the knowledge that his daughter is a whore who bedded a traitor might well be enough to kill him on the spot. Assuming he survives, the damage to the Franken name would destroy your family's business. You could live your life as an outcast in some distant city, I suppose."

"Damn you." She said it so softly he barely heard. "Why are you still trying to ruin my life?"

Otto nearly laughed. "Since the moment we met, you've been trying to make your problems my fault. Need I remind you; our wedding wasn't my idea. I was perfectly content to have nothing whatsoever to do with you. Since our marriage, you've cheated on me, conceived a child with another man, tried to convince me that it was mine, and now you tried to sic the captain of the palace guard on me. What, other than having the misfortune to be born into the Shenk family, have I ever done to you to deserve this hate?"

She didn't seem to have an answer and at this point he wouldn't have really cared if she did.

"You understand now what's at stake. If you do anything to make my life even a fraction more difficult, I swear before all the angels in Heaven and all the demons in Hell that I will destroy you and the brat you value so highly. Do you understand?"

She stayed silent.

"Look at me!"

Annamaria turned her head a fraction so he could see the despair in her eyes.

"Do. You. Understand?"

"I do. Now leave me alone."

"With pleasure."

Otto marched out, dissolving his spells as he went. With any luck he'd never have to speak to her again. And if he did, heaven help her.

CHAPTER 32

Axel and his men had searched every border town and found them all equally devoid of life. The retreating Straken forces had killed everything between them and the border. The unnecessary murder left Axel in such a rage he could hardly think as they rode back to camp. Fortunately, by the time they reached the first pickets, his temper had cooled enough that he was able to make his report to General Varchi in a professional manner.

Now he stood, hands clasped behind his back, while his commander considered the information with his eyes closed and a smoking pipe clamped between his teeth. He seemed so calm, sitting on his wobbly folding camp chair that Axel wanted to grab him and shake him with both hands while screaming that the people he'd sworn to protect, people he'd promised to return and rescue, had been cut down like cattle in a slaughterhouse.

Not that doing so would accomplish anything besides making Axel feel a tiny bit better. He understood deep down that the general had to make decisions without letting his emotions get the better of him, but that didn't mean he had to like it.

At last, the general opened his eyes and focused on Axel. "I know you want revenge, but our orders are to avoid any unnecessary casualties. King Wolfric intends to rule the kingdom and slaughtering the people will not make that any easier. You understand?"

"Yes, General," Axel said. He understood perfectly and he hated it.

"I don't like it any better than you," General Varchi said as if reading his mind. "But killing innocent people won't bring our citizens back to life. The enemy army is bound to make a stand eventually. When they do, we'll make them pay for what they've done."

"I understand, sir. What are our orders?"

"I want you to take your scouts, along with the First Legion, across the border. Secure as many towns as you can and prepare a location for us to set up and begin our conquest. Should you face resistance, take prisoners and show restraint."

"What will the Second and Third Legions be doing?" Axel asked.

"Waiting. I had word yesterday that your brother as well as a number of his new recruits will be arriving within a few days. I want to get the wizards integrated into our forces before we advance. Your job is to prepare the way for our arrival."

"Understood, sir. We'll have a place all set up when you arrive." Axel saluted and backed out of the tent.

So, Otto and his wizards were on the way. Axel wasn't entirely sure how having wizards in the army was going to work out, but having seen the power of his brother's magic, he had high hopes for their results. He was less enamored with being ordered to show restraint and take prisoners. He understood the king's point of view, but someone needed to pay for what they'd done to those villagers.

It was a short walk to the scouts' campsite. He found Cobb pacing when he arrived, a deep scowl creasing the sergeant's bearded face.

Axel barely got within shouting distance before Cobb demanded, "What did he say?"

"No revenge. We are advancing with the First Legion to secure a foothold for the invasion. Our orders are to go easy on the locals. It seems the king doesn't want to anger his future subjects."

Cobb barked a laugh. "Any of his future subjects in Straken would be happy to plunge a dagger into his heart and no amount of going easy will change that. They hate us over there and the feeling is mutual. The best thing we could do would be to slaughter them all and let Garenlanders resettle the land."

"Maybe, but we have our orders. Get the men up and ready, we go in an hour."

Cobb marched off grumbling to himself, not bothering with a salute. Axel kept his mouth shut and let him go. After what they'd seen he and all the men deserved better than the general had given them.

○

Just past midday, Axel and his scouts led the First Legion into the nearest Straken village. It was as silent and empty as the villages on the Garenland side had been. The log cabins, piles of cut and split firewood leaning against their rear walls, could have been picked up and placed there from the opposite side of the border.

Considering how similar the people were, it was a wonder the two countries hated each other so much. On the other hand, perhaps each side recognized in the other what was most wrong with themselves.

"Fan out by squads and search door-to-door," Axel said. "It looks like they evacuated everyone, but we don't want to run into a trap."

As the squads broke off and began their search, Cobb moved up beside him and said, "I can't believe the general gave you overall command of the advance unit. I can't think that went over well with the leader of the First Legion."

"I don't believe anyone asked him what he thought," Axel said. "This job is closer to scouting than it is fighting a war. So I suppose it makes a certain amount of sense for me to be in charge. Not that I intend to rub the colonel's nose in it or anything. We all have a job to do and I assume we can be professional in getting it done."

Their discussion was cut off by a shout and the clash of steel on steel. Axel drew his sword and ran toward the sound of battle. He arrived to find an infantryman dead and four villagers armed with axes lying on the ground, two wounded and two dead.

"What happened?" Axel asked.

"These four jumped us out of nowhere," the sergeant in command of the squad said. "They took down Johan before we had a chance to react."

"Tie up the survivors and bind their wounds. Once the village is secure, I'll have some questions."

The sergeant nodded and began barking orders.

"Those weren't soldiers," Cobb said.

"No, they weren't. Probably some diehards that refused to evacuate. Straken knew we were coming and moved their people out of our path. It seems they were smart enough to know what we were likely to do after their actions in our villages."

It took most of an hour, but the soldiers finally finished searching the village. They took eight more prisoners with no further losses on their side. Without the element of surprise, untrained villagers were no match for soldiers of the legion. When they were finished, it became clear that it wasn't only the villagers that had been moved. All the food, grain, and anything else that might be of value to the invaders had been taken away as well. Foraging, it seemed, was going to be a problem.

"What now, my lord?" Cobb asked.

"Now we have a chat with our prisoners."

The eight men they'd captured sat in a circle with their backs together and their arms bound behind them. As big and bearded as any soldier in the Straken army, the prisoners greeted them with hard looks and bared teeth. One glance at them told Axel he was going to have trouble extracting any information out of them. Still, it couldn't hurt to ask.

"Where has your army fled?"

"You'll get nothing from us, Garenland filth," one of the prisoners said.

Cobb stepped past Axel and kicked the prisoner square in the face. He fell over, blood staining his beard. "When Lord Shenk asks you a question, you answer it."

The prisoner sat up and spat a line of blood into the dirt. He glared at Cobb but remained silent.

Cobb drew back to hit him again, but Axel laid a restraining hand on his shoulder. "We'll get nothing from them today. Let them rot for a while and we'll try again later. Make sure they are kept under guard."

The muscle in Cobb's jaw bunched but he nodded and said, "Yes, my lord."

Axel left Cobb to his work and went to find the legion commander. He hadn't seen fit to join Axel in searching the village; no doubt he thought it beneath him. And given that he had seven thousand men under his command, it probably was. According to the rules, Axel wasn't supposed to lead from the front either, but he found it easier to get a feel for the battle if he was a part of it. Besides, ordering men into battle from the safety of the rear didn't suit him.

Now that they'd cleared the first village, Axel had a real sense of what they were dealing with when the king said they were conquering the country. How many times would they have to perform this same task? And how would they do it if the next village was full of women and children?

He didn't know and wasn't eager to find out.

CHAPTER 33

O tto never imagined he'd find himself back at Axel's
fort, but here he was. At least this time it wasn't
under siege. Though given the number of soldiers
camped around it, you would have been forgiven for thinking
otherwise.

The Northern Army, a large portion of it anyway, was
camped out around the fort and apparently General Varchi
had set up his headquarters inside. Otto knew how many men
served in the army but seeing them spread out before him
really drove it home.

The trip north had been a long, bumpy, miserable journey
that he would have happily avoided. But considering how
valuable the magical armor was, he didn't dare let Hans and
the men travel alone. Four days into the trip he was hoping
someone would attack just so he could take his boredom out
on them. As it was, they arrived safely without encountering
another soul.

When they had moved to within a quarter mile of the camp,
Otto reached out through the ether. He concentrated on the

apprentice rings he'd given to the squad commanders that came ahead of him. It took only a moment to find their position about twenty yards from the fort on the southern side.

As the wagons clattered their way through the camp, the soldiers looked them over. No one tried to stop the wagons or even questioned them about their purpose. Otto assumed it was because they came from the south and were driving standard-issue army wagons. They probably thought he was bringing supplies. Which he was, after a fashion. Still, it wouldn't hurt to point out to the general that his security was rather lax.

"Here is fine," Otto said.

Hans reined in and brought the wagon to a halt. Wizards emerged from the half-dozen tents that made up their camp. Someone had found uniforms for them. That was smart. He hadn't given it a thought, but naturally they'd want to blend in with the rest of the soldiers.

One of the squad leaders, a young woman in her early thirties that if he recalled correctly wielded ten threads. Her mithril ring flashed in the light as she saluted and said, "Welcome, Lord Shenk. We weren't sure when you'd arrive. The general has been waiting for you to begin his advance."

"It looks like some of the army has already advanced."

"The First Legion is preparing the way. They don't seem to expect much trouble until we move deeper into Straken."

Otto suspected they were right. Straken was a rough, mountainous, forested country with only a few places suitable for large-scale battle. Otto didn't know which one they'd choose, but in one of those spots they would surely be waiting for the Northern Army to arrive. Straken's forces were going to get a real surprise when they saw what his wizards could do.

"Hans, get the men settled. I need to go speak with General Varchi."

Otto climbed down from the wagon and turned toward the fort. He stuck to the paths between the rows of tents and soon reached the front gate. A squad of soldiers was on duty though they seemed more interested in chatting than security. Which wasn't a surprise given that they were surrounded by an army of over ten thousand soldiers.

The sergeant in command held out his hand as Otto approached. "Name and business?"

"Otto Shenk to see General Varchi."

The men scrambled to attention. "I didn't recognize you, my lord. Please, go right in. We've been expecting you for a few days."

Otto nodded as he passed and walked through the open gate. The walls and courtyard were filled with soldiers far more alert than those outside. Otto had never seen them, but they had to be the general's personal guard. He'd heard they were the finest soldiers in the army.

Before he could choose a soldier from whom to ask directions, a man about twenty came hurrying over. He stopped directly in front of Otto and touched his fist to his heart. "Lord Shenk?"

"Do I know you?" Otto asked.

"No, my lord. I was on leave when King Wolfric announced that you were to be his chief advisor. Since I know what you look like, General Varchi asked me to keep an eye out for you. If you follow me, I can take you to his office."

"By all means, lead on."

He followed the soldier inside and up a flight of stairs lined with shields and battle flags. The soldier knocked on a closed door and a moment later a muffled voice said, "Enter."

"There you are, my lord." The soldier opened the door for him and stepped aside.

The general looked up as Otto entered. His steel-gray hair was cropped close and his uniform was rumpled with an ink stain on the front. Otto smiled, happy to see he was dealing with a working man and not someone a step removed from the nobility. Despite being a member of that group, Otto didn't care for most of them.

"Lord Shenk," General Varchi said. "It's a pleasure to have you join us. I'm eager to see what you and your wizards can do."

Otto seriously doubted anyone associated with the army for as long as the general had been was eager to go into battle with wizards, but he put on a good face. "Thank you, General. I read the most recent reports. It seems your march so far has met with little opposition. Since Straken doesn't have a reputation for cowardice, what do you suppose they're planning?"

The general pointed at an empty chair and Otto sat. "I can't say anything for certain, but our assumption is that they didn't expect such massive opposition so soon. We believe they sent at most two legions to invade the northern province. Assuming that's correct, we had them badly outnumbered. Retreat and regroup was the most sensible decision. However, the bastards made sure to murder their way out."

"Oh?"

"According to your brother's last report, they slaughtered everyone they had taken for slave labor. Their families as well. I know His Majesty wants us to go easy on them, but given what they've done…"

"I understand how you feel, but the civilians you want to take your revenge on aren't the ones responsible for killing our people. Defeating their army, taking the capital, and freeing them from Uther's tyrannical rule is the best thing we could do. It will take time, but eventually the people will come to appreciate life under Garenland's more enlightened laws."

The general's laugh held not a trace of humor. "If you think any Straken citizen will ever appreciate anything associated with Garenland, then you don't know Straken. Uther might be a tyrant, but he's their tyrant. King Wolfric will never be anything more than an invader."

"You take a rather grim view, General. Surely the parents of those who might become wizards will welcome us knowing their sons and daughters will no longer be slaughtered."

"They might," General Varchi allowed. "But how many people is that, a few score at most? Hardly enough to secure the country. No, I fear we're in for a long, hard slog bringing this miserable country to heel."

"I hope you're wrong, but if you're not, we can still use them as slave labor in the mithril mines. When do we go to meet Axel?"

"The army marches first thing in the morning."

"If you don't mind, I'd like to take my team and go ahead. There are some magical things we need to get set up."

"That's fine. If you leave now you should make it before dark. The engineers have been building a proper road so we can get supplies through."

Otto stood and they shook hands. The general was hard-headed and practical. Otto hoped they'd get along well.

CHAPTER 34

Calling what the engineers had built a road was far too generous in Otto's opinion. He, Hans, and the rest of the squad had been rattling down the shaded path for hours. The guys weren't thrilled when he said they were setting out again, but Otto wanted to find Axel and commandeer some of his prisoners before the rest of the army caught up. Many would find what he had to do to empower the enchanted armor troubling and he preferred as few witnesses as possible.

It was an hour before dawn when they reached the edge of the Straken village. A picket of soldiers greeted them with leveled spears. It seemed his brother took camp security more seriously than the general. No surprise there. He and Axel had both received the same brutal training from Father. A poorly set picket would have gotten both of them black eyes.

When the formalities were complete, Otto asked the sergeant in charge, "Where can I find Axel Shenk?"

"The commander has just returned from pacifying another

Straken village in preparation for the General's arrival tomorrow. We weren't expecting anyone until midday at the earliest."

"I just arrived from the capital and was eager to see my brother," Otto said. "Can you supply me with a guide?"

"You won't have any trouble finding him. Just look for the tent flying the Garenland flag. He'll be inside."

"My thanks, Sergeant." Otto settled back in his seat and once the simple barricade of sharpened stakes was moved out of the way Hans urged the wagon through.

Even a single legion looked too big to be occupying the border village. Tents and men and cook fires filled every space. The scent of stew simmering reminded Otto that he hadn't eaten since breakfast that morning. He silenced his grumbling stomach and focused. Food would keep until he finished his work. Getting the armor up and operational so Hans and the others could practice before an actual battle was vital.

They found the flag waving above the largest canvas tent in the camp. Otto jumped down as soon as Hans stopped the wagon and strode over. The four guards on duty gave him a serious looking over before one of them, a man about twenty-five wearing a mottled green and black uniform, took a step back and said, "Lord Shenk?"

"Have we met?" Otto asked.

"Not face to face, but I was one of the scouts you rescued. I never got a chance to offer my thanks. We were all more grateful than we could say."

"I was just doing my duty, the same as you. Is my brother in?"

"Of course." The scout pulled the tent flap open for Otto. "Go right in, my lord."

"Thanks."

Otto stepped into the dim interior. A pair of Lux crystals hung from tent poles and illuminated a table in the center of the tent. Axel stood beside it with another, older man. They were both studying a map covered with markers.

Otto cleared his throat and both of them looked up. Axel grinned and said, "Finally made it to the front, little brother. Took you long enough."

"Yes, well, unlike you I haven't been strolling through empty fields and forests. I've been hunting bandits and spies. Have you gotten the latest report?"

"The last report we got was one ordering us to go easy on the enemy. Why, what's happened?"

"Rolan has seized about thirty miles of the southern province."

"What?!" the second man demanded.

Otto shifted his gaze a fraction and raised an eyebrow.

"Otto," Axel said. "Let me introduce Legion Commander Zoltan, leader of the First Legion. Zoltan, this is my brother, Otto, First Counselor to King Wolfric. You were saying?"

"Rolan has taken control of the border and about thirty miles of our territory. We've struck a deal to avoid a fight, for now at least. Until Straken is brought to heel, we can't divide our attention. How go things here?"

"I'll leave you to bring your brother up to speed," Zoltan said. "If you'll excuse me."

When Zoltan had gone Otto said, "He's a charmer. Reminds me a little of Stephan."

"He's not that bad. Zoltan's in charge of the legion, but General Varchi has given me overall command of the advance mission. Since I'm about ten years younger he took it as a personal insult."

"Welcome to my world. Do you have any idea how difficult it is to convince people to take me seriously at my age? Fortunately, the magic makes up for my youth. Now, about your invasion."

"Right, we've cleared every village within twenty miles of here and taken eighty prisoners." Axel spat those last two words like they tasted bad. "We've seen no sign of the main enemy force. I know they're around, but where is the question."

"I can help you with that later. For now, how would you like to see fifty of your prisoners die horribly for a good cause?"

"What cause?"

"A magical ritual. I need fifty sacrifices to activate the weapons I brought. I came early in the hopes that you'd have enough for me."

"That's not exactly going easy on the locals," Axel said, though from his tone, Otto got the impression he didn't object too much. "What about our orders?"

"Have you actually reported how many prisoners you've taken?"

"Not officially, though plenty of people know."

"They're Straken." Otto shrugged. "Do you think anyone will really care as long as we win the war?"

"I don't care even if we lose the war. They can all rot."

"Interesting choice of words. Where are they being held?"

"At the edge of camp. I've got my scouts guarding them so there'll be no trouble. Come on, I'll take you."

They left the command tent, collected Otto's squad and the wagons, and made their way west toward the edge of camp. A crude stockade had been set up and in the dying light Otto could see figures moving around behind the wooden barrier. A stocky man with a beard approached and saluted Axel. He looked familiar, probably someone Otto had seen at the fort.

"What brings you out here, Lord Shenk?"

Otto shot Axel a look. When he joined the military, Axel had given up any claim to his noble rank.

His brother ignored him and said, "Change of plans, Cobb. Seems at least a few of our prisoners are going to get what they deserve."

Cobb spat to the side. "Glad someone came to their senses. What do you want us to do?"

Axel looked at Otto who said, "Give us a moment to get set up then we'll need them in groups of ten. Hans, let's get the cage put together."

The men got to work assembling the mithril cage and five minutes later it was ready. "Okay, Axel."

Cobb and some scouts dragged ten men out at sword point and drove them toward the cage. Otto conjured light so they could see better what they were doing. The prisoners had received some rough treatment. Many of them had blackened eyes and walked with a limp.

As they were herded into the cage one of them asked, "What the hell's going on?"

Cobb punched him in the face and shoved him through the door. Clearly no love was lost between Axel's subordinate and the people of Straken.

When the last one was in, Hans bolted the door shut. Otto went to the wagon and opened the wooden case they'd brought from the armory. Inside were five purple crystals about eight inches long and five in diameter. At the top of the cage was a tripod designed specifically to hold them. A tentacle of ether carried the crystal into place.

When it was secure, Otto took a deep breath to center himself. This was where it got tricky.

He summoned ten threads of ether and sent them into the crystal until it started to give off purple light so dark it was almost black. Once that was done, he pulled one of the first threads back out and used it to connect one of the prisoners to the crystal.

The instant the thread touched his flesh, the man stiffened and arched his back. A low moan slipped past his lips, but he clenched his jaw, clearly determined not to give them any satisfaction. Otto admired the man's courage, but it would take more than courage to withstand what was coming.

One after another he connected each of the prisoners to the crystal. When all ten were linked, he conjured ten more threads and ran them from the prisoners to the crystal creating a complete loop.

The moment the final connections were complete, purplish black energy raced down the first thread and pierced the man it was connected to. The screams that came were worse than anything Otto had ever heard from his father's torture chamber. It sounded like the men's souls were howling as the crystals ripped them apart.

After a few seconds, golden light flowed out of the prisoners and back to the crystal through the second thread. It took about five minutes for the crystal to drain every drop of life from the ten prisoners. When it was done, the crystal pulsed with bright, purple energy. An aura of ethereal magic surrounded it, connecting the crystal to the ether itself.

The prisoners had been reduced to little more than fine gray powder. Otto carefully removed the activated crystal from the tripod. The ritual hadn't weakened him as much as he expected. The crystal did most of the work once he connected it. Charging the other four should be a simple enough process.

As he carried the crystal back to its resting place in the chest, Axel stalked over to him. "What the hell was that? You said you were going to execute them, not do whatever that was."

"You wanted them to pay for their crimes," Otto said before placing the crystal in a padded slot. "I'd say they paid. What's the problem?"

"What did you do to them?" Axel asked again.

Otto turned to face his brother. "I drained their life force to charge the crystal. I only need to do it once. It's now connected to the ether directly. If you would get the next ten, I'm ready to continue."

Axel stared at him. "Even Father wouldn't do this. I thought you were the sane one in the family."

"What difference does it make if we kill them this way or cut their heads off after burning them with hot pokers? At least now they'll serve the greater good. These men would never have accepted Garenland's rule. I suspect most of them stayed behind knowing they would probably die. You're a soldier, Axel. Surely you've seen men die badly before."

"When a soldier kills it's eye to eye and sword to sword. Not by some crazy magic. It's wrong, Otto. Evil."

Otto offered a silent prayer for patience. "Magic isn't good or evil, it just is. One sort of painful death is no different than another. If my ritual is offending your delicate sensibilities, you can go. My men and I can manage from here."

"No. As the commander of this mission I have a responsibility to bear witness even if I can't stop you. Do what you have to and do it quickly. I want this over with."

"As do I. I promise you killing gives me no pleasure. But I

won't flinch from doing what's necessary to secure Garen-land's future."

Axel nodded once and they got back to work. An hour of screams in the darkness and it was done. In the morning they could begin training in earnest. Otto could hardly wait to see the armor operational. It was going to be a sight to behold.

CHAPTER 35

Wolfric sat in his throne and listened with growing irritation as Captain Kelten outlined what he'd learned from his so-called investigation into the assassin Lothair. There was a great deal of garbage mixed in with the occasional tidbit that proved nothing. He was no further ahead than he had been when he set out weeks ago to uncover the truth, whatever he imagined that to be. It was time to shut him down before he lucked into something really damaging.

The two of them were alone at the moment as Wolfric wanted no one else to hear what his captain of the guard was wasting his time on. He also didn't want the nobility getting the idea that he didn't have complete control of his subjects, especially the one in charge of keeping him safe.

When Kelten finally paused for a breath Wolfric said, "Let me see if I understand. In the month-plus you've been chasing ghosts, you've learned that Lothair had a few minor run-ins with the watch, but nothing more than childish pranks. He worked briefly for one of the wealthiest families in the city before leaving for no discernible reason. After that you lost track of him. Is that correct?"

"Yes, Majesty, though when you put it like that you make it sound like I haven't accomplished anything. I feel like with a little more time I might find out why he decided to leave the Franken's service. That was an easy job with excellent pay. Who walks away from that? Considering that he left around the same time Lord Shenk arrived in the city, I can't discount the possibility that he was somehow involved."

Wolfric stood, his purple robe falling down behind him. "Are you accusing my chief advisor and most trusted friend of being involved in the murder of my father? If not for your excellent record of service, I'd have you shipped out to the front lines this instant."

"I meant no offense, Majesty. It just seemed too much—"

"Enough! This farce has gone on long enough. Did it ever occur to you, Captain, that the reason Lothair left the Frankens' service was because his masters decided it was time to move against us directly? Would that not be the simple explanation?"

"It feels wrong." Kelten spoke barely above a whisper.

"You'd best get over it. I'm ordering an end to your inquiries. As far as the Crown is concerned, this matter is closed. Should I get word that you are still pursuing these matters or that you've pestered anyone else, especially Otto or his family, I will have you shipped north naked to lead the first charge against Marduke's walls. Do I make myself clear?"

"Perfectly, Majesty. I shall devote myself to my duties and thank you for indulging my investigation. I'm sure you're right. I only wish I didn't have so many questions."

"And I wish my father was still alive." Wolfric didn't have to fake the emotion that made his voice shake. He really did wish he hadn't had to remove his father from the throne. "But he isn't and we must both deal with the world as it is and not how we'd like it."

Kelten bowed deeply. "If I caused you any additional hurt, it wasn't my intention. Rest assured I will continue to serve to the best of my ability."

He sounded contrite, but Wolfric heard an undercurrent of dissatisfaction. Maybe Otto was right and they should have arranged an accident for Captain Kelten. It wasn't too late to do so, but for now he'd settle for watching and waiting.

⟲

K elten strode out of the throne room calmly and with his head held high. Inside he seethed. He was so close to a breakthrough, he knew it, but if he continued his investigations, it would be directly against the king's wishes. It was one thing to work at it on his free days, especially when he had the king's blessing, even if it was reluctantly given. But now...

In all his years of service, he'd never disobeyed the king, never even felt tempted, but here he was, barely dismissed from King Wolfric's presence, and already he was considering how best to work around the command he'd just received. He served the throne more than the man, yet he found he didn't respect Wolfric the way he had his father. Was it just the new king's youth that brought out his disobedient side?

He liked to think there was more to it, some gut instinct that made him so certain there was more to learn. But deep down maybe he thought he knew more than a barely twenty-year-old boy who now sat on the throne and was advised by another boy two years his junior.

Kelten nearly laughed at his arrogance. Wolfric and to a

lesser extent Otto had been trained their entire lives to lead men and make decisions. The nobility might be lax in some ways, but when it came to training their heirs, they were careful to make sure they knew what they needed to from a young age. Kelten was a commoner that was good with a sword and loyal. That's how he rose through the ranks to his current position. If he lost half his qualifications, maybe he had no business serving as the captain of the guard.

If he couldn't follow his king's command, the honorable thing to do would be to quit and continue on his own. But without his position, he'd have no sway with the rich and powerful and his instincts screamed that someone powerful was behind this murder, maybe even the king's advisor, assuming he wasn't reading too much in to Annamaria's letter.

He rounded the bend that carried him from the throne room and slammed his fist into the wall. What was he supposed to do?

Kelten blew out a long sigh. Right now, he had no more leads to follow anyway. He'd bide his time and keep his eyes open. If something came up, fine, if not, he'd have to be satisfied with what he'd accomplished.

CHAPTER 36

Immediately after a bland breakfast of oatmeal and biscuits, Otto, Hans, and the rest of the squad gathered at the wagons to begin the first test of the enchanted armor. Axel and General Varchi were the only audience for this first effort which suited Otto fine. If there was a problem, the fewer people who saw them falling all over themselves the better. That said, there was no way five suits of ten-foot-tall armor stomping around wasn't going to attract attention.

The tarps were pulled back, revealing the armor to their guests. General Varchi drew in a sharp breath. "Who on earth made those things?"

"I believe they were made by Lord Karonin, at least I stole them from one of her armories." Technically Otto had permission to take them, but he wasn't about to point out that he was in regular contact with the spirit of a long-dead Arcane Lord. "Ready to begin, Hans?"

"Ready as we'll ever be, Lord Shenk."

Otto grinned and retrieved one of the glowing purple crystals from the storage chest. There was a slot in the chest plate that accepted the crystal. He slid it in and a moment later the thin lines of mithril running from the slot to the arms and legs of the armor began to glow the same color as the crystal. That was the sign that it was ready to use.

Reaching through the ether, Otto seized control of the armor and had it gently climb down out of the wagon. Guiding it with the crystal in place took far less of his energy. Once it was out, Otto had the chest plate slide up, revealing the space where the operator stood. There were places for the arms and legs to slip in as well as padding to protect from impact.

"Climb aboard, Hans. Show everyone how it's done."

Hans shot Otto a dubious look. "I wish someone would tell me how it's done."

"Just strap yourself in and the magic will do the rest. These were designed to be used by soldiers not wizards so it should be simple enough to control them."

Hans didn't look convinced, but he climbed up the right leg and backed into the armor. His legs went easily into the correct openings then his arms and hands found homes. When he leaned back, the front plate clanked down into position, hiding him from view. The armor's visor glowed with purple light.

"Lord Shenk!" Hans sounded both awed and terrified. "This is… This is…"

"Take a breath and tell me what you see," Otto said.

"I can see out the visor, but I can't see the chest plate in front of me."

"That's good. The magic has integrated your senses into the armor. My voice should sound like it's coming from the helmet as well."

"It does. This is very… odd."

"You'll get used to it. Now try raising your arms one at a time."

It wasn't smooth or steady, but both arms went up then back down. So far so good. Now for the big test.

"Take a step, slowly."

Han's foot rose, wobbled, and came slamming down. The left foot followed and then he started walking in a slow circle. After two circuits Hans said, "It feels as natural as walking on my own if I were dressed in heavy armor. I can't believe it. It's like the armor and I are one."

Otto grinned. This was going better than he'd ever dared hope. "That's exactly how it's supposed to work. Keep practicing your movement while I get the others operational."

"An impressive display." General Varchi's voice startled Otto. He'd been so focused on his work he'd forgotten the older man was there. "Though they're so slow I can't imagine they'd be much use on the battlefield."

"Just wait until we get going, General. You'll see how useful they can be."

Twenty minutes later, all five suits were up and stomping around. Soldiers had gathered at a safe distance. When it was clear that Hans and his men had the units under control Otto said, "Let's take a walk down to the forest and I'll show you just what they can do."

The general nodded and the group strolled to the edge of the woods.

"Hans." Otto pointed at a pine tree about ten inches around. "Rip that tree out by the roots."

Hans stomped over, wrapped his arms around the trunk, and heaved.

The tree resisted for a second, then the mithril lines glowed brighter and snapped it off at the base. That wasn't exactly what Otto was hoping for, but you couldn't say it wasn't impressive.

Hans tossed the shattered tree aside.

Otto pointed at a boulder jutting out of the earth. "Cord, pick that rock up and throw it as far as you can."

Another suit bent and heaved. The rock came loose and went flying a moment later, only crashing into the earth a hundred-plus yards away.

"You see, General, with this armor, no enemy fortification will last an hour. Did you notice the swords on their backs? Imagine a cavalry charge running into those weapons swung about four feet above the ground. I'll grant you the armor might be less than effective in melee combat, but in the right place, they'll be absolutely devastating."

"An impressive display, certainly," the general said with considerably less enthusiasm than Otto expected. "I suppose we could use them as mobile siege equipment. Now if you'll excuse me, I need to plan our next move."

"The general's old fashioned," Axel said. "Anything new will take time to win him over. Frankly, I can imagine winning a battle just by letting the enemy see those things. I sure as hell wouldn't want to go up against them."

"Once he sees them fight, old fashioned or not, he'll come around. The real fun will come when I show him the wizards' magic."

"Having seen what you can do on your own, I'm sure it will be impressive. I need to catch up. He'll want me to go out scouting soon enough."

"How would you like to know right where to look? I can show you if you can spare me ten minutes."

CHAPTER 37

Axel had to hand it to his little brother, the enemy position was exactly where he said it would be. Unfortunately, that was the only good thing about their situation. On the plains ahead of him, the Straken army had built a massive fortification that stretched from tree line to tree line.

There were trenches filled with spikes, walls topped with more spikes behind which lurked hundreds of archers. Catapults and ballistae were just visible, the tops of their frames barely jutting above the wall. It reminded Axel of the earthen fort they took weeks ago only on a huge scale. There was absolutely no way past it unless they retreated and marched hundreds of miles out of their way and even then they'd have a huge army at their backs as they approached the capital.

General Varchi had said that when they finally met the enemy in battle, it would be decisive. Axel figured he was right. Getting past their position was going to be next to impossible. They lost hundreds of soldiers taking the small fort; this one could easily break the army, leaving them with no choice but to retreat. He hoped whatever tricks Otto and his wizards had in store were good ones. They were going to need every advantage they could get.

"How many men you reckon in there, my lord?" Cobb asked.

"A lot. Three legions at least, maybe four. Say twenty thousand plus."

"So they've got us outnumbered and a strong defensive location. Think your brother's toys can get us through that?"

"No, I don't. Impressive as they are, five suits of giant armor wouldn't stand a chance against a force that size."

"And what are we going to do?"

Axel shook his head. "I'm going to be grateful I'm not General Varchi and you're going to follow whatever orders come down."

Cobb snorted and they slipped back to join the rest of the scouts. The main force was two hours behind. For all his indifference to the armor, General Varchi had taken Otto's word about the enemy's location.

Axel didn't pause as he retreated, just waving his men to fall in behind him. They reached the army an hour later. The general rode in the lead with Otto nearby.

"You found them?" General Varchi asked.

"Yes, sir. There's a sprawling fortification exactly where Otto said it would be. The walls are high enough that I can't see the entire force, but given the size, I'd guess at least twenty thousand."

The general nodded and said, "Fall in and we'll have a look."

Axel and his men guided their horses into line and the army set out again. Nothing troubled them as they approached the plains and around noon they stopped at the edge of the grass.

General Varchi didn't speak for long minutes then at last he said, "Isn't this something. All forces deploy. Defensive positions. Get settled in for the night. There isn't time for an attack today."

Axel, Otto, General Varchi, and the command staff stayed mounted while the rest of the soldiers got to work setting up the camp. They were well out of catapult range so there was no danger of getting crushed by a stray boulder. They still had five hours of daylight, so Axel was surprised they weren't making at least one run at the enemy. Not that it was his place to say. The men could certainly do with a rest before the first strike, though how any of them would sleep Axel didn't know.

He was just considering getting down to help the men set up when the drawbridge on the fort lowered across their spike trench. "General, company."

"Finally. I was wondering how long their commander was going to keep us waiting." General Varchi nudged his horse and rode a hundred yards or so into the prairie.

Axel and Otto shared a look before going to join him. A small force of ten mounted soldiers emerged from the fort, a white flag flying over their heads. At the front of the group rode a mountain of a man on the back of a horse that had to measure twenty hands tall. He wore furs and dark armor as seemed to be the style in Straken.

"Do you know the enemy general, sir?" Axel asked.

"No, though I suspected whoever was in charge would come out to parley, exchange a few threats, that sort of thing. From what I've read this sort of preseige ritual was common back before the Portal Compact ended our wars. I assume whoever he is has read those books as well."

"Other than a desire not to be rude, is there some reason we don't just kill them all right now?" Otto asked.

"We're not savages," General Varchi said. "Besides, if he's

smart, he's got a second who's talented enough to take over should we break protocol. Now keep quiet and let me do the talking."

Otto bristled and given his current rank and status Axel understood why. Fortunately, Otto had more self-control than Father and after a glare at the general's back settled in to watch.

"Greetings," General Varchi said. "I assume you wish to discuss terms."

"Terms?" the Straken commander said. "No, I'm here to offer you one chance to withdraw from Straken. You can't possibly defeat my force. We have the stronger position and greater numbers. Don't throw your men's lives away needlessly. Retreating before a superior force isn't cowardly."

"I assume you're authorized to speak for King Uther and that you'll be promising not to return to Garenland? Anything less than that and we'll be forced to continue on our way to Marduke."

"Even if I did, would you trust my word?"

"No." General Varchi shrugged. "I suppose my men will see yours on the walls in the morning."

"They'll be cut down long before they reach the walls. You should never have come to Straken." The enemy contingent turned their mounts and rode back to the fort.

"That was a waste of time," Axel said.

"Yes, as most formalities are." General Varchi nodded. "Staff meeting in the command tent as soon as it's up. You'll both be joining us of course."

Otto nodded as the general rode off.

"You were staring awfully hard at the Straken general," Axel said.

"I was memorizing his features. That way I'll be sure to kill the right person tonight. Your General Varchi might be content to swallow the arrogant fool's insults, but I'm not. Assuming he's right, there's someone else ready to take over anyway."

Axel watched his little brother ride toward where the wizards had begun setting up their tents. Every time Axel saw him, Otto reminded him more and more of Father. Considering how powerful he was now, that couldn't be good for anyone.

CHAPTER 38

The sun had risen an hour ago and now Otto found himself standing at the front of the Northern Army with his wizards on either side of him. Fifteen thousand men were watching and counting on them to soften a seemingly unbeatable enemy. Yesterday at the staff meeting Otto had argued that they should be allowed to strike first, that was why they'd come after all. Once the melee began, their spells would be far less effective. Or at least more difficult to target.

General Varchi had agreed though with a considerable lack of enthusiasm. The old fool still didn't appreciate what they brought to the battlefield. In fact, like most people, he probably still thought wizards should be little better than slaves, their rights constrained and controlled by idiots who didn't understand what they were capable of. Today, at last, he would learn exactly how wrong he was.

Otto drew his mithril sword and leveled it at the fort. "Fireballs ready! Squad leaders, don't forget to channel through your rings. We want maximum damage. Target their siege equipment with the first volley."

With the order given, Otto channeled twenty threads' worth of ether through the blade of his sword. The sphere he formed soon filled with orange energy. All around him he felt the others building up their spells. Otto charged the sphere until he felt the wall begin to vibrate. The result was a blue-white sphere as large as his head.

"Fire when ready!" Otto sent a targeting thread to the battlements directly above the gate where a pair of ballistae sat ready to slaughter anyone getting close.

The moment his thread was in place, the fireball streaked along it.

His spell detonated with more force than he'd anticipated. Hot wind caressed his face as the roar savaged his ears. Through the smoke and debris he couldn't see how much damage the spell did.

As he peered ahead, more, smaller explosions sounded up and down the line.

They waited to assess the damage.

They didn't have long to wait. When the smoke cleared it was apparent that the first volley had been effective. Where Otto's spell had struck, little remained beyond a few charred bits of wood and chunks of flesh that had once been men. He'd destroyed a section of wall about thirty feet long making a gap plenty wide for the infantry to enter.

To his left and right, catapults burned and enemy soldiers screamed as their comrades tried to put them out. The others hadn't done as much damage as Otto, but the results were still impressive.

Nevertheless, there were still many thousand soldiers

unharmed as well as scores of siege weapons. Their work had only begun.

"Pick your targets and fire at will. Should you feel fatigued, fall back to the aid station."

Otto shifted his strategy this time, conjuring three smaller fireballs and sending them exploding into three different targets. The damage was still impressive if not as total. Now that there was an opening for the eventual assault, destroying catapults and killing archers was more important.

He would have liked to hear what the enemy's new commander—he'd made good on his threat to kill the one that spoke to them last night—was saying to rally his men. It must have been good since Otto couldn't see anyone running for it. Not that he could see much.

A dozen fireballs later Otto was starting to feel drained. He figured one more round and he'd be finished for a while. Best to stop before that. Being powerless in enemy territory was a good way to get killed.

He glanced left and right. The others had already fallen back which wasn't a surprise. Even with their training, none of the war wizards had broken through their personal barriers. Otto had no intention of teaching them how either. He wanted followers not competitors.

With the magical bombardment complete, Otto waved to Hans and his squad. They were strapped into the magical armor and each of them carried heavy, wooden gangplanks about eight feet wide and twelve feet long. Their job was to drop the planks across the spike trench then deal with any archers still near the opening Otto blasted in the wall. It was the armor's first chance to shine in real combat and Otto was anxious. If it went badly, he'd lose what little confidence he'd gained from General Varchi.

It was too late to worry about it now. The five suits went clanking out, each hoisting a plank that was actually more like a section of wall and carrying it with no difficulty. As they approached the enemy position, a few archers shook off the shock and fired a barrage of arrows. A handful stuck in the wood without doing any damage.

Their lack of success didn't discourage the enemy archers. They kept up their useless barrage until the planks went down across the trench. A few arrows pinged off the heavy steel plate, doing even less damage than they did to the wood.

Hans reached over his shoulder and drew the massive sword attached to his back. A single swing sliced three archers who leaned too far out of the fort in half. Two other squad members slammed their massive gauntlets into the wall and ripped the opening wider so it would be easier for the infantry. Walls that had looked so sturdy a moment ago crumbled like dry cake under the armor's powerful gauntlets.

A horn sounded and the Second and Third Legions advanced around him. They marched at a steady pace, turtled up to avoid any incoming arrows. A few came arcing in, but it appeared most of the archers had had enough. When the soldiers reached the edge of the trench, Hans and the others moved their armor aside to allow the regulars through.

Otto had seen all he needed to. If the Second and Third couldn't wrap this up with a minimum of losses, he didn't know what more he could do to help. He fell back to the rear command position. Three-quarters of the way there he spotted Axel and General Varchi watching the army's progress from a safe distance. He angled their way.

"An impressive display," Axel said. "War will never be the same after this."

"Hardly seems fair though," the general said. "There's little honor to be found in such a slaughter. Hopefully the Straken commander will do the wise thing and surrender."

"There was little honor in Straken slaughtering helpless villagers before they retreated," Axel said, drawing a glare from the general.

Otto kept his thoughts to himself. The more he heard from General Varchi, the more he thought Wolfric needed to replace him. Honor had no place in war. Otto would have happily killed every Straken soldier with magic had he the power. The only lives that interested him were those of Garenland citizens. The honorable dead were of no use to anyone.

"Ideally," Otto said. "Word of what happened here will spread and the next time we show up somewhere the enemy will simply surrender and no one will have to die."

"That is beyond naive," General Varchi said. "No matter the odds, when you invade a country, the citizens will fight. It's unavoidable."

Finally, something they agreed on. How nice.

CHAPTER 39

The Lady in Red stood as calmly as she could in the courtyard in front of Castle Marduke. A light dusting of snow had fallen the night before, little more than an annoyance for the moment, but anyone that had lived in Straken for as long as she had knew the real storms weren't far off. She offered a silent prayer to any power that might be listening that the snows would come early this year. Let the miserable Garenlanders get bogged down to their knees in it. Let them starve in the cold.

Her curses were all well and good, but they accomplished nothing. She grimaced and pulled the fur-lined hood of her cloak up. She was expecting one of her message riders any time now. The last report she'd received indicated that the enemy army was within days of the Saber Plains.

It would all come down to that. If the combined armies could either defeat outright or at least badly damage Garenland's forces, they had a chance that they wouldn't reach the capital this year. A draw or heaven forbid a rout and she'd have to find some way to convince Uther to allow her to seek aid from the other nations of the alliance.

She shivered and not from the chill northern breeze. Uther hated anything that smacked of weakness, but her hope was that he hated the idea of his capital city getting sacked even more.

A faint sound drew her attention and sure enough the messenger was thundering across the drawbridge. Sweat lathered his horse's chest and flanks. It looked like the beast was near death. She tried not to take that as an omen.

The rider, dressed in dark leather and furs, leapt off his mount and offered her a scroll. She didn't bother asking him any questions. The scroll was at least three riders removed from whoever first received it. Instead she broke the seal and started reading.

She felt the blood drain from her face. The fort had fallen and the combined army was devastated. Thousands dead and thousands more taken prisoner. Half a legion had managed to break out and escape. They were making their way north and would continue toward the capital unless they received orders to the contrary. The enemy's losses were estimated at less than a thousand.

The Lady in Red almost screamed. A thousand! The Garenlanders had lost nearly that many in the first skirmish with a force a tenth the size of the one they faced here. It wasn't possible!

Forcing herself to calm down she resumed reading the letter. The reason for their loss was magic. Garenland's wizards had finally made an appearance on the battlefield and what an appearance they made. Fire rained down from the sky, destroying siege equipment and killing men by the hundreds. Giant suits of armor bridged the trenches and broke the fort's walls. The magic broke their soldiers' will and many surrendered at once. Others weren't killed outright but wounded and unable to fight.

The message wasn't signed by either the army's general or his sub-commander but rather by a lieutenant whose name she'd never seen before. If he was the highest-ranking officer still alive, there was no hope for a counterattack. Not that she had much hope for one anyway after reading the note.

She realized the rider was still waiting before her, panting for breath. "Go. Rest and eat. You did well getting this to me."

"Ma'am." He led his horse toward the stables leaving her alone in the snow.

After reading this there was no chance Uther could deny they needed help, magical help, as well as soldiers. She hated wizards as much as any right-thinking person and this did nothing to change her mind about how dangerous they were, but sometimes you had to fight fire with fire.

A brief walk through the cold dark halls of Castle Marduke brought her to the nearly empty throne room. Uther sat with one leg slung over the arm of his throne, a flagon in his hand, and not a guard in sight. At least his sword was near to hand.

The king smiled when he saw her and eyed the scroll in her hand. "News from the front? How badly did we crush the Garenland fools?"

"We lost. Our forces were nearly wiped out. Half a legion survived and is making their way here. It seems Garenland brought their wizards with them."

Uther's smile turned to a scowl. "Wizards! I can't believe they trusted those unnatural monsters on the battlefield. I always knew Garenland was full of weaklings and this proves it. If good steel can't do the job they resort to magic. Pathetic!"

"Yes, Majesty. However distasteful such means are, it is

difficult to deny the effectiveness of their wizards. If Straken is to survive, we'll need help, including wizards of our own."

Uther surged out of his throne and hurled his flagon across the room. "You dare speak to me of bringing wizards here, to Straken, to fight our battles for us. You think I need the help of those horse-lovers in Rolan? Or the arrogant fools in Tharanault? Why not suggest we take out a loan from the bankers in Lasil while you're at it?"

The Lady in Red weathered the storm of Uther's anger just as she had many times previously. In truth he had little temper for ruling, though she couldn't deny he had cunning and a cruel streak a mile wide. There were no doubt better men to serve as king in Straken, but she only had Uther to deal with.

"Majesty, I know my suggestion displeases you. I knew it would before I spoke. However, the facts are this. All our remaining men under arms number less than what we lost on the Saber Plains. Even if we could recall them in time to reach Marduke before the Garenlanders, they would be torn apart by the enemy's magic just as our other army was. If we want to win, I see no other way forward."

Uther snarled and glared around the room. Unfortunately, there was nothing there for him to vent his rage on. At last he slumped back onto his throne. "They got me good. I had the invasion all planned out. We'd take the northern province before winter and march on Garen City in the spring. As long as their weakling king was in charge, I could have had my way with the miserable country. Then he had to go and get himself killed and his brat took over."

"It was certainly inconvenient, Majesty." Uther had accepted the necessity of her reasoning; she knew him well enough to recognize that. Now it was just a matter of letting him vent until he gave her permission to carry out the mission.

"That's putting it mildly. By all rights a boy king with no experience should be an easier opponent. So much for that." At last he blew out a long sigh. "Go and do what you must. Straken must survive if we're to avenge this insult."

The Lady in Red bowed. "The portal opens in Rolan in two hours. If I hurry, I can be packed and on my way by then. I won't fail you, Majesty."

His smile returned, melancholy this time. "You never have. Good luck."

She bowed and hurried out of the throne room. She had packing and planning to do. Convincing their so-called partners to help wasn't going to be easy.

But she'd do it. There was no question in her mind. She would save Straken no matter what it took.

CHAPTER 40

Captain Kelten completed his rounds, checking every guard post in the castle and finding all exactly as it should be. He made the journey twice a day and had done so every day since assuming his position as captain of the royal guard. He took his job and the oath to obey the king seriously.

Yet deep down he couldn't deny a part of him still wasn't satisfied with how he'd left his investigation into the late king's assassination. He had missed something, he knew it, but what that something was he had no idea. He'd kept his word to King Wolfric not to pursue the matter further, both because of his oath and because he simply didn't have anywhere else to search.

Kelten sighed and rounded the corner to his office. The hole-in-the-wall was little bigger than a closet in the king's chambers, but that was fine. It was really just a quiet place out of everyone's way where he could read reports and think. Unlike merchants with their ostentatious carved desks and leather chairs, he had no one to impress.

As he approached the smooth, plain door he froze. A piece of rolled-up parchment had been tucked through the iron hoop of his knocker. No one had ever left him a message before. If one of his men needed something, they'd say so when he checked their post and an off-duty guard would simply wait and speak to him when he arrived. They all knew his schedule well enough to predict within half an hour when he'd be in his office.

He shrugged and reached for the note. Maybe it would be something to take his mind off the investigation he wasn't supposed to be thinking about.

Kelten unrolled the scroll and groaned. It was from Commander Trask. As promised, the watch had continued to keep an ear open for any news relating to the assassination, Lothair, or anything else out of the ordinary. Apparently they had a witness that saw a battle between a small army of thugs and a group of mercenaries. The battle ended when a wizard fitting Lord Shenk's description turned up and wiped the thugs out. There were no details or any mention of Lothair. Trask ended the letter by inviting him to call on watch head-quarters if he wanted to know more.

He certainly did want to know more, but he couldn't leave his post until tonight. While he usually took his meals with the men in the barrack's mess hall, he could certainly skip one night without drawing any comment. But if he did visit Trask, he would be going against his king for the first time since joining the castle guard.

Was finding out what happened worth breaking his promise? Kelten liked to think it was and that just because he broke his oath this one time for something extremely important, he wouldn't do it again. But then again why not? If the king gave him an order and he decided he knew better, what was to keep him from following his own path the next time?

Kelten didn't know, but he did know that if Trask had found out something new about the assassination, he had to know what. His mind would never be at ease until he knew the whole truth.

⟳

The sun had long since set when Kelten finally got away from the castle. Making his way through the city at night was an odd feeling. The forges were quiet and the streets largely empty. Warm light and the sounds of happy people laughing emerged from a tavern he passed. While he didn't spend enough time in the city to know what it was generally like, tonight at least, everything felt right. You could be forgiven for forgetting that there was a war going on far to the north. And going well from what Kelten had heard.

The last message the king received indicated that the Northern Army was preparing to make the final approach to Marduke and that little stood in their way beyond the city's walls. That note had come from Lord Shenk who had joined the army, along with a group of his newly trained wizards, for the final assault on the Straken capital. The king had been well pleased with the report as had the nobles when he read it to them.

Kelten had no desire to bring His Majesty bad news, but depending on what Trask had to tell him, he might have no choice.

Watch headquarters was well lit at night and a full shift of watchmen were on duty at all times. Hopefully, Trask worked late but if he didn't, whoever was on the night shift should be able to direct him to the commander's home. He pushed through the front doors and strode into the large open floor where the watch processed criminals, wrote reports, and generally did their jobs. It was quiet tonight with only a pair of drunks snoring in one of the holding cells.

On the left side of the room, a desk with a tremendously fat man behind it served as a greeting area for anyone that needed to report something. Mercifully, there was no line. Kelten hadn't bothered changing out of his uniform and one look at it got the man's attention.

"How can I be of service, sir?" the duty sergeant asked.

"Commander Trask requested that I join him when I was able. I know it's late, but I hoped he might still be in."

"That he is, sir. Do you know the way to his office or should I get one of the pages to show you?"

"I know where it is, thank you." Kelten nodded to the sergeant and made his way to the back of the building.

Trask's office was in the northeasternmost corner, away from the hustle and noise of the processing floor. Kelten caught a few passing glances as he made his way back, but no one bothered him. That was one of the reasons he most liked wearing his uniform. No one ever wanted to bother someone associated with the palace.

He knocked and a moment later Trask's gruff voice said, "Come."

Kelten stepped inside and shut the door behind him. "I got your message."

"I figured you'd be along sometime tonight." Trask stood, held out his remaining hand, and they shook. "It was just dumb luck we found the guy. Have a seat."

Kelten eased himself into one of the guest chairs. "What happened?"

"A watch patrol was doing a regular sweep through some of the rougher parts of the city, you know, just to let them know we hadn't forgotten about them. Anyway, the guys found this drunk staggering around talking to the air about a secret war and a wizard that hurled lightning. He clearly had no business being on the streets, so they brought him in. I was talking with one of my lieutenants when he came in and overheard his rambling. When he described the wizard, it was a perfect likeness of Otto Shenk."

"If there was a fight like you described in your note, how could no one else have noticed?"

"In the part of the city where it happened, people have learned to see nothing, hear nothing, and most importantly say nothing. Besides, the thugs went in ahead of time and cleared the locals out. Our witness just slipped through the cracks. Anyway, I questioned him closely and it turns out Lord Shenk and the mercenaries took a few of the attackers prisoner. You'll never guess who one of them was."

"Lothair."

"Correct. And the other two match the description of Allen and his bartender. What do you think about that?"

"If Lord Shenk had Lothair in custody before the assassination, how did he escape? And were the thugs Straken assets or just regular criminals? Finally, what were all these people doing in a rough part of the city?"

"Those, my friend, are all excellent questions. Now, I doubt we'll have any luck questioning Lord Shenk, but Allen and the bartender are another matter. How about we head over to the Thirsty Sprite and see what he has to say about this?"

"That sounds like an excellent idea." Kelten stood, more

convinced than ever that Lord Shenk was involved in the king's assassination. Not that his belief would be enough to convince King Wolfric. He needed proof, something more than the word of a crazy drunk.

Nothing less would save him when Wolfric found out that he had disobeyed a direct order.

CHAPTER 41

There was a good crowd in the Thirsty Sprite, the best Allen had seen in weeks. Everyone was celebrating the Northern Army's success and the ale was flowing freely. Word had spread quickly when a messenger arrived with tales of victory. From the sound of it, the wizards had proven their worth as well. Lord Shenk would be pleased. And a happy Lord Shenk was something Allen very much liked to see.

He shivered. How could a teenager be so intimidating? Under other circumstances, Otto Shenk was the sort of person Allen would've kicked in the ass and sent scrambling.

It was the magic of course. Nothing like being able to electrocute someone to death from half a city away to make them fear you.

Allen shook off his worry. Lord Shenk was a thousand miles away and certainly too busy to be thinking about him. He might as well focus on the tavern finally making a bit of gold for a change. He scanned the room just to make sure no one was up to anything sketchy. He didn't think about it anymore, it was a habit after running the place for the last few years.

Speaking of sketchy, Sin walked through the door and caught his eye at once. She'd swapped her black leather for a simple green smock and plain wool cloak. Sin would have caught his eye at any time, but tonight she wasn't giving him the sort of look he liked to get from a beautiful woman. This was more of a "we're in trouble" kind of look.

Allen nodded toward his office door and started working his way through the crowd. He had to be cursed. How long had it been since something went his way for more than a day at a time?

"What is it?" Allen asked when she reached him.

"One of my people got arrested and while he was in processing overheard the commander interrogating some crazy drunk who claimed to have seen a street battle that ended with a wizard killing most of the combatants before taking a trio hostage. He gave a pretty good description of you and your foreign friend. The third guy sounded a lot like a certain assassin."

Allen cursed every demon in hell. They'd cleared that neighborhood. No one should have been there to see anything. How could they have missed a crazy drunk?

Not that it mattered. He'd be having company soon enough. "Thanks for the warning. I'll be sure to pass along word of your good work to the boss when he returns."

"There's more."

Allen suppressed a groan. Of course there was. "Let me have it."

"When I got word of what happened, I stationed a man outside watch headquarters. Not long ago, Captain Kelten of the palace guard went in. How much you want to bet I know what they were talking about?"

"No bet. I need to make myself scarce. Thanks again."

Allen waved to get Ulf's attention. He needed a place they could hide out in for a few days. Hopefully things would blow over by then. He'd leave the serving girls to run the tavern for tonight. They'd all worked for him for a while, so they'd manage. After that, it was just a matter of waiting.

While Ulf finished pouring a drink, Allen flicked a glance at Sin who had settled on a stool. He'd expected the thief to disappear the moment her message was delivered. "Are you waiting for anything in particular?"

Her smile was hot enough to melt steel. "I'm curious to see what happens when the hunters find their prey missing. We should arrange a meeting for tomorrow."

"Yeah, how about by the portal, say around noon?"

"Perfect, that's a nice short walk from my place. You'd best get going."

Ulf finally finished with his customer and joined them. He raised an eyebrow.

"Trouble coming. Tell the girls they're in charge and meet me out back."

Ulf nodded and Allen slipped through the kitchen door. His cook looked up from the stew pot he was tending. Allen offered no explanation, instead hurried past and out the rear door.

The night was cool and quiet with no sign of watchmen. That was all he could hope for at the moment. The question now was, where did he go to hole up? The answer came to him a moment later. Erin and Eric had returned home for the night. They'd been staying with him long enough. It was time for them to return the favor.

The moment Ulf emerged from the tavern they set out. The mercenaries lived all the way across the city. Right now, that sounded like a very good place to be.

⌒

T he walk from watch headquarters to the Thirsty Sprite took about ten minutes and Kelten resented every minute. It felt like the squad of watchmen they'd brought with them was dragging their feet, but Kelten knew it was only his anxiety talking. These were good men and he wouldn't think ill of them.

Allen, on the other hand, well, when he got his hands on that lying tavern keeper…

He forced himself to relax. The truth was, their eyewitness wasn't exactly reliable. Their only hope was to make it sound like he wasn't a half-crazed drunk and hope they could intimidate Allen into telling the truth. It seemed a dim hope, but you never knew what might happen when you got someone alone in an interrogation room.

When they finally arrived, the tavern was filled with a raucous crowd. He'd hoped to find the place less busy, but that wasn't going to stop him. Trask deployed his men to surround the tavern in case there were any back doors or secret exits.

When that was done the two men shared a look and Kelten led the way inside. Every table was packed with laughing, half-drunk patrons. Attractive servers in revealing uniforms carried trays back and forth from the bar and kitchen. Another pretty girl stood behind the bar serving drinks and laughing with the men seated on stools. There was no sign of Allen or his friend.

It seemed impossible that neither of them was here on such

a busy night. Kelten made his way to the bar and waved the bartender over.

"What can I get you, sir?" she asked.

"Your boss."

Kelten couldn't deny her pout was adorable. "Allen went out on some business or other a few minutes ago. He took Ulf with him and left us to do all the work, the skunk. At least we won't have to share our tips. If you want to leave a message, I'll see that he gets it."

"It's something we need to discuss in person. Do you know where they went?"

She laughed and shook her head. "Allen doesn't tell me anything. You can wait if you like."

"No, I'll try again another time. Thank you."

Kelten left the bar and rejoined Trask. "He slipped out ahead of us."

"I checked the common room," Trask said. "They're not hiding here. There's an upstairs room, but I doubt he'd be dumb enough to hide there either. Someone must have warned him we were coming. Did you tell anyone about this?"

"Not a soul. Could it have been a watchman on the take?"

"I like to think not, but I can't guarantee it. We're not going to find him tonight. I'll tell my people to keep an eye out. Soon enough he'll poke his head out of whatever hole he's crawled into and when he does, we'll grab him."

Kelten hated waiting, but Trask was right. They'd blown their chance tonight.

CHAPTER 42

The Lady in Red, along with an honor guard of six burly infantrymen led by her chief security officer Mal, and her personal servant, a mute girl named Anna, stepped through the portal and emerged an instant later in Rolan City, the capital of Rolan. The moment they did, warmth rolled over them. They were over a thousand miles south of Marduke and the temperature difference was considerable, and welcome if she was honest. Cold, long winters might breed powerful warriors, but they had little else to recommend them.

Normally, when she went to call on one of Straken's allies, things were set up days in advance. A special envoy would be waiting to meet her and usher her to the royal palace. Today they were going to have to make the trip their own.

They moved quickly out of the way to make room for the dozen merchant wagons passing through. War or not, business never stopped. That was one of the few things she loved about merchants, their focus. As long as there was coin to be made, they were making the effort to get it.

"What now?" Mal asked.

"Now we head to the castle and hope the king is in a reasonable mood."

She wasn't at all confident that he would be. King Villares had a reputation for many things, but reasonableness wasn't among them. Fortunately, he was terrified of Uther. That should aid her diplomacy a great deal.

The country of Rolan was flat for the most part. There were a few small forests near the northern border and a range of hills to the southwest, but other than that it was level grassland crisscrossed by rivers and dotted with lakes. The combination of good land, plenty of water, and a long growing season made Rolan the largest agricultural producer on the continent. They were also the owners of the finest cavalry the world had ever seen. That was what the Lady needed. Straken's own cavalry was a sad, meager collection of horses ridden by the few men they could find small enough not to break their backs.

The Lady walked in the center of her guards, which obscured her view of the city. Not that there was much to see. Everything was done in shades of brown, including the people and their clothes. It was a fifteen-minute walk to the castle gates and when they arrived, Mal stepped aside to let her approach.

The castle was surrounded by a fifteen-foot stone wall with an iron portcullis guarding the entrance. The stone and iron had both come from Straken, gifts to cement their alliance from Uther's grandfather to Villares's. The time and effort to build the bloody thing had been horrendous, but it had forged the two kingdoms' bond into something strong. Hopefully Villares would remember that.

She'd been here often enough that the guards on duty

snapped to attention at her approach. They wore mail covered with a tabard emblazoned with a rearing stallion. "We had no word you were coming, ma'am. Please forgive the lack of an escort."

She smiled her best smile, the one that made men's knees go weak, and said, "It was a sudden decision. I need to speak with King Villares on an urgent matter. If you could send word?"

"Right away, ma'am." The youngest of the four guards went running toward the castle.

Twenty minutes later she found herself seated across a polished brass table from King Villares, a steaming cup of tea on a saucer in front of her. The king was dressed in fine gray robes, but that did nothing to take away from the worn and weathered look that made it clear he'd spent his share of days in the saddle.

"What brings such a beautiful guest to visit me so suddenly?" King Villares asked.

"Frankly, Your Majesty, I'm here to ask for your help. The Garenlanders have forced our army back across the border and they've brought their wizards with them. Their magic has proven very effective, to the tune of thousands dead. If you could spare us a legion of cavalry and as many wizards as possible, Uther would be most grateful."

King Villares's smile had slowly faded while she spoke. "Uther assured me, assured all of us, when we agreed to support his move against Garenland, that they wouldn't be a problem. Straken was to get the northern province, and we were to get the southern. Now you're telling me your king was wrong about your ability to carry out your plans and you need me to save you. Is that correct?"

"Yes, it is. When Uther made his plans, he made several assumptions that turned out to be wrong. The death of the former king puts his more aggressive son in command and no one could have guessed that they'd allow wizards to fight with the army. Wizards haven't been permitted to use offensive magic since the forging of the compact."

"And once we kicked Garenland out of the compact, they no longer saw any reason to hold back," Villares said. "It seems Uther didn't think his plan through as thoroughly as he claimed. I see no reason why we should help you. Our efforts in the south are going well. My agent has already struck a deal with Garenland that basically allows us to keep what we've taken as long as we make no more aggressive moves. I believe I'll pocket those extra thirty miles of territory and not push my luck."

The Lady's heart sank. She'd hoped to manage this without threats, but Villares wasn't giving her much choice.

"You're a wise man, Majesty, so I'm sure you know that the reason Garenland is allowing you to keep that territory is because they're busy fighting us. Should Straken fall, you can be certain they'll be coming for those thirty miles in your pocket. If you'd seen the reports I have, you'd be eager to avoid fighting in your own territory with no allies. Believe me when I say it isn't a winning strategy."

The king scratched his goatee. "You make a compelling point. Straken is truly in danger of falling?"

"I say with all honesty that without the aid of you and Tharanault, Marduke will be taken before the snows."

King Villares frowned and said, "It will take time to gather my forces but expect us within the week. I don't know how much our wizards know about war, but they'll learn or die."

The Lady in Red bowed her head in acknowledgment. The first step was taken. With Rolan on board, it would be easier to convince Tharanault. With more forces and wizards of their own, Straken would be able to fight Garenland on even terms.

So let them come. They would find Marduke a far tougher nut to crack than they expected.

CHAPTER 43

Kelten received the king's summons before he'd even begun his rounds. A member of the royal guard had appeared at the barracks with an official parchment signed by King Wolfric and bearing the royal seal. His heart lurched when he read the note. There wasn't much really, just a command to follow the bearer immediately. Kelten wasn't a political person, but he understood at once that ignoring this command would end with his head on a spike.

And so he marched off behind the silent guard, through the familiar halls, to the throne room. The two men on duty outside the doors weren't members of the palace guard. Kelten knew all his people and even if he hadn't, they were dressed in black tabards with the royal griffin on the chest. More than the official note, seeing strangers on guard duty told him exactly how much trouble he was in.

Inside, King Wolfric sat on his throne with Commander Borden at his side. The leader of the royal guard wore a grim scowl on his generally humorless face. His hand never strayed more than a few inches from the hilt of his sword. Kelten considered and immediately dismissed the question of whether he could defeat Borden in a fight. The notion that they might cross swords was ridiculous.

Kelten stopped ten feet from the throne and bowed. "You summoned me, Majesty?"

"I did. I have one question, Kelten. Was I at all unclear in my order to drop your pointless investigation into my father's murder?"

"No, you were perfectly clear, Majesty."

"Excellent. I'm pleased to hear that we agree on that at least. Now, given that my order was clear, why, exactly, are you still working with the city watch on this matter?"

Kelten winced then frowned. "Did you have me followed, Majesty?"

"Yes. Now answer my question."

Of all the responses Kelten had expected a blunt admission wasn't one of them. "Trask got a new lead on the assassin and reached out to me. I didn't believe hearing him out on my own time would be a violation of your order."

"And joining him on a raid, a failed raid mind you, that didn't violate my order either?"

"I have to know, Majesty. The uncertainty is driving me mad."

"No, Kelten." The king leaned forward and stared hard into Kelten's eyes. "What you had to do was obey. Since you appear incapable of doing that, I'm relieving you of your command, your rank, and your position in the castle. You will leave your uniform, armor, and weapons behind. Orders have been given that you are no longer welcome in the palace. Borden will be taking over your duties. The palace guard will be folded into the royal guard. Should any of your men prove as disloyal as you, they will join you on the street."

Kelten could only stare in dumb shock. All his life had been dedicated to serving the Crown. He couldn't conceive of a life outside of that.

"Borden, see this disloyal swine out of my castle."

"Majesty." Borden strode down from the dais, stopped in front of Kelten, and raised an eyebrow.

Kelten turned silently and trudged out. As they passed various guard stations, his men called out to him, but Kelten couldn't find words to answer them.

He wasn't their commander anymore.

He wasn't anything.

Back at the barracks, Borden watched him strip off his gear and change into civilian clothes. His meager personal possessions fit into a small satchel.

At the side gate Borden shoved him through and said, "I hope it was worth it. Don't come back. The archers have orders to shoot on sight."

With that final warning, Borden turned on his heel and marched back to the castle, leaving Kelten alone in the street.

Wolfric wiped the sweat from his brow and shrugged out of his purple robe. It was a relief to have Kelten gone. Having him digging around in matters that didn't concern him was stress Wolfric didn't need. Things were going well in Straken and the merchants and nobles were happy about the bandits being eliminated. For the first time since he took his father's throne, Wolfric felt like he had a good handle on his kingdom. There was still the matter of Rolan, but their defeat would come soon enough. Otto was right, one thing at a time.

The throne room door opened and Borden strode in. "He's gone."

If there was one thing Wolfric liked about Borden it was his complete lack of formality. He was also one of the few that knew Otto had helped him plan the removal of his father from the throne. Unlike Kelten, Borden had little use for Father's maneuvering and subtlety. While Wolfric had no issues with either of those things, he knew they couldn't solve every problem. Some problems required steel and blood.

"Good. Are the palace guards giving you any trouble?"

"They aren't thrilled about their commander losing his position, but no one has questioned my orders yet. Anyone that does will find themselves on the street with Kelten."

"Agreed. People need to accept that I'm king now not my father. The sooner they do that the better. You sent the letter to Commander Trask?"

"First thing this morning. He wasn't happy either but agreed to drop the investigation."

Wolfric nodded. "Have someone keep an eye on him. I don't want any nasty surprises."

"Maybe we should just kill them both."

"If it comes to that, fine, but the king's death rattled the people. Should the watch commander and the captain of the palace guard both fall as well, only months later..." Wolfric shook his head. "I might be king, but I can't rule if I lose the confidence of the people and the nobility. The deaths of more prominent people, especially right after I gave them orders they didn't like, would invite too many questions. Should they defy me again or move against the throne, that's another matter."

"As you wish. There are a few petitioners this morning. Do

you want to see them or should I have them return tomorrow?"

"I'll see them. No sense giving the impression that anything's changed."

Borden nodded and headed for the door.

Wolfric slipped his robe back on and adjusted his crown. It was time to listen to some complaints and show off his wisdom. He smiled to himself. Maybe he should be one of those kings that led the army personally.

At least he wouldn't die of boredom.

CHAPTER 44

Kelten sat in the dark corner of a tavern no one bothered to name and sipped weak ale. Four days had passed since he was dismissed from his position as Captain of the Palace Guard. His civilian tunic felt strange and he missed the weight of his mail coat. He'd gambled everything and lost it all. He had no idea what the future held for him and no particular desire to find out. He had coin enough to hold him over for a few months at least, assuming he was careful. Maybe he'd get a job guarding caravans come spring.

A bitter laugh drew a few curious looks, but this wasn't the sort of place that people asked questions and the curious soon returned to their drinks. To go from a protector of kings to a protector of produce, quite a step down. There were plenty who would laugh at his fall. He had earned derision for his actions. His duty had been to the living not the dead.

He sighed and took another sip.

A man in a dark cloak slid into the seat across from him. Kelten had been so distracted he hadn't even noticed the stranger approaching. That was a good way to get his throat cut.

"You look like something I stepped in on my way here and scraped off my boot."

Kelten blinked. "Trask? What are you doing here?"

"Keep your voice down." Trask looked around, but no one was paying them the least attention. "I'm risking my job even talking to you. Word came down from the king that we were to drop our investigation into the assassination. Officially I have, but my people still keep their eyes open. Allen and his friend have surfaced at last. I can't go after them, but you can. What more do you have to lose?"

Kelten scowled. He'd take considerable pleasure beating the miserable tavern keeper to a pulp. "Where is he?"

"Back at his place if you can believe it. He opened last night like nothing happened. Someone must have gotten word to him that the watch wasn't looking for him anymore. Like you said, I think I have a leak in my office. But that's my problem. What are you going to do?"

"Talk to Allen. One way or another I will find out the truth."

Trask nodded. "I was hoping you'd say that. I've ordered all patrols to avoid the area tomorrow between noon and three. You can make your move then. I'm sorry I can't do more."

"There is one more thing you can do. I need a sword."

Trask shifted around and leather scraped on metal. He pulled his sheathed blade out from under his cloak. "Here, it's standard issue to the watch and the most common design sold in Garen."

Kelten hefted the sword and smiled his first genuine smile in weeks.

⌒

Allen leaned on the bar and smiled to himself. It was good to be home and even better to escape Eric and Erin's dingy little flat. The place was a tight fit for two people and four was ridiculous. When Sin had finally informed him that the hunt had been called off his sigh of relief had been loud indeed. Ulf had simply shrugged and said he'd seen worse. For that, among many other things, he pitied his friend.

The real shocker had come when Sin revealed the king himself had ordered the watch to drop their search. Deep down he suspected Lord Shenk must have had a hand in it, but as far as Allen knew, their employer hadn't been back from the front in weeks. Given that he could travel by magic and had no reason to tell Allen about his comings and goings, Lord Shenk could have visited a dozen times.

As he was happily surveying his recovered domain, someone knocked on the front door. It was barely after noon and they didn't open for hours. Who could be bothering them this early?

Allen touched the mark Lord Shenk had put on the back of his neck. If he had returned, they'd best not keep him waiting.

"Ulf? Would you get that?"

Ulf stood up from the pot he'd been tending and walked silently to the door. He slid the bolt open and the instant he did, the door crashed into him, sending the slender man sprawling.

Captain Kelten strode through, a sword bare in his hands. He kicked the door shut and put the tip of the blade to Ulf's throat. "You will answer all my questions or your friend dies."

Allen stared in disbelief. "You again. What demon lord did I offend that he should sic you on me?"

"I know you were seen in the company of the assassin Lothair and that a wizard fitting Lord Shenk's description captured you all." Allen's stomach twisted. This couldn't possibly end well. "Was he involved in the king's murder?"

"I don't know."

Kelten pushed the tip of his sword harder into Ulf's throat. "That is not an acceptable answer. Try again."

"Look, yes, Lord Shenk captured the three of us. After a thorough questioning, he made Ulf and I a proposal, work for him putting together a spy network and live. Or hang. It wasn't a hard choice. He let us go but kept Lothair along with a pair of Straken spies. What happened after we left, I can't say and don't want to know."

"Why would Lord Shenk trust you when you were working for the enemy hours before?"

Allen turned slowly and lifted his hair off the back of his neck. "See that mark? It's magic. Lord Shenk can use it to find us anywhere in the world and kill us. Let's just say betraying him wouldn't be in our best interest."

"Lord Shenk couldn't have been acting alone. Who was with him?"

Allen turned back, keeping his hands visible. The nearest weapon was his sword and it was hanging from a hook at the end of the bar. Even if he could reach it, Ulf would be dead before he could do anything.

"If you mean the soldiers that were trying to kill us, I didn't get a formal introduction. There were five of them dressed in unremarkable mercenary gear, lots of leather and steel."

"Describe them."

Allen racked his brain. He'd been focused on other things at the time, like staying alive. He'd only paid attention to the man that threatened him, and that was Lord Shenk. "The leader of the mercenaries was maybe forty, scruffy beard, a little shorter than me with a broken nose. He had a rough, scratchy voice, though that might have been from yelling orders during the fight. I believe Lord Shenk said his name was Hans."

At the mention of that name, a light went on for Kelten. Allen had made a career of reading people and that man had just learned something that interested him. Hopefully it wouldn't be something that got Allen killed when Lord Shenk found out he let it slip.

"Lothair was still in chains when you were released?"

Allen nodded.

"What about the other prisoners? Tell me about them."

"I didn't know them well. From what I heard I judged they were Straken spies and when they were hanged as such a few days later it was confirmed. I swear I knew them only as customers. Had I known their true allegiance, I never would have sold them information." He withheld a silent "probably" since if they'd offered enough coin, Allen certainly wouldn't have thought much about their plans before taking the gold.

Kelten was silent for so long Allen finally asked, "What happens now?"

"Nothing, everything, I don't know. Don't follow me." Kelten bolted for the door and was gone.

Allen walked around the bar and helped Ulf to his feet. "We need to install a door with a peep hole."

"Or hire a doorman." Ulf touched his neck where the tip of Kelten's sword had left a small crease. "What do you think he's going to do?"

"I don't want to know. Just pray he doesn't come back or mention to Lord Shenk everything we told him. Either of those is liable to end poorly for us."

ↄ

Kelten remembered nothing about his journey from the tavern to his flat. He threw his borrowed sword on the table and slumped into his lone chair. It all made sense to him now. How the assassin had reached the king, why Wolfric wanted to end the investigation, all of it.

Hans was the key. Kelten had met him a few times. He was one of Wolfric's most loyal supporters. There was no way he wasn't keeping his master informed about Otto's plans. That meant Wolfric was aware of and probably approved of having his father killed. Whether you called it regicide or patricide, it was still murder. How could he have done it? The late king was the kindest man Kelten had ever known and Wolfric never showed any sign of wanting power, at least not in Kelten's view.

Father and son did quarrel after Garenland was cast out of the compact. Kelten didn't know the details, but there were rumors that Wolfric didn't approve of his father's weak response to the Straken invasion. Considering that the first thing he did after being crowned king was deploy the Northern Army, it wasn't impossible to imagine he'd believed he was doing the right thing by removing his father.

Kelten couldn't judge Wolfric's motives, only his actions. He was clearly involved with his father's murder, along with Otto, Hans, and his men. They needed to be held responsible for their actions. Not that there was anyone in a position to punish them. Who exactly did one complain to when the king broke the law? You could even argue that since the king decided what the laws were, he couldn't break them.

No, if Wolfric and his conspirators were going to pay for

what they did, it was up to Kelten and whoever else he could convince to aid him to make things right.

He smiled. A weight had lifted from his chest. All the stress and anxiety he'd felt over not knowing the truth was gone. What he'd learned was horrible, but now he knew what he had to do. He would probably die doing it, but that didn't matter. The right thing was worth dying for. Justice was worth dying for.

But he had to act quickly. With Otto and Hans at the front, Wolfric was alone and vulnerable. He had no hope of besting the wizard, but if he could defeat Wolfric and expose his crimes, all the nobles would rally to the cause of hunting Otto and the others down and seeing them pay.

Wolfric was the key. Kelten still had people loyal to him in the palace guard. It wouldn't take many of them to capture an unblooded boy.

Kelten leapt to his feet. The night shift was off duty and a handful lived outside the palace.

It was time to get started. It was time to put things right.

CHAPTER 45

The worst thing about their overwhelming victory, at least as far as Otto was concerned, was the prisoners. They'd taken a ton of them and now they needed to feed and guard them. He was fairly sure that Wolfric only wanted them to go easy on civilians, not soldiers, but General Varchi was in charge and he'd decided to interpret the king's command as widely as possible.

Which was strange considering earlier he'd seemed to resent them. Perhaps he was just being difficult to punish Otto and the wizards for their large part in the army's success. Tempting as it was to simply execute the prisoners all while the general slept, he wasn't ready for that confrontation yet.

Day after day the army crawled ahead at a snail's pace while scores of units traveled east and west to forage for supplies to keep them all fed. Worst of all, they'd already had the first snow of the year. Only a dusting, but it was enough to remind them of what was coming. At their current pace, it would be a miracle if they got within sight of Marduke before they were buried in snow. At best they'd have two shots at the city. Fail and it was back to Garenland for the winter.

Much as he disliked the idea of retreating, they'd accomplished far more than Otto had dared hope when the war began. At a minimum, they'd eliminated any threat from Straken for years. And even if they failed to take the capital, when the Northern Army returned in the spring, they'd face a far smaller opposing force. No, whatever else happened, Otto couldn't consider the campaign anything but a success.

And it might be even more than that if his hunch proved correct. Lord Karonin, when she told him about the armory in Garenland had kind of hinted that there were more. He took it as a challenge that she hadn't told him exactly how many more or where they were. His theory was that one might be hiding in Straken. Since he didn't have anything better to do while they were slogging toward Marduke, he figured he might as well look for it.

Otto urged his horse over beside Hans's wagon. "Do you need something, my lord?"

"I'm going to do some scouting and I can't guide the horse at the same time." Hans brought his wagon to a halt, Otto tied his horse to the back gate, then climbed up beside him. "I'll still be able to hear you, so if there's trouble let me know."

"Understood."

Otto closed his eyes and sent his vision soaring. Usually he didn't focus on the ether when he went searching, but today he needed to if he wanted to find his target. When he shifted his perception, the ether appeared, brighter and richer to his magical vision than when he was seeing through his physical eyes. This was close to what he experienced when he became one with the ether.

The colors, swirls, and lines were terribly distracting.

Searching for an enemy position with all this going on around him would have been pointless. He assumed if there was an armory in Straken, it would have a different marker than the one in Garenland, but just to be sure he focused on the rune Lord Karonin had shown him in the tower all those months ago.

Even at this distance he could vaguely sense it to the south. As he feared there was nothing closer with that mark. How was he supposed to separate all the background energy from what he sought?

As he considered the problem, he turned a slow circle. Three-quarters of the way around he stopped and stared. A straight streak of energy flashed past. Otto followed it as far as he could but ran out of threads before he got to the end. Still, that was far enough to realize what he saw was something traveling through the portal to Marduke.

The moment he recognized it, he knew how to find the armory, assuming there was one here. The ether around him was chaotic and random swirls. When a wizard worked the energy, it took on an ordered, regular appearance. That was what he needed to search for.

Determined now, he kept his senses focused on anything straight or geometric. It took over an hour, but he finally found it. At the foot of a mountain, as far east as his extended senses would reach, he found a sealed area where his sight couldn't penetrate. That had to be what he was looking for.

He flew down for a closer look. The space warded against his entrance was about a hundred feet square at the base of a sheer cliff. He'd wager his sword that an illusion disguised an entrance of some sort there. He marked a clear spot fifty feet from the ward and snapped back to his body.

"Anything happen while I was gone?" Otto rolled his shoulders and worked his neck from side to side. Whenever he was out of his body for any length of time, he ended up stiff.

"Nothing, Lord Shenk. You'd think they'd send raiders to harass us or something."

"They don't have the men to spare. For Straken, the capital city will be all or nothing. There was nothing moving besides us for twenty miles."

"I wish they'd try something. Using that armor is addicting. The power is unlike anything I've ever felt."

"Interesting. Perhaps you're getting a small taste of what wizards feel when we work magic. It's called the Bliss."

"That's a fine name for it. Small wonder that wizards enjoy magic so much if that's what you feel."

"I've located something interesting. If there's trouble, you know how to use the coin. I'll return after camp is set tonight. Place the coin in a clear space in my tent and make sure no one enters. Understood?"

"Yes, my lord. If I may ask, what did you find?"

"I'm not sure yet, but it's old and magical and therefore interesting." Otto focused and became one with the ether.

CHAPTER 46

O tto followed his marking thread back to the cliff wall he was certain hid another armory. When he emerged from the ether he held his breath and listened. Aside from a few chirping birds, he could have been alone in the world. If this armory was anything like the one in Garenland, there would certainly be some sort of trap protecting the entrance. Hopefully it worked like the first one and he'd be able to open it with no trouble.

Tentacles of ether formed at his command and began probing the cliff wall. They instantly sank beneath the illusion and settled on the actual door. At least there was something here, that was good. Now how to get in.

Otto closed his eyes and sent his vision along one of the tentacles. The door hidden behind the illusion was different than the armory he'd visited earlier. Instead of smooth wood and steel, this one had a bronze beast head in the center. It looked a little like a bear, but he couldn't be sure.

Since no runes or other markings marred the metal sculpture, Otto assumed it was just a decoration and resumed his search. He soon found the source of the illusion in the form of a collection of runes running along the door's frame. He covered the runes with ether and the illusion vanished. So far it was working just as he hoped.

He returned his sight to his body and gave the door a closer look. Why would Lord Karonin have put such an ugly and garish decoration on the door of her armory? He doubted it was simply for appearances. But if it wasn't, he couldn't figure out what it meant.

Otto shrugged and sent his tentacles into the door, quickly finding the hinges and pouring ether into them. The door slid silently into the ceiling. That was different as well. Beyond the door, a rune glowed in the center of the chamber.

Caution warred with curiosity and lost badly. Conjuring a light, Otto stepped inside. He managed three strides before the door slammed back down with a rather final-sounding thud. Alarming as it was, he didn't let it rattle him. He knew how to get back out after all.

He put an extra thread's worth of ether into his light and sent it up to the ceiling. There were no bookshelves in this armory, or weapons for that matter. Instead six pits ran the diameter of the single chamber. The wall held four unoccupied sets of manacles. There was also a heavy chain ending with an iron collar on the side opposite the manacles.

What the hell had he stumbled into, a weird torture chamber? What kind of torture chamber didn't have tools? A wizard's might not. Otto could do a fair job of torturing someone with just magic so what could Lord Karonin have managed?

He shivered just thinking about her questioning prisoners in this grim chamber.

He walked to the edge of one of the pits and looked down.

It was about twenty feet deep and fifteen feet around, not huge, but big enough to hold a prisoner easily enough. Something lined the bottom, but he couldn't make out what. His first guess was straw, but why would his master bother with bedding for a prisoner she was planning to torture?

A tentacle of ether brought a handful of the stuff up for a closer inspection. It wasn't straw after all, but fur, coarse, brown fur unlike anything Otto had seen before. He tossed it back and moved on. All the pits were the same, some had more fur at the bottom than others, but that was the only thing that distinguished them.

Hours passed while he checked every surface for hidden doors or anything else of value, but he came up empty. Whatever Lord Karonin did here, it was a mystery to Otto. He sighed and moved to the center of the chamber. At least his search broke up the tedium of the long march north.

He was about to enter the ether and rejoin Hans when a vibration from one of his runes jangled his nerves. He focused and traced it back toward Garenland. Since no one knew about the one hidden in his suite in Franken Manor, it had to be Wolfric in the palace. His friend wouldn't be calling out unless he was in trouble.

Otto became one with the ether and rushed south. Hopefully he didn't arrive too late.

↻

It took three days of talking and planning, but Kelten finally had his team, seven men, all loyal and determined to do the right thing. He was very careful who he selected. Even one person letting something slip at the wrong time could doom them all. He hadn't reached out to Trask either. The Watch

Commander had risked enough. If their effort failed, Kelten didn't want anything to happen to the one remaining man who might be able to oppose what he feared Wolfric and Otto intended.

As he stood in the long shadows of an evergreen with a view of the palace's side entrance, Kelten steeled himself for what was to come. Some good, honest men might die today. Many would see what he was doing as a betrayal of the Crown and would try to stop him. They didn't know the truth and might not believe it if Kelten told them. He wished he didn't believe it. He wished he could go back to his blind loyalty, but he couldn't. The murder of the old king had broken his faith.

Across the street a lantern flashed.

That was the signal. He ran across the street and ducked under the portcullis. Two of Borden's men lay unconscious on the ground. The first thing Kelten's replacement had done was put men loyal to him at all the entrances. But he hadn't increased their number which made them easy to deal with.

"So far so good, Captain," Sergeant Timothy said.

"The others are in place?"

"Yes, sir. Wolfric has retired early. Our people should have cleared a path to his private chambers."

So it was just Wolfric now, no honorific, no respect. Well, he couldn't blame them. It was harder to betray someone you respected.

"Then let's not keep him waiting." Kelten drew his sword and set out with Timothy and his partner trailing behind.

The familiar twists and turns of the castle took on a sinister feel. Despite the assurance Timothy offered, Kelten assumed enemies waited around every corner.

After the first bend they found two of their comrades standing over the bodies of the guards on duty. A shallow pool of blood was spreading under them. Those weren't Borden's men, but palace guards that once served under his command. That they had to die was a tragedy, one he placed directly at Wolfric's feet. How many deaths would the boy king have to answer for by the time they reached his private chamber?

The next two guard posts had been subdued without any loss of life. When they reached the doors to Wolfric's bedchamber they found the final two members of the group on duty. They were the key to this whole thing going off without a hitch. If anyone else pounded on his door, Wolfric would be on alert.

Kelten nodded, not daring to speak lest Wolfric hear him.

The right-hand guard rapped on the bedroom door. "Majesty, a messenger has arrived."

"I'll deal with them in the morning, now keep silent." Wolfric's voice was muffled by the doors, but his annoyance came through loud and clear.

The guards looked to Kelten who mouthed the words, "It's from Lord Shenk."

"It's from Lord Shenk, Majesty. Some trouble at the front."

There was a noise from behind the door and Kelten tensed. Any second now.

The door opened a crack. "What?"

Kelten lashed out with a front kick, slamming the door into Wolfric.

The king staggered back but didn't fall.

He dodged a thrust and leapt over the bed, putting it between them. Before Kelten could do anything else, Wolfric yanked a pull cord dangling beside the bed.

"They won't get here in time," Kelten said.

Wolfric grinned. "We've made a few changes since you left."

From outside came shouts and the thunder of pounding

armored feet rushing down the hall. How did they respond so fast?

"A squad of Borden's finest are stationed around the corner in a converted closet. We didn't announce the change, just in case."

Kelten grimaced. All Wolfric had to do was delay long enough for his soldiers to arrive and this would all be for nothing.

"We'll hold them, sir." Thomas slammed the door, sealing him in with Wolfric.

"Surrender and I promise your execution will be painless," Wolfric said.

"If I die, it will only be after I've killed you. Wolfric von Garen, for the crime of regicide, I sentence you to death."

Wolfric shook his head. "He wasn't supposed to die. I loved my father, but I loved my country more. If we hadn't removed him, Garenland would have fallen to Straken. We only intended to wound him so he couldn't rule for a few months, long enough for the invaders to be driven back across the border. But luck wasn't with us and a clot formed during the night."

"That wasn't your decision to make." Kelten shifted left and Wolfric matched him to the right.

"Wasn't it? You saw what Father had become. He was delusional, believing talk would accomplish anything at this point. How many innocent citizens would you have consigned to death while he tried to make up his mind to fight? Was his life worth more than the scores or maybe hundreds or thousands of innocents that would have died? Tell me, Captain, would you have come here to take my life on their behalf if I had done nothing?"

Outside the muffled crashes and thuds grew louder.

Wolfric was trying to delay him so his guards could come to the rescue. Still, he raised a point that Kelten hadn't considered. Was the king's life worth more than a hundred commoners? A thousand? He couldn't say.

"I'm not here to debate what might have been. Protecting your father was my charge. Since I failed, avenging him is all I have left."

Kelten lunged across the bed.

Wolfric scrambled around to the other side and sprinted toward the closet. If he got in there and locked the door, Kelten had no chance of reaching him before his men were overwhelmed.

He lashed out with a kick that grazed Wolfric as he passed, staggering but not stopping him.

The king yanked the closet door open.

Kelten was right on his heels.

The door started to close, but Kelten jammed the fingers of his left hand into the gap. He winced as they were crushed between the frame and the heavy wood.

Snarling away the pain, he wrenched the door open.

He was just in time to see Wolfric pounding on a strange, glowing mark with a hammer.

Kelten's moment of confusion cost him dearly.

Before he could react, a blinding light filled the closet. When his vision cleared, Otto stood directly above the mark.

Their eyes met and lightning crashed into Kelten's chest.

Darkness claimed him.

CHAPTER 47

Otto stared down at Kelten's unmoving body. He'd made sure to only use enough lightning to render him unconscious, not kill him. There were questions that needed answering and dead men were notoriously difficult to question. He flicked a glance at Wolfric's wardrobe then settled his gaze on the king, still dressed in purple silk pajamas.

Putting the marking rune in his giant closet had seemed silly when Wolfric suggested it, but it worked out well today. "Are you okay?"

"Yes." Wolfric's voice was still a little shaky, but considering he'd nearly been killed it was pretty steady. "I should have taken your advice and had him killed. I can't believe Kelten would do this. And how could he have figured out everything we did?"

"A lot of it was probably guesswork. We'll find out for sure once we interrogate him." Otto was about to say more when the bedroom door burst in.

Borden and a dozen armed and bloody soldiers rushed in.

The commander took one look at the situation and motioned for his men to sheathe their weapons.

"We've dealt with the traitors outside." Borden nodded toward Kelten. "Do you wish me to dispose of this trash?"

"Take him to the dungeon," Wolfric said. "We'll have questions for him when he wakes up. Make sure only people you're certain of are guarding him."

Borden bowed. "I'll make sure. And I beg you forgive me for this failure. I suspected there were sympathizers, but I wanted to give them a chance."

Wolfric waved a hand as if nearly getting killed by his former captain of the guard was no big deal. "What's done is done. The important thing is to make sure it doesn't happen again. We'll need to purge the guard to make sure no more disloyal men remain."

"I'll see to it personally," Borden said.

"No." Otto stepped out of the closet and moved closer to Borden. "I will see to it personally. Every guard working in the palace will be interviewed and cleared by me before they even get close to the king."

"I assure you my men are loyal." Borden took a breath to argue more but Wolfric raised a hand.

"Otto will make sure. I trust you personally, Borden, but better safe than sorry. Get Kelten to the dungeon before he wakes up."

"Yes, Majesty."

The soldiers dragged Kelten away leaving Otto and Wolfric alone.

"I can interview enough guards tonight to ensure your safety," Otto said. "We'll question Kelten in the morning if that's okay."

Wolfric nodded then asked, "What about the army? Don't you need to get back?"

Otto shook his head. "At the rate they're moving, it will be a miracle if we reach Marduke before the first major storm. The prisoners are slowing us terribly. I suggested to the general that we could leave them behind with a small guard force or execute them, but he said the first wasn't safe and the second went against your orders. It would be a huge help if you could write a letter explaining that the order to go easy on the people didn't apply to enemy soldiers."

"It obviously doesn't," Wolfric said. "General Varchi should realize that."

Otto shrugged. "He may have refused simply because I suggested it. The general doesn't like wizards. Seems he regards killing with magic as dishonorable. As if the men are somehow more dead if you stab them. I knew there were going to be problems integrating wizards into the army, but I must admit I didn't expect the general himself would be part of them. I mean, what sort of leader doesn't want to win with as few casualties as possible?"

"The old-fashioned sort." Wolfric blew out a long sigh. "He may need to be replaced or at least be reminded that the goal is to win, honor be damned. I'm going to put you in overall command. Varchi can consult on strategy and carry out your orders."

"I'm not sure that's a good idea. For all his faults, the soldiers look up to him. Undercutting him will hurt morale. I think what you need to do is clarify that getting to Marduke before winter is most important and that enemy soldiers don't need to be treated gently. That should be enough to accomplish our goals."

Wolfric smiled and went to his desk. "This is why I chose

you as my advisor. Any other man would have jumped at the chance to lead the army, but you take the time to consider what's best for Garenland instead of what's best for you. Oh, and thank you for saving my life."

"My pleasure. I'll leave you to write. I need to conduct some interviews before I return. May I suggest letting Kelten rot for a while? We can speak to him together once things in Straken are settled."

"Agreed. Letting the bastard hang in the dungeon will soften him up."

Otto withdrew to begin his interrogations. He'd come far too close to losing his best ally. If Wolfric had gotten killed, it would have set his project back years at least. He couldn't let something like this happen again.

CHAPTER 48

The city of Marduke was very much like everything else in Straken, huge and powerful looking. Otto studied the sixty-foot-high thirty-foot-thick walls from a safe distance while the army deployed. After rescuing Wolfric and assuring himself of the loyalty of at least a third of the guards in the palace, Otto had rushed back with a message to get the army moving.

General Varchi, bless his obedient heart, had ordered the army into high gear, which still wasn't very fast, but at least doubled their pace. Any prisoner that failed to keep up was put to the sword, which kept them moving at a good clip.

And now here they were, facing the capital of Straken, three inches of snow covering the killing field between the walls and the forest surrounding the city. Taking the city was going to be a challenge, even with magic. There were only two entrances, both sealed by massive, iron-bound gates. Smashing their way through them would take heaven only knew how long, even with the enchanted armor.

"Quite a sight." Axel eased his mount up beside Otto.

"Indeed. Any thoughts about how we get inside?"

Axel quirked an eyebrow. "I assumed you and your wizards would blast the walls to gravel and we'd just march in."

"Funny. Magic's much better against living targets than solid stone walls, at least my magic is. What an Arcane Lord might have done I couldn't say. I figure our best bet is to lob fireballs over the wall and burn the city to the ground. When everyone's dead, one of your scouts can climb over and open the gate for us."

"You think it'll be that simple?"

"Of course not. If we've got more than two weeks to get this done, I'll be shocked. The best we can hope for is to do as much damage as possible in preparation for next year. When spring arrives, we'll be back to finish the job."

"The king's not going to like that."

"Wolfric was always overly optimistic about this campaign. Given that the Northern Army didn't even deploy until the end of summer, it's a miracle we made it this far. Once he thinks about it, he will understand. Besides, there's plenty to be done back home."

"That's right, you've got a kid on the way. I almost forgot. When is the baby due?"

Otto grimaced. He had no desire to discuss Annamaria or Lothair's spawn. Still, best to play the part of an interested father-to-be. "Not until early spring. I'll probably be on the march right after the little one is born."

Axel grinned. "Mother will be thrilled to have another grandchild. You'll have to squeeze in a trip home to show her."

"Maybe Mother can come to Garen. Annamaria had an ugly run-in with Stephan last time and I doubt she'll be willing to return to Shenk Castle."

"I can't blame her. I'm not anxious to return either. Though in my case it's because Father wants to kill me."

Otto laughed. "You know, I've heard people claim that their greatest joy in life is family. What do you suppose that's like?"

"Beats me. Stay safe, little brother."

"You too, Axel."

When his brother had ridden off to rejoin his men, Otto closed his eyes and sent his vision soaring over the city walls for a look around. Just inside the gate, a huge force had gathered. There were thousands of cavalry and heavy infantry mixed with archers. How could Straken have so many soldiers left?

He flew down for a closer look.

Something smashed his ethereal construct to pieces. Otto's sight instantly snapped back to his body, leaving his vision blurry.

What in Straken could have detected his spell much less broken it? They had no wizards, that was well known by everyone. It couldn't have been a magical device; they'd still need a wizard to activate whatever they found.

Curious now, Otto rebuilt the construct and this time sent it out wide of the city so he could approach the area in front of the main gate from the rear. He made it, this time keeping his distance in the hopes that he wouldn't draw attention. In the mustering area, the huge force he'd glimpsed before hadn't moved.

A closer look revealed that they wore different uniforms. The cavalry wore Rolan's brown with a horse on the chest. The infantry was a mix of Tharanault's midnight blue and gray and Straken's black with fur trim. As he'd feared, Straken had brought in reinforcements. The streak he'd seen when he was one with the ether must have been soldiers arriving through the gate.

Otto inched closer. Two smaller groups didn't look like fighters. Every other one had the ethereal glow he associated with a wizard using magic in some way. Next to each wizard was a soldier with a bare dagger in his hand.

He didn't need much to understand the implications of that. Having seen how effective Garenland's wizards were, Straken had brought in some of their own. He counted a hundred wizards before giving up.

His twenty had no chance against them. If they all cast at once, the Northern Army was doomed.

CHAPTER 49

The instant Otto's vision cleared, he twisted his horse's head around and kicked its ribs. The wizards had set up at the rear of the army, thankfully near the command tent. If the Northern Army was going to survive what was coming, he didn't have long.

Soldiers stared as he thundered past. Otto ignored them, his sole focus on getting the army ready.

He reined in just short of a half-erected tent. One of his squad leaders, the man's name escaped Otto at the moment, looked up at him. "Lord Shenk?"

"Master Enoch taught you defensive magic, right?"

"Only the most basic. He said if we hit an incoming spell with a thread of ether it would break apart. We didn't really practice. All our focus was on offensive magic."

"Well, you're about to get all the practice you'll need. Straken's brought in about a hundred wizards from other nations. I need you to take the others and gather at the front. Stop as many incoming spells as you can. Watch the front gate. As soon as it opens, send up a single-thread fireball to let me know. Understand?"

"Are they coming now?"

"They're gathering as we speak. Hurry!"

"Yes, my lord."

Otto left him to gather the others and continued on to the nearby wagons. Hans and his men were setting up the tent they shared when he arrived. "Forget that and get your armor ready. We'll need you to break up the cavalry charge."

"What's going on?" Hans asked.

Otto repeated what he'd seen. "You'll need to hold them while the rest of the army retreats. There's no way we can take them with our wizards so badly outnumbered."

"We're on it, Lord Shenk." Hans ran off bellowing orders and waving his hands.

Now if only General Varchi would be as quick to see reason. There was no time for a debate.

Otto raced to the command tent and leapt off his horse. The guards on duty outside started to speak, but Otto ignored them. There was no time.

Inside, the general and his seconds, including Axel, were gathered around a crude map of Marduke. They all looked over as Otto entered.

"We need to get the men assembled and ready to fall back to the forest. Straken's brought in reinforcements along with wizards, a lot of wizards."

"That's absurd," General Varchi said. "They would never leave the safety of their walls, not when the weather will end the siege for them in weeks."

"I'm telling you they're mustering right now. I've got look-outs in place. Every second we wait means lives lost. If I've made a mistake you can mock me later. Right now we need to move."

"Ready the legions," General Varchi said. "Prepare for a controlled withdrawal."

"We should drive the prisoners to the front and use them as shields to break the enemy charge," Axel said.

"Good idea," Otto said. "It's not like we can take them—"

An explosion cut him off mid-agreement. Otto darted outside in time to see the last sparks fading above the army.

"What was that?" General Varchi asked.

"My spotter. The enemy's coming."

As if to hammer the point home one of Axel's scouts came riding up. "The gates are opening, sir."

"Get everyone formed up!" the general bellowed. "Where's my armor? Why is everyone standing around? Move!"

"I'll join my men up front," Otto said. "We'll deflect as much of their magic as we can."

"We'll get the enemy prisoners into position," Axel said. "Good luck, brother."

"See you on the other side." Otto held out his hand and Axel shook it.

They parted ways and Otto hurried back to the front of the army. His wizards were spread out in a line, their eyes peeled for incoming spells. It would have been simple enough to escape through the ether and return to Garen, but if he fled, the defense would have no hope and they'd probably end up losing most of the army. That loss might break Wolfric's will to fight.

The wizards all looked to Otto but he immediately pointed back toward the slowly emerging enemy force. "Watch for spells. You know what to do. Anything that looks like it will miss the main body of the army can be ignored. This is where we show them that wizards are indispensable. When we save the Northern Army, no one will ever question a wizard's worth again."

They all nodded and turned back just as the first targeting threads came streaking in.

Otto conjured an ethereal wall as tall and wide as he could. Score of threads struck it and dissolved. As long as they could stop those threads, enemy spells couldn't strike home. He said a silent thank you to whoever wrote that book on war magic. The author was about to save their lives.

The targeting threads changed trajectory, arcing up over his wall. He didn't have power enough to expand his wall.

The first fireball came streaking in only to get blasted apart by one of the others. The longer path gave them time to counter at least.

The ground shook as Hans and his men came clanking up in their magical armor. "Orders, Lord Shenk?"

"Hold fast for now. When the cavalry charge comes, use your swords to break their formation." Another fireball exploded above them. "And be sure to stay behind me until then."

"Understood." Hans and the others took a knee to Otto's left and right.

A tense few minutes passed as enemy spells were broken. The main Straken force continued to advance. They were half a mile away when Axel finally arrived with the prisoners. He didn't even look at Otto, he just drove them on like a herder pushing sheep to slaughter.

When they were a hundred yards ahead of Otto, Axel turned and rode back the way he'd come, throwing a salute as he passed. Now they had a wall of flesh and a wall of ether to protect them from incoming spells.

"If any of them come this way, cut them down," Otto said to Hans.

All five armored units stood and drew their swords. Otto let the ethereal wall go, trusting that the wizards wouldn't do anything to threaten the prisoners.

"Here they come!" one of the wizards shouted.

Thousands of cavalry thundered toward Otto. The soldiers of Rolan showed no great restraint, knocking down or trampling prisoners as they approached.

Hans and his men strode forward, six-foot swords swinging. Watching them was like watching a farmer harvest wheat. Each swing of the massive blades felled half a dozen men and horses. Cavalrymen tried to counterattack, but their curved swords just shattered against the massive enchanted armor.

In the end they decided to just ride around them. When they did, they were met with fire and lightning. At such close range, the enemy wizards could do nothing to stop the onslaught.

"How's the retreat going?" Otto asked.

One of the wizards turned to look. "Most of them are into the forest. Another minute I think."

"Alright, you lot get going. I'll cover your withdrawal." Otto pulled all the ether he could manage and wove heat into it. "Hans! Fall back."

The armored warriors disengaged and withdrew. As soon as they were clear of the enemy line Otto hurled the gathered ether, raising a huge wall of flames. Threads connected the spell to the ether so it wouldn't go out until the enemy wizards broke them.

Otto staggered, drained by that final spell.

Hans bent down and picked him up in an oversized gauntlet. "I've got you, my lord."

Otto was only vaguely aware of the reassurance. As Hans clanked away from the flames, Otto devoutly hoped that the enemy didn't give chase, at least not for a few hours.

The war was over for Garenland. Now it was just a matter of getting home in one piece.

CHAPTER 50

Otto woke up and was surprised to find he wasn't moving. The last thing he remembered was nodding off in the grasp of Hans's armor as they fled the battlefield. He stared up at the evergreens and beyond them the leaden sky. How long had he been out? It felt like moments, but he suspected it was considerably more.

He tossed his blanket aside and sat up.

"Morning, my lord."

Otto looked to his left and found Hans tending a fire with a bubbling pot over it. He couldn't smell anything over the smoke that filled the air, but whatever he was cooking would be welcome if it quieted his rumbling stomach.

"What happened?" Otto's heart skipped a beat when he remembered that the armor could only function for eight hours at a time. "The enchanted armor?"

"It's fine. Some of your brother's scouts brought our wagons. You've been out for twenty hours; we were starting to get worried. That wall of fire was quite a sight. It let us get the stragglers to safety. You made a lot of friends in the army today, you and the other wizards. Hungry?"

"Starving." Hans ladled out a bowl of thick...something and handed it to Otto. He took a bite of bland oatmeal and grimaced. "Thanks."

"We'll be breaking camp soon, but I wanted to have something ready in case you woke."

Otto nodded and tried to show a little more enthusiasm. "Bring me up to date."

"Not much to tell. After we reached the forest, the enemy returned to Marduke. We haven't seen anything of them since. Doesn't seem likely they'd just let us go, but so far that's exactly what they've done."

"I doubt Rolan and Tharanault have any desire to order their troops to go tromping across Straken hunting a force that might turn on them at any moment. I'll wager if they haven't already returned to their home nations, they will soon."

"Maybe you should tell General Varchi. We could turn around and try again."

Otto scraped up the last of his breakfast and handed the bowl back. "There's no point. They could simply bring them back through the portal at the first sign of trouble. I didn't take that into account when I made my plans. I knew the three countries were allied, but I didn't realize they were close enough that they'd offer military assistance. I never even considered the implications of the portals beyond knowing we couldn't starve them out in a traditional siege. We'll need to rethink our entire strategy for next year."

Hans grunted and put the now-clean bowl back in his kit. "I'll leave that to you and the other higher-ups. Just point me at who you want killed."

Otto grinned and wished he could take such a simple position. But of course he couldn't. Figuring out the portal problem would be his task. Luckily it was one he'd been thinking about for a little while. He suspected he'd be spending a good deal of time in consultation with Lord Karonin this winter. But if his plan worked, it would change the world forever.

⟳

The Lady in Red stood beside a snarling Uther as they watched the last of the Tharanault heavy infantry vanish into the portal. As they'd hoped, their allies had turned the tide of the war, especially the wizards, but now that Marduke was secure, they had no desire to linger.

Uther had argued that they needed to chase down and finish off the Garenlanders. The two commanders had listened then explained that they both had orders not to commit to any action beyond securing the city. And nothing Uther could say would change their mind.

Not that they could complain. She had no doubt Straken would now be under new rulership and her and Uther's heads would be adorning pikes if their allies had refused to help. So they stood and watched until the portal closed. As least they had promises of more aid should Garenland threaten the city again. That and nothing more.

"Idiots, the lot of them," Uther said. "We should have crushed Garenland together when we had them on the run."

She nodded as Uther vented. He knew as well as she did that just because Garenland had fled a losing position, didn't mean that they they might not turn and counterattack if given the opportunity. She'd seen enough of their magical capabilities to know the damage they could do in such a situation would be considerable.

"We should start preparing for spring as soon as possible," she said. "You know they'll be back."

"I do and we will. Damn all wizards to hell! There must be some way to overcome them without relying on outsiders. Assassins maybe. Do you think we could sneak some across the border and have them kill any wizards they find?"

"It's something to consider, but I don't really have many people suited for that sort of thing. Our soldiers tend to stand out in a crowd." That was putting it mildly. The average Straken man was a good hand taller than the people of the other nations. And now that Garenland was on guard, they'd likely just be sending their people to die. "I'll think about it some more, Majesty."

"You do that. I need a drink."

Uther left her alone in the softly falling snow. Some way to defeat wizards without using other wizards. That was a problem she doubted even her scheming could solve.

CHAPTER 51

Otto rode with the Northern Army for three days, both to regain his strength and to make sure Straken didn't make any moves against them. As he expected they didn't. For now, at least, it seemed both sides were done with fighting. That was fine with Otto, he didn't especially like fighting, especially when he wasn't in a position to win.

Once he was satisfied that nothing was going to happen, he teleported back to the city, appearing in Franken Manor instead of the palace, mostly because appearing in Wolfric's bedchamber was a little awkward. That and after a week in the field, he was in desperate need of a bath and change of clothes. Since he had no desire to advertise his return, the bath would have to wait. The servants, bless their hearts, kept a pitcher of clean water beside his bed. Otto washed up with that, changed into something clean, and felt human again.

Reasonably presentable, he turned invisible and worked his way toward the servants' exit. He only had to avoid a single chambermaid laden with fresh laundry. As soon as he found a spot with no one around he reappeared and turned toward the side entrance to the palace. It was an hour before noon and he badly wanted some of the palace chef's delicious cooking for lunch. There was nothing like army food to make you appreciate fine dining.

At the entrance he was met with surprised looks followed by quick salutes. "Welcome back, Lord Shenk," the elder guard said.

"Thank you. I trust all has been quiet since I left?"

"Perfectly, my lord. Whatever traitors there were have learned their lesson. His Majesty will have nothing to worry about now." The guard gestured to someone inside and the portcullis started to rise.

Otto appreciated the man's confidence but doubted matters would be tied up so quickly. Kelten was well known and according to Wolfric well liked. His execution should finish the job of smoking out any traitors. But first Otto needed to have a nice long chat with him.

He ducked under the portcullis and made his way down the familiar halls. Guards saluted as he passed and servants bowed. Otto nodded back and hurried on toward the throne room. Even if court wasn't in session, the guards there could tell him where to find the king.

As luck would have it, court was in session when he arrived. The guards weren't technically supposed to allow anyone in after the doors closed, but they knew better than to hold Otto up. Not because he would do anything to them, but rather because Wolfric would. Standing orders were to let him through no matter the circumstances.

They opened the doors just enough for Otto to slip inside. The throne was half filled with nobles who all had their eyes riveted to the scene up front. A middle-aged bald man in a fancy silk and lace outfit was on his knees before the throne where an enraged Wolfric stood looking down at him. Behind the throne, Borden and a dozen of his men kept a wary eye on the crowd.

"Tell me how it is," Wolfric demanded, "that you're here when your barony has fallen under the control of an enemy nation? Why are you not back in your castle plotting how best to wrest control of the portion of our southern province seized by Rolan? Why did I find out a chunk of my kingdom had been usurped by Rolan not by the baron responsible for ruling it, but by my chief councilor who was traveling around cleaning up messes left by my nobles instead of being here to advise me? And lastly, my lord, why did my guards have to drag you out of a cheap whorehouse to face this inquisition instead of you showing up on your own as is your duty?"

Wolfric's voice had been rising with each question until the last one was shouted at full volume. The nobles in front of Otto were muttering in low, nervous voices. Perhaps this was the first time they'd heard about the loss of territory in the south.

"Your Majesty, I often spend my time in the capital so I can be close to court. My seneschal has always managed my territory with skill and wisdom. I trusted him to handle any problems that might arise in my absence. It seems I erred in my judgement. Please forgive me and let me prove that I deserve my position."

"Very well," Wolfric said. "When the time comes to reclaim your territory, you shall lead the charge against the invaders."

"Lead the charge?" The question came out as a squeak.

"Absolutely. Think how inspired our soldiers will be to see such a brave noble leading the way. In the meantime, you'll be my guest here at the palace."

The nobleman lowered his head. "Yes, Your Majesty."

Wolfric finally looked up to see what effect his words had on the crowd. His gaze landed on Otto and he waved him forward.

"Welcome back, my friend."

Otto bowed when he reached the throne. "Majesty. It is good to be back."

"Please, give our fellow nobles the latest news from the front."

Otto knew better than to give them all the news. "The Northern Army has reclaimed all the territory taken by Straken and delivered a heavy blow to their forces. There can be no fear of them returning next year to try and take back what they've lost. Unfortunately, the snows have begun and we were unable to take Marduke. The army is on its way home. When spring arrives, we will return and finish what we started."

The assembled nobles gave a great cheer.

When they quieted, Wolfric said, "Spread word of our victory far and wide. Court is finished for today and I'm ordering three days of celebrations."

There was another cheer and the nobles began filing out.

When they'd all gone and the doors were sealed Wolfric asked, "How are things truly?"

"Everything I said just now is true. However, it wasn't snow that kept us from taking Marduke. Rolan and Tharanault sent help through the portal, including nearly a hundred wizards. There was no way we could defeat them with what we had so I encouraged the general to retreat. He wasn't pleased, but there was only a week or two at most before winter arrived in earnest, so it wasn't worth the risk."

Wolfric's scowl was deep and went all the way to his

eyebrows. "I thought you told me the wizards would rise up and help us, not fight for their masters."

"Every wizard had a soldier beside him with a drawn blade and I assume they have families back in their home countries. Even so there was no way they attacked with their full strength. Anyway, the wizards aren't the real problem. Once our team is complete, we'll be able to defeat them in battle. The real problem is the portals. As long as they can bring in food and soldiers instantly from all their allies, we can't wear them down enough to win."

"The portals are beyond our control."

"Not necessarily. I've been studying how they work and I believe there's a way to seize control of them. I'll be spending the winter researching my theories, but if I'm right, we'll be able to swoop in and take control of all the nations' capitals in one shot. Whether I can do it or not is the big question. Time will tell. In the meantime, we have a prisoner that needs interrogating."

Wolfric brightened. "I've been so busy with foolish nobles I'd forgotten about Kelten. Questioning him will do me good."

"Perhaps after lunch? I'm starving."

Wolfric laughed. "Of course, my friend. It's not like he's going anywhere."

Stuffed with delicious food, Otto, Wolfric, and Commander Borden descended to the palace dungeon. There weren't actually that many prisoners. Aside from Kelten, there was a butler that was caught stealing and a guard accused of rape who was due to go on trial in a few weeks. Those two were kept well away from the star prisoner, mostly so he couldn't poison them against the king, not that anyone really cared about a pair of criminals' opinions. It was easier to keep them apart than risk them hearing too much and having to kill them.

The dungeon itself was far nicer than the one under Castle Shenk. There was no mold on the walls, or water running along the smooth stone floor. At the end of a short hall was the torture chamber. Two guards had strapped Kelten to an X-shaped vertical rack and removed his tunic. Kelten had lost weight during his stay and his ribs were clearly visible. His hair was ragged and filthy. Only his eyes showed signs of life as they stared holes through Otto and Wolfric.

"I don't care what you do," Kelten said. "You'll not get a word out of me."

"Shall I heat the pokers?" Borden asked.

Otto looked from Kelten to Borden and back. "I'm not sure what you two think is going to happen here. Torture is such a crude means of extracting information. Mental manipulation through magic is much more effective."

He bound Kelten's eyelids open and conjured thin but dense threads of ether. Unlike when he hypnotized Lothair, Otto wasn't trying to program Kelten, he just wanted to unlock his memories. Opening his mind wasn't all that different than picking a lock. You just inserted ether into the correct part of his brain and twist at the right moment.

"How did you find out about Wolfric's involvement in his father's assassination?" Otto asked.

In his magical vision a tiny point in Kelten's brain lit up. That was the memory he needed. Two needles of ether acted like pry bars and pulled the information out through Kelten's mouth.

"During my interrogation of the tavern keeper Allen, he

mentioned the name Hans. I knew Hans was one of Wolfric's most trusted soldiers. There was no way he was involved without his master's permission."

It seemed Otto was going to have to have a chat with Allen later about being more careful with his words.

"Who else knows about this?" Otto asked.

"Commander Trask of the city watch. He helped me find Allen so I could question him again and he also found the witness that detailed the battle in the slums where you and Hans captured Lothair."

"I ordered Trask to drop the investigation," Wolfric muttered. "I'll have to replace him."

"He is quite old," Otto said. "Old people die all the time. Tomorrow morning someone will be getting a promotion, hopefully someone more loyal."

"I know the perfect person," Borden said.

Wolfric nodded. "See to it."

"Leave him alone!" Kelten shouted. "Trask is a good man just doing his duty."

Wolfric lashed out, punching Kelten in the jaw. "His duty is the same as yours was, obey your king. How hard is that? I'm not asking you to bring about world peace or swim across the bloody ocean, just do as you're told."

"There is no honor in obeying an illegitimate king," Kelten said.

Wolfric punched him a second time.

Before the king could scramble their prisoner's brains any more than he had Otto asked, "Do you have any other questions? If you want to beat him to death it's okay with me but getting information out of a damaged brain is harder."

Wolfric glanced at Borden who shook his head. "I think

we're good." He turned to Otto. "You'll take care of Commander Trask?"

"Of course. I'll make it look like he died in his sleep. No one will know otherwise. If you'll excuse me, I have a few other matters that require my attention." Otto bowed and withdrew. While he was no longer sickened by it, he still didn't have a taste for torture and was just as happy to leave before matters got too unpleasant.

Besides, a ton of work required his attention before he could go consult with his master about the portal issue. The sooner he got started on that the better the odds that he'd figure it out by spring.

CHAPTER 52

A full day later than he'd hoped, Otto appeared in the large chamber at the top of his master's hidden tower. The room was an unchanging sanctuary, a place where the many problems of the world could be forgotten, or at least ignored for a while. He'd spoken to Allen and was convinced that he'd had no intention to betray them to Captain Kelten. He just spouted one word too many. When someone had a sword to the throat of your friend, things like that happened.

His punishment had been to order Allen to write down everything that happened while Otto was out of the city. It should make for interesting reading. Killing Trask had been a simple matter. A single thread of lightning directly into his heart had killed the man in his sleep without a sound. Right now, Borden should be installing his chosen replacement into the vacant position. With any luck, this purge should be the move that fully secured Wolfric's rule. It would be nice to have the homeland under control so Otto could focus on external foes.

He turned and found his master's green-tinged face filling her magical mirror. Otto bowed to her with a great deal more sincerity than he did to Wolfric.

"You have that look in your eye, Apprentice," she said.

"What look is that, Master?"

"The hungry one that tells me you have many questions."

Otto smiled. Was he really that obvious? "I won't deny it. We've made great progress, but our final victory in the north was cut off by reinforcements that arrived by portal. I have a theory about the portals, but I don't understand them well enough to know for sure if I'm right."

"Tell me."

"I thought that there should be some way to transfer control of the portals from the one in Markane to the one in Garen while at the same time reactivating our own portal. If we could do that, it would be easy to swoop in and seize control of the other nations' capitals and at the same time prevent anyone from sending reinforcements."

"Given what you've told me about how Valtan has altered the portals' functions, I believe you are correct." Otto's heart leapt. "However, the process will be a long and difficult one. And once you've secured control, there's nothing preventing your enemies from taking it back through the same process."

"I never believed it would be easy," Otto said. "But if it can be done, the work doesn't deter me."

"Excellent answer. Shall I begin explaining what needs to happen to turn the pig Valtan's greatest accomplishment against him?"

"One more quick question if I may. When I was in Straken, I found a hidden workshop, something far different from the armory. It had pits and shackles. I'd never seen anything similar."

"You found my fleshpits. I never imagined you'd stumble on them. That workshop was used for shaping flesh and creating monsters. I never had great talent for the process despite Lord Azteca's personal training. Those skills are still far too advanced for you. Best if you focus on bringing the continent under your control then completing your transition to Arcane Lord. Once that's done, you'll have all the time in the world to master any magic you desire."

Otto grinned. He liked the sound of that.

He took an empty notebook out of his satchel along with a writing kit. "I'm ready when you are, Master."

"Then let us begin."

AUTHOR NOTE

Hello everyone and thanks for reading The Great Northern War. I hope you're enjoying Otto's story. Things only get worse in the next book when he's forced to give up the thing he values most, control.

The Portal Thieves follows some of Garenland's top spies as they try to infiltrate the other nations and complete a dangerous mission.

I hope you'll check it out.

James

ABOUT THE AUTHOR

James E. Wisher is a writer of science fiction and fantasy novels. He's been writing since high school and reading everything he could get his hands on for as long as he can remember.

To learn more:
www.jamesewisher.com
james@jamesewisher.com